THE INJUN

LANNY BLEDSOE

BLEDSOE PUBLISHING

1

The sign in front of the old building on the bank of the Chattahoochee River had one word on it – Whiskey. That was enough for Floyd Wimms. He'd been on the river for two weeks sleeping on the ground under a tarp and he was ready for a drink. He beached the boat, picked his pistol up off the middle seat and stuck it in his belt. He stepped out, tied up the boat and walked up the bank toward the building.

He looked around as he always did when coming to a new place. He didn't see anybody outside. Two boats were tied up at the landing so he figured there would be people inside. He walked up on the porch, pushed the door open, stepped inside and scanned the room. There were three men at a table on the left side of the room, all with drinks in front of them. A woman was standing behind the bar on the far side of the room. All talking stopped when Floyd walked in, and every eye was on him. The men at the table and the woman looked him over from head to foot, their eyes focused on the pistol stuck in his belt. He looked at the woman as he walked across the room to the bar.

She eyed him as he approached. "What you want?" she said.

"Whiskey," he said, his eyes on her face. He judged her to be in her thirties, dark hair with a bit of gray and not bad looking.

"I got shine."

Floyd nodded. "That'll do."

She reached behind the bar, got a glass, then looked back at him. "Ain't never seen you in here afore."

"Ain't never been here," said Floyd. "Went past some years back but didn't stop."

"Where you be from?"

"Downriver."

She smiled and cut her eyes at him. "Where be you going? Upriver?"

Floyd nodded.

She laughed. "Thought that be what you'd say," she said as she poured his drink. "You be dressed like a damn injun," she said, her eyes on his outfit of buckskin and beads. She didn't seem unfriendly, just curious and making talk.

He cut his eyes at her. "Do it bother you what I be wearin'?"

She shrugged. "I don't give a damn how you be dressed. Don't matter to me none."

He took a sip of the drink and looked around. "This yo' place?"

She frowned and stared at him for a moment. "You sho' do ask a lot of questions. Ain't none of yo' business bout whose it be but it be mine."

"You got any places to sleep here?" he said. "I ain't slept in a bed in a while."

She looked at him and shook her head. "I got one bed, that be all I got."

He cut his eyes at her again. "I don't take up much room," he said, watching her reaction.

She smiled and nodded toward a table on the other side of the room. "You be about a bold bastard; I'll sho' say that for you. Best you go sit down with yo' drink before you say too much and git me riled."

Floyd smiled, took his drink, walked to the table and sat down with his back to the wall.

The men at the far table had listened to his conversation with the woman and seemed to figure he wasn't a threat. They settled down and went back to their talking and drinking.

Floyd stretched his legs out in the chair and relaxed. It felt good to have a drink and a place to sit down. The last few days had been a challenge. He hadn't planned to be upriver at this time, but after he shot those two men downriver, it seemed the best thing to do. The shooting was self-defense, but the family of the men he'd shot wouldn't see it that way and there were a lot of them.

The shooting came about because he'd helped a woman in trouble. At the time he'd thought it was the right thing to do. Afterward, she thought it only fair that she thanked him by sharing her bed with him. Her husband caught them and didn't agree with her method of payment. He and his brother came after Floyd with pistols and the shooting started. He wounded both men and left the house with his clothes under his arm, the woman standing at the door asking him when he was coming back.

He got to his house and quickly packed his belongings. He dressed in the buckskins he'd worn when he'd wintered with the Cherokees years before, got in the boat and headed upriver. He'd reached the boat just ahead of the posse.

He camped at a long bend of the river for two days and watched to see if anyone was following him, but nobody came. Under the circumstances he decided that he might as well go back to the mountains and winter with the Cherokees again. That seemed the safest thing to do.

He had plenty of time before the snow came so he could take his time going upriver. He could stop and get a drink when he wanted to, so he ended up here. He looked at the bartender. After seeing her, he thought this might be a good place to spend the night or maybe more than one night. She seemed friendly, and he took that as a sign that she might be cooperative.

He was sipping on his second drink when the door opened, and two men and a young girl walked in. They stopped just inside the door and looked around. One of the men was holding the girl by the arm in a way that caught Floyd's attention. It looked to him that she wasn't with the men. She seemed to be their prisoner. The men looked at the three men at the table and then glanced toward Floyd.

He kept watching them. They were like most men you saw on the river, bearded, rough looking men with unfriendly faces. Both were young and had pistols stuck in their belts. The girl looked to be about twenty or so with a dirty face, greasy hair and filthy clothes. Cleaned up she might look all right but right now she looked to be as rough as the two men.

Floyd had seen men like these before in other places and had dealt with them. Their kind usually meant trouble. As was his practice when he sensed danger or felt threatened, he pulled his pistol out of his belt and held it in his hand under the table. He had no idea that they would start anything, but he wanted to be ready. He never wanted to be surprised and at a disadvantage. He sipped on his drink with his left hand and watched them.

The men at the table across the room were also watching the strangers as they walked across the floor to the bar. The girl looked at them. She took several more steps and then her eyes swept across the room toward Floyd. He could see that she was scared; it was written all over her face. The look in her eyes reminded him of a deer about to break and run. The man holding her arm saw her looking at Floyd and jerked her around. The girl cried out in pain.

"I done told you to stay with me and not start nothin' to cause trouble," he said. He looked at Floyd as he said this.

The woman behind the bar looked at them as she put glasses on the bar. "What you want?" she asked. She looked at the girl, sensing that something wasn't right with her.

"We want whiskey."

The bartender looked at the girl. "What do you want, honey?".

"She don't want nothin'," said the man.

The bartender glanced up at him for a moment and then poured two drinks.

They quickly downed the drinks and asked for another.

Floyd leaned back in the chair and watched them as they stood at the bar. He didn't know why the girl was with these two, but nothing about it felt right. She was obviously scared, and he figured given half a chance she would run. It seemed the men she was with thought the same thing and that was why they were holding on to her.

Everything about these people bothered Floyd and he thought about getting up and walking out before something happened. He'd been around situations like this in the past and could sense trouble brewing. But he stayed seated. Something about the way the girl had looked at him, her eyes pleading for help kept him in his seat.

Both men quickly downed their drinks and asked for a third. The woman poured the drinks and again looked at the girl. "You sure you don't want some water or something,' honey? You look like you could use somethin'."

The man turned and pointed his finger in her face. "Listen, bitch," he said, leaning over the bar toward her, "I done told you she don't want nothin'. It be best you keep yo' mouth shut before I teach you how to keep yo' mouth shut."

The bartender's face reddened, and her lips tightened. She stared at him. Her right hand was under the bar and when she pulled it out, she was holding a pistol. She leaned over the bar and pointed the pistol in the man's face. "You bastard," she said, "you ain't gonna talk to me like that. You say one more word to me and I'll send yo' sorry ass to hell where it belongs."

Wide eyed, he stepped back and held up both hands. "Whoa there, woman. Ain't no need to get all tore up bout this. I didn't mean nothin' by what I said. You put up that pistol. I don't want no trouble."

She stared at him for a moment, then slowly lowered the pistol, her eyes on him. She stepped back, the pistol still in her hand. "Y'all finish yo' drinks and get the hell out of here. I don't want yo' business." She reached under the bar and handed the girl a cold soda. "You look like you need this, honey."

The girl looked up at the man that was holding her, hesitantly took the soda and clutched it to her chest. "I need to go to the outhouse, Trip," she said. "I gotta go pee."

Trip started to say something, glanced at the woman behind the bar and thought better of it. He looked at the other man. "Go with her, Whit. Watch 'er or she'll run."

Whit nodded, grabbed the girl's arm and led her out the back door.

Floyd sat quietly at the table and watched as all this took place. He admired the woman behind the bar for standing up to the man's treatment. But he also knew that she'd put Trip down and his kind didn't like that kind of treatment. Given half a chance, he would come back at her. The retaliation came quickly, much faster than Floyd had expected.

The woman turned away from the bar for an instant to get a glass and Trip came after her. He jumped halfway over the bar, grabbed a handful of her hair and snatched her back toward him. She screamed as she hit hard against the rough wood on the edge of the bar. Trip grabbed her arm with his other hand and jerked her around where she was facing him. He turned her hair loose with his right hand and slapped her hard on the side of her face. The blow stunned her, almost knocking her out.

"I'm gonna teach you a lesson, bitch," he said as he drew back and hit her in the face with his fist. The blow burst her lip and blood flowed down her chin. He drew his arm back to hit her again.

Floyd stood up, his pistol in his hand at his side. "Turn the woman loose," he said in a loud voice.

Still holding the woman, Trip twisted around and looked at Floyd. He held the woman's arm with his left hand. "This ain't none of yo' damn business, injun. You better stay out of it."

Floyd stepped away from the table toward the bar. "I ain't gonna tell you again to let her go."

Trip turned her arm loose. At the same time, he turned to face Floyd and reached for his pistol with his right hand. The woman, semi-conscious, was unable to hold on to the bar and slumped to the floor.

Trip's pistol was halfway out of his belt when Floyd shot him in the chest. The force of the bullet knocked him back against the bar. He was stumbling and trying to get his balance to turn back toward

Floyd when the second bullet hit him in the neck. He was dead before he collapsed on the floor.

Floyd glanced toward the men at the other table. When they saw him look their way, they all held up their hands and sat back in their chairs.

Suddenly, the back door was flung open, and Whit rushed in, dragging the girl by the arm behind him. He had a pistol in his right hand as he came around the end of the bar. He looked at Trip's body lying on the floor in front of the bar and turned the girl loose. He glanced at the men at the other table and then turned toward Floyd. As he raised his pistol Floyd shot him in his chest. He put his hand on the bar to keep from falling and when he turned around Floyd killed him. He collapsed to the floor.

Shocked by the events, the girl stared down at Whit lying on the floor beside her and then looked across at Trip's body lying in front of the bar. She was wide-eyed and her face questioning as she turned and stared at Floyd. "You done kilt both of 'em," she said. She walked over to Trip's body, looked down and spat on him. "You sorry bastard," she screamed. "You needed to be kilt fir what you done to me."

She looked back at Floyd and started walking toward him. "I thank you fir killin' 'em," she said as she walked nearer to him. "You done saved me from 'em. I be goin' with you now and I gonna be yo' woman."

Floyd, surprised by her statement, shook his head. "I don't know who the hell you are, girl, or what you be talkin' bout, but you ain't goin' nowhere with me. I didn't kill 'em on account of you."

"I be Sister," she replied. "I be yo' woman now. That be the right thang fir me to do cause you done saved me."

Floyd shook his head as he stared at her. "I done told you that ain't gonna happen, girl. I be bout to leave here and you damn well ain't goin' with me."

The woman behind the bar got up holding her head and trying to gather her senses. She walked around the end of the bar, stared at the two bodies and looked at Floyd. "By God, you done a good day's work, mister, killin' them two. They was bad trouble." She walked over to him. "Ain't nobody gonna miss 'em. I be Nell. I owe you fir what you done."

He shook his head and looked at her and the girl. "I didn't want none of this to start with. Neither of y'all don't owe me nothin. Damn it, all I wanted was a drink." He started walking toward the door.

One of the men at the other table spoke up. "You had a right to kill 'em," he said. "We'll all back you up bout that when the law gits here."

Floyd looked at him. "You can say what you want to but I ain't waitin' for no law. I be leavin' right now and ain't nobody gonna stop me." He looked at the girl. "Ain't nobody goin' with me neither." He walked toward the door.

The girl ran after him. "I wanna go with you, mister. I ain't got no other place to go. I done been with a man, so I know about it. I can be yo' woman whatever you want."

Floyd looked at the woman who had said her name was Nell. "You want to do somethin' for me?" He pointed at the girl. "You take care of her and keep her the hell away from me."

Nell turned to Sister. "Where'd you come from, Sister?" she asked.

"I lived upriver with my folks till my mama died," said Sister, "then I runned away from home. My daddy sent them two to get me but they was bad to me." She stared at the bodies. "I be glad they be dead."

"You can stay here with me if you want to," said Nell.

Sister pointed at Floyd. "I want to go with 'im."

Nell laughed. "Hell, girl, I'd like to go with 'im too." She smiled as she looked at Floyd. "I'll keep 'er, she can help me."

"Don't matter with me," said Floyd, "as long as she's not with me."

"They had a boat," Sister said. "It be parked right outside. I can run it and follow you. I won't be no trouble and I can cook."

Floyd looked at Nell and then at Sister. "Damn it, girl, ain't you got no sense? You ain't goin' with me nowhere." He looked back at Nell. "She can sell the boat; it be hers now. Then she'll have some money. You look after her." He turned and walked out the door. He walked to the landing, got in his boat and looked back at the building to make sure the girl wasn't following him. Then he cranked up and headed up the river.

He rode for an hour, landed and pulled his boat up on the bank in some bushes. He watched downriver, half expecting the girl to show up, but she didn't. He set up his tarp and made camp.

Later he ate a cold supper of ham left over from breakfast, put down his bedroll and crawled in. As he lay on the hard ground, he thought about what had happened earlier. He didn't give a damn about shooting the two men. They had caused the trouble. What he regretted was that if they hadn't showed up, he would probably be in Nell's bed right now instead of sleeping on this riverbank.

2

Sister watched Floyd as he walked to his boat. He got in and headed up the river. She was tempted to go after him, but he had made it clear that he didn't want her with him. She would have to think on that later, but right now she had to do something. She looked back at Nell. "Who was that man?"

Nell shook her head. "Damn if I know. I ain't never seen 'im afore he come walkin' in the door." She grunted. "He be a sho'nuff bad son'abitch though. He done kilt them two fore they knew what was happenin'."

Nell walked over to the body of the man Sister had called Whit, picked up his pistol and laid it on the bar. She went through his pockets and put what money she found with the pistol. She looked at Sister and nodded toward the other body.

"Go through his pockets, Sister. What you find is yore's, he ain't gonna need it no more. I figger it be yore's the way they treated you. Pull off his boots too, we can sell 'em."

Sister didn't hesitate. She knelt beside the body and went through the pockets. When she pulled off the boots, she stepped back and held her nose. "Damn, he sho' stinks."

Nell looked at the three men sitting at the table. "Y'all drag these two outta here and throw 'em in the river. They be bleedin' all over my floor."

"Ain't you gonna call the law?" said one of the men.

Nell frowned. "Why would I do that? What the hell fir? They'll just come in here and start a fuss and ask me questions. I ain't got no time fir 'em. I don't know who these two be anyway. Hell, we don't even know who that man was what kilt 'em."

The man shook his head. "This don't seem right to just toss 'em in the river."

"Right?" said Nell, cutting her eyes at him. "Who gives a damn about what's right? They come in here and started trouble and got their ass kilt. There ain't no right." She glared at him. "Y'all drag these two asses outta here and dump 'em in the river fore I get mad and shoot yo' ass. When y'all git through I'll give you a drink."

The men jumped forward, picked up the legs of the two bodies, dragged them out the door and across the yard to the riverbank. Nell stood on the porch with Sister and watched them roll them into the water. Both bodies floated for a piece down the river and then sank.

The three men came back inside, and Nell poured them a drink. "I reckon y'all ought not say a damn word bout this," she said staring at them.

They all nodded, downed their drinks and went out the door. Nell turned to Sister. "What am I supposed to do with you?"

Sister shrugged. "I don't reckon you gotta do nothin' with me. I can look after myself."

Nell laughed. "Sho' you can. I done seen the mess you got in with them two men what brought you in here."

"They snuck up on me. I couldn't fight both of 'em, they be too strong."

"So, what do you do now?" said Nell, staring at her.

"I got their boat. I can go down the river cause ain't nobody after me now."

"You got any money?"

"I got four dollars out of Trip's pocket, and I got his boots and pistol."

Nell smiled. "Why don't you stay with me for a few days and then decide what you want to do? You can work for me and earn some money fir when you go down the river."

Sister thought as she looked at Nell. "I reckon I could do that. I ain't never worked in no place like this. I just worked on the farm."

"You got any more clothes?"

Sister shook her head. "I ain't got nothin' more. I run away and didn't have no time to git no clothes."

Nell walked over to the bar, reached underneath and handed Sister a bar of soap. "I got some clothes that oughta fit you. But fore I give you any clean clothes, you take this soap and wash off in the river. You're dirty and stink like a polecat. There's a towel on the porch. Go get cleaned up and wrap up in it. There ain't nobody around to see you naked so you wash all over. You might be right decent lookin' if you git all that dirt off you."

Sister took the soap, grabbed the towel and went to the landing. She stripped off her clothes and jumped in the water. She soaped up all over, rinsed off and climbed up the bank. She dried off, wrapped herself in the towel and walked back inside.

Nell pointed to a table. "I put clothes over there. You see what might fit you."

Sister walked over, tossed the towel aside and started looking through the clothes Nell had put out.

Nell stared at her standing there naked. "Damn girl. With that dirt off you be a sho'nuff good-lookin' woman. With a body like you got, you oughta not have no trouble findin' a man to look after you."

Sister cut her eyes at her. "I don't want no man to look after me. I be gonna look after myself." She walked over to where Nell was standing. "I saw that pistol you put in Trip's face and scared the hell outta 'im. I want to get me one of them pistols. You show me how to shoot it and ain't no man ever gonna bother me cept I want 'im to."

Nell laughed. "You got a lot to learn girl. You stay with me, and I'll show you bout thangs." She walked over and looked Sister over as she stood naked in front of her. "You stay with me and work here in the bar. When I dress you right and the men around here see you, business will pick up. You want to do that?"

Sister shrugged. "Don't matter to me. You tell me what to do."

~

Nell's forecast was correct, within a week her business had doubled. She dressed Sister in a short, tight dress with the front cut low. The outfit showed her body off with little left to the imagination and the reaction was immediate. Sister learned the business quickly. She took full advantage of the attention given her by the men she served. She didn't wear a bra and learned that bending over and showing her breasts got the men's attention. Allowing them to stuff tips down the front of her dress increased her income. She let them touch and fondle her as much as they wanted if they paid for the privilege. After what Trip and Whit had done to her, these men weren't a bother at all.

Nell had never paid attention to the way she dressed and looked, but after she saw Sister in action, she followed suit. She combed her hair, painted up and dressed to draw attention. Within a week she had two proposals of marriage and several requests to share her bed. She kept refusing these advances, but the offers kept going up until she was seriously considering expanding her business to include trips to the back room.

The attention Sister got from customers resulted in several fights and daily confrontations until Nell was forced to hire a local ruffian to keep order. Rufus, the new bouncer, had a reputation in the area for fighting and he was glad to get paid for what he had always done for free. He immediately fell in love with Sister and protected her as if he was her knight.

A local farm girl named Tillie heard about what was going on at Nell's place and came looking for a job. She figured anything would be better than milking cows and slopping hogs every day. Nell was glad to have her, since she and Sister now needed some help. Tillie wasn't as pretty as Sister, but she had ample endowments and the men weren't picky, so she did fine. She fit right in. She watched how Sister dressed and how she acted with the men, and she did the same. Later Nell converted a storeroom in the back of the building into a bedroom for Tillie. It wasn't long before Tillie was augmenting her income by having visitors for the night in her bed.

Sister saw what Tillie was doing but she continued to avoid any relationships although she had ample opportunities. While she was grateful to Nell for allowing her to stay and earn money, this life wasn't what she wanted. She knew there was another world out there and she wanted to see it. She also thought about the man that had saved her. She still felt indebted to him.

The next week Tillie brought her sister to Nell, and she was hired. With two other girls helping now, Sister felt it was time for her to leave. She told Nell how she felt; Nell understood and told her to do what she wanted.

The next morning Sister hugged Nell and Tillie, got her few belongings and loaded them in the boat. She got in, looked upriver and then downriver, not sure which way she should go. Finally, she cranked the motor and left the landing.

3

F loyd Wimms left Nell's place and headed upriver. He was born thirty-three years earlier in a cabin on the Chattahoochee River just south of the cotton mill town of River Bluff, Alabama. His family was worse than dirt poor, they had nothing. His daddy tried to eke out a living catfishing but did poorly, hardly making enough to keep himself in whiskey.

Floyd's mother died when he was eight and his life went from bad to worse. Without any guidance at home, he was headed for a life of crime and jail when he met two young men from River Bluff. He met them when they caught him stealing fishing gear out of their boat. Jim Hawke, one of the men, took off his belt right then and gave him a whipping that he never forgot.

They gave him a choice, either act as they told him, or they would turn him over to the town constable. He agreed to do as they wanted him to.

Jim and his friend, John Gill were some years older, but they took him under their wing and after that day, he was their constant companion. If he got out of line, they didn't hesitate to discipline him. Before long he wasn't a problem.

Jim lived on an island on the river. He fished for a living and did well, mainly fishing baskets for catfish. Basket fishing was illegal, but many people did it. Despite his vocation, he was well thought of by the people in town.

John Gill was different. His family owned the mill and the town, so they were well off. John's daddy didn't want him to feel that he was better than the regular mill folk, so he sent him to the local school instead of to a boarding school as he had done. Since John was involved in the town's regular life as an equal, he was accepted. This would help him later when he took over the leadership at the mill.

As Floyd grew up, having these two to guide him kept him out of serious trouble. Jim Hawke was his main mentor since he lived on the river and that life was what Floyd wanted. Jim taught him all he knew about the river. Floyd was a good student and soaked up the knowledge.

Floyd's life changed when he was drafted in the army at age eighteen in the midst of World War One. He had never been ten miles away from home before then. He went to boot camp for training and soon after was sent to the trenches in France. Here he saw part of the hell of war. He saw people killed, he killed people and he was good at it. When he returned to River Bluff, he was no longer the innocent youth he had been when he left. Like many of the other young returning veterans of the war he was wilder than a goat and he quickly earned a reputation as a troublemaker.

He was a good-looking young man. He had learned about women in France, and he brought that learning home with him. Soon after he returned home several fathers told him to stay away from their house and their daughters.

After a while he grew tired of working in the mill and the life in River Bluff, got in his boat and headed upriver. He ended up in the mountains of North Carolina and stayed with the Cherokees for two winters. He liked that life and was headed back there now.

During his latest return to town, he'd had an experience that still stayed with him. He'd met a young woman that he had known years earlier. Their first meeting had been when he returned from the army and hadn't gone well for him.

She was a young schoolteacher and had just arrived in River Bluff. She'd recently graduated from college, and it was her first teaching job. She was from a quiet town in north Alabama. Floyd was standing in the middle of town with some of his buddies when he saw her for the first time. She was walking to the dormitory where the women teachers lived and passed in front of the crowd. She was pretty and Floyd decided to be cute and impress his friends.

Alva Tinney had passed this group on another occasion and remembered the crude comments and whistles directed at her as she walked past. She had not wanted to run the gauntlet again but had no choice. She hoped they wouldn't notice her but that wasn't the case. When she heard the first comment, she started walking faster but then Floyd was standing in front of her.

She was already nervous but now she was terrified. By nature, a shy person, she'd never in all her life faced a man like Floyd. He grinned suggestively at her and told her in his crude way that he'd decided she was the woman for him. He went on to say that if she'd go with him in his car, they'd go to the river and park.

Alva heard no more. She burst into tears, pushed past him and ran all the way to the dormitory. She went in her room and didn't come out for two days.

Floyd watched her run away crying, shrugged and went back with his buddies. He didn't care how she'd reacted to his attention. He thought nothing more about it.

Several days later he again saw her coming out the street and walked out to meet her. When she saw him coming, she turned and ran the other way. He wondered what was wrong with her. Women didn't normally act that way with him.

After several years, their second meeting had occurred recently. He came back to River Bluff for the first time in years and had no place to stay. John Gill gave him a room in the dormitory for a few days. The room was down the hall from Alva's room. He came out of his room and Alva was coming toward him. He recognized her immediately and was struck with how attractive she was. She was older now and looked even better than she had when younger.

She didn't recognize him and wondered what a man was doing in the dormitory, only women lived here. Floyd was older now, had long hair and a beard so it was understandable that she didn't know him. "What are you doing in the dormitory?" she asked. As always, she was friendly but concerned.

"I'll be staying here for a few days," he answered. "I just got into town and John Gill let me stay here."

Alva nodded. If John Gill had allowed him to stay here, then he must be all right. She noticed he was a nice-looking man despite the long hair and beard.

Floyd saw that she had no idea who he was. "You don't recognize me, do you Alva?"

She was puzzled, she was sure she'd never seen him. She shook her head. "I don't. Have I met you before?"

"I'm Floyd Wimms, Alva. I met you years ago."

Alva did remember him. She remembered standing in the middle of the street and him offering to take her to the river and park. All the hurt and embarrassment she'd felt then boiled over in her mind. Her face reddened and her lips tightened as she stared in his face. She nodded. "I do remember you," she said. "You're the most despicable, hateful man I've never known. I don't know where you've been all these years, but I wish you'd stayed there." She turned, ran to her room and slammed the door.

Floyd was dumbfounded. He searched his brain for what he'd done that was so terrible she would have remembered it all these years. Later he mentioned to his friend, Walt that he wanted to talk to Alva and clear up whatever problem he had with her.

Walt shook his head and laughed. "You trying to get Miss Alva to like you? You better pick out somebody else. She's a straight arrow and you ain't got a chance with her, not with yo' reputation. Miss Alva's a lady. She goes to church ever Sunday, she don't drink and ain't gonna be around them that do." He smiled as he looked at Floyd. "Look at yo' long hair and scraggly beard and dirty clothes. Them river women you run with ain't like Miss Alva." He chuckled. "You better get cleaned up and start going to church if you want to talk to her. Otherwise, you ain't got no prayer."

After some thought, Floyd decided to take Walt's advice. He went to the barber shop, got a haircut and his beard trimmed. Then he went to the general store and bought nice clothes. Lastly, he went to the drugstore and bought Alva a present. The next time he saw her he was dressed nicely, apologized for what he'd done and gave her the present.

It took several such times before she would talk to him. Finally, she relented and went to the movie with him. He had been on his best behavior, and after several dates she allowed him to kiss her but stopped him when his hands started to wander. She knew his reputation with women.

Alva made it clear to him that they had no future without marriage. She was not going to live on the river but in town. Also, she went to church every Sunday and would expect him to do the same. He would have to stop drinking. If he wanted to get in her bed, these were the rules.

He liked her more than any woman he'd ever been with. He might even be *in love* with her. But her demands and requirements as to how he should act were too much and sadly he walked away. Soon afterward he got with another woman and that's when the shooting started.

Floyd was two weeks upriver from Nell's place when he rounded a bend and saw a ferry barge in the middle of the river. It was attached to a cable that ran across the river from the right bank to the left bank. A car was loaded on it and being slowly carried across. He slowed down and watched. The barge reached the bank and the car drove off.

He saw buildings and houses on the right side of the river, looking like a small town. He needed supplies so he landed, tied up his boat and walked up the bank to the road. There was a building that seemed to be a general store up the street, so he walked to it. Up the street on the right side was another building with a sign out front that said, Tub's – Beer and Whiskey. That sign reminded him that he hadn't had a drink since he left Nell's place so that had priority. He would come back and get supplies later.

He walked on up to Tub's and went in. It was a typical beer joint but larger than Nell's place. There were two men sitting at a table and one at the bar. As he walked across the floor, he thought back to what had happened at Nell's and decided he'd get a quick drink and be gone. The men at the table were already looking at his outfit and making comments.

He ordered a beer, stood at the bar, drank it and ordered another. The bartender eyed him but didn't comment. He took the beer, walked to the end of the bar and sat on a stool where he could see the entire room.

He was halfway finished with the beer when a door behind the bar opened, and a woman came out. She saw Floyd and headed for him. She was dressed as most women in these type joints dressed, showing as much of her body as she could. She walked up to him and leaned over the bar. She was older than most and somewhat attractive.

"Want to buy me a drink, honey?" she said.

Floyd stared at her and shook his head. "I got to go. I be just finishing this beer," he said.

She frowned. "What's the matter with you. You thank you're too good to drink with me?"

He looked at her, reached in his pocket and took out a bill. "I don't want no trouble," he said as he tucked the bill in the front of her dress. He stared in her eyes. "I ain't got time to stay with you but if you say another word, I'm gonna wreck this place and you with it." He put his hand on his pistol in his belt and took the last swallow of the beer. "Now you step aside and don't say nothin' else." He stood up, his eyes on her face.

Wide-eyed, she stared up at him. "I didn't mean nothin' by it," she said. "I was just bein' friendly."

He nodded, walked past her and went out the door.

She looked at the bartender. "Did you hear what that bastard said to me?"

F loyd walked down the street to the general store, went inside and bought a few supplies. He didn't speak to another person as he walked back to the boat. The ferry was docked right above his boat and an old man was sitting in a chair and eyeing him.

"I ain't seen you before," he said. "You just come upriver?"

Floyd looked up at him as he put the supplies in the boat. "Just got here." He said.

The old man leaned over and spat tobacco juice in the water. "You plannin' to go on upriver?"

Floyd nodded. "That be what I be planning on doin'."

"How fir you be goin'?"

"All the way to the mountains," said Floyd.

The old man laughed. "That be a long ways."

Floyd threw up his hand at him, cranked up and headed up the river.

T wo days later he rounded a bend and saw a large dock and buildings on the right bank of the river. He was surprised, this hadn't been here the last time he came down the river. There were two large boats, similar to tugboats he'd seen at ocean ports where he'd been, tied up at the dock.

There were several men, black and white, loading sacks and boxes on these boats. It seemed to be a large operation. As he neared the dock, he saw a two-story southern plantation home sitting atop a hill a hundred yards from the river. The porch stretching across the front had large white columns like he'd seen on such houses in Virginia. He'd noticed this house in the past but had not stopped and looked at it. It was impressive and he wondered what it was doing here in the backwoods of Georgia.

He beached the boat on the bank below the dock and got out. He was ready for a break and wanted to find out what all this activity was about. He walked up on the end of the dock and noticed a man watching him intently. This struck Floyd as odd. He seemed to the in charge of the workers but now his attention was directed at him. The man walked toward him, stopped and looked him up and down. "How about you stand right there till I get back," he said, his eyes on Floyd's face.

Floyd stared at him, wondering what he was talking about. He'd never seen him before.

The man turned, hurriedly went to the building and went inside. Shortly he came out the door with a young woman walking behind him. He pointed at Floyd and said something to the woman.

She looked at Floyd, nodded her head and thanked the man.

Floyd was puzzled as to what was going on.

The woman walked toward Floyd. "We've been watching for you," she said. "We figured you'd get here eventually."

Floyd didn't know what to say; he'd never seen this woman and wondered why she'd been watching for him. He frowned as he looked at her.

She smiled when she saw his confusion. "You don't have any idea what I'm talking about, do you?"

He shook his head. "I sho' don't."

"A rider came here several days back and told me that a man dressed like an Indian had killed two men downriver at Nell's place. He said the two men were mistreating a girl, this man came to her defense and the shooting started." She looked at him. "You're dressed sort of like an Indian, with the leather and beads, so I figure you are the man from Nell's place. Am I right?"

Floyd hesitated. She was asking him to admit he'd killed two men. He didn't know where this was leading or why she was so interested in him. "Why you be lookin' for me and why you be askin' me all these questions?"

She laughed and held out her hand. "I'm Virginia Mann. I'm sure

I have confused you but when I heard the story about the shooting, I thought you might be a man I wanted to talk to."

He watched her face as he shook her hand. Standing this close to her he saw that she was a beautiful woman. However, all she'd said to this point didn't make any sense to him. If she knew that he'd shot those men, why would she want to talk to him? He frowned and looked at her. "I don't know what you be talkin' bout."

"My family owns this farm," she said. "My father, who has run it for many years, has had a heart attack and is not in good health. So, the job has fallen to me to keep everything going. There's no one else to help me."

Floyd kept his eyes on her face as she talked. He understood what she was saying but had no idea why she was telling him all this. He knew he didn't have anything to do with whatever she was talking about.

"When I heard this about you, and what you did, I sent a man to talk to Nell. She said she'd never seen you before and had no idea who you were, but you weren't a man to fool with. She'd seen you in action and knew what you can do. She also said that after the shooting, you were concerned about the girl's welfare. You acted honestly about her future. Nell was impressed with you."

Floyd shook his head. "I hear what you be saying but why do you care bout what I done? I ain't really been proud of it myself."

"There are people that are trying to take advantage of me with my father sick. Some of these people are bad people and will do anything. I'm alone here and need somebody that I can depend on to back me up. I need a strong person on my side. I realize this sounds strange since I don't know anything about you, but I'd like to talk to you and see if you could be that person." She paused. "What is your name?"

Floyd shook his head. "I ain't trying to be rude or nothin', but this be bout the craziest thang I've ever heard of. I shot 'em two men at Nell's place cause I didn't like the way they was doin' that girl. They drawed on me. But that don't make me nothin' like what you be wantin'. I'm goin' up the river and winter with the Cherokees. I don't know nothin' bout yo' troubles but they ain't my troubles."

Virginia nodded. "I agree it's crazy, but I don't have much choice. I thought there might be a chance you would fit in." She smiled. "Would you at least tell me your name and where you're from?"

Floyd didn't like being questioned. He rubbed his hand across his face as he looked at her. "I be Floyd Wimms and I come from a little town downriver called River Bluff. There ain't much else to know bout me."

"That's so strange," she said. "I know about River Bluff. I have a friend from Atlanta that I went to school with named Karen Hogan. Her family owns Shoal Creek. It's a farm across the river from River Bluff. I've been to Shoal Creek with her."

Floyd, surprised at this news, stared at her. "I know Karen Hogan. I did some fishing for Shoal Creek and met her over there."

"Let me ask you this, Floyd," her eyes watching his face. "Will you have supper with my daddy and me tonight and at least talk about what I've said?"

He stared at her as he thought about what she was asking. He wasn't sure what her problems were, but he'd always tried to stay out of other people's troubles.

She saw his hesitation. "I tell you what. You've been living on the river for a while and probably could use a night sleeping in a real bed. I have a guest house up the hill and you can stay in it for tonight or longer if you wish. You can get a bath and have a real meal too. Regardless of what happens, that should be something you would like."

Floyd nodded. A bath, a good home-cooked meal and a night in a real bed did sound good. He could do that and then leave tomorrow. He nodded. "That sounds good to me."

She smiled and again he was impressed with how attractive she was. "Get your things and I'll show you to the house." She stopped and looked at him, staring at his outfit. "I'm not trying to pry but do you have clothes other than what you have on?"

He pursed his lips and nodded. "I have some more clothes."

"I didn't mean any offense, but what you're wearing is sort of strange, with all the leather and beads."

"Several people have told me that," he said.

She laughed. "I would think so."

"You said you been lookin' for a man that was at Nell's place dressed like a injun. Them folks at Nell's remembered me fir the way I be dressed." He looked at her. "They remembered what I done, and they told other people bout me."

She nodded. "So, the man dressed like a injun, as you say it, is somebody they don't want to fool with. You have that reputation."

"That be it. When folks see me, they leave me alone."

She nodded. "I understand. However, you've been on the river for a while, and I doubt you.ve done much bathing. You're dirty and you smell. I'll send a woman over to get your dirty clothes and wash them. When they're clean, you can wear what you want."

"I thank you," he said. Then he walked to his boat, got his belongings and followed her up the hill to the guest house. It sat across the street in front of the big house. She got to the house, opened the front door and went inside.

"You make yourself at home," she said. "I'll give you time to get ready and then I'll knock on the door for supper." She turned and walked away.

He watched her leave and wondered why she didn't have a man to look after her. With her looks he figured she could have whoever she wanted. He went through the house. The house was nicer than anything he'd been in in a long time. He stored his gear and found the bathroom. He bathed and then dressed in the clothes he'd worn the last time he'd gone out with Alva.

He walked in the front room and sat in a nice soft chair. He thought about what had happened and what was happening. He still had no idea how all this had come about but at the moment he was going to enjoy it. It surely was better than sleeping on the ground on the riverbank.

4

S ister sat in the boat at Nell's landing. She looked downriver and
then up, trying to decide what her next move should be. She
knew there was a small settlement downriver about two days away.
That was where she was when Trip and Whit found her. She had no
idea what was below that point.

She turned and looked upriver. Her daddy's place was in that
direction. He had sent the two bastards after her and she would never
forgive him for doing that. She had the pistol Nell had given her and
Nell had taught her how to shoot it. She had thought about returning
home and facing her daddy. The thought of shooting him had
crossed her mind more than once. The more she thought about it
and remembered what Trip had done to her, the more she thought it
should be done.

Then she thought about the man that saved her. He was
somebody that she would like to be with; he was a real man. If she
was with him, she would be his woman and he would look after her.
That was what she wanted. She made her decision, cranked the
motor and started upriver. She knew that he had started over a week
ahead of her, and she'd have to hurry to catch him.

As she rode, she thought about the injun, that was how she

thought of him now. He said he was heading to the mountains and planned to winter with the Cherokees. Her plan was to catch up with him. He would be camping alone on the river and once she found him, she would do whatever necessary to get with him.

Dealing with the men at Neal's place had shown that men liked her. Nell had told her that she was pretty and numerous men had proven that to be true. Most every night men had offered her money to be with them in the back room. She felt that when she caught up with the injun and offered to get in his bed, he wouldn't refuse her.

T hree days later she reached her daddy's place. It was midday; the sun was straight overhead. She hadn't seen any sign of the injun but she hadn't expected to this soon; he was still several days ahead of her. She landed, tied up and walked toward the house. She had the pistol in her hand but hadn't decided what she would do when she saw her daddy.

She walked up on the porch, pushed the front door open and peered inside. The front room was empty. She heard pans rattling in the back of the house toward the kitchen. She held the pistol by her side and walked down the hall toward the noise. She peered around the doorframe. A woman was standing at the stove on the far side of the room. She was taking a skillet of cornbread out of the oven. The smell filled the room and Sister remembered she hadn't eaten since yesterday.

She recognized the woman; Gert Body was her name. She lived about a mile away on the road toward town. Her family had a place there where they raised chickens. Gert was about thirty or so, ugly and skinny as a rail. Sister had never known her to have a boyfriend, but with her here cooking in her daddy's house, it seemed she'd done got him.

"What you be doing' here, Gert?" she asked as she stepped in the room.

Surprised by the noise, Gert wheeled about and stared at Sister. "Damn, Sister," she said as she set the skillet on the stove. "You done bout scared me to death. Where'd you come from?" As she said that she saw the pistol in her hand. "What you doin' with that there gun?"

Sister ignored her question. "What are you doin' here?"

"I be with yo' daddy now," she said. "I be his woman now."

Sister shook her head. "Both of you are sho' nuff bad off," she said. "Where does daddy be?"

Gert's eyes were on the pistol. "He be out in back." Her eyes came up to Sister's face. "How come you got that gun?"

"I intend to shoot his sorry ass," said Sister as she turned and walked out of the kitchen. She walked to the back door, opened it and stepped outside in the yard. She could hear Gert screaming behind her. Then Gert walked out behind her and stood by the door

She saw her daddy walking toward the house from the barn. He had a bucket in his hand. He stopped when he saw Sister. She could see the surprise on his face as he stared at her.

Sister raised the pistol and fired. The bullet knocked up dirt beside her daddy's foot.

"Sister, what the hell are you doin'?" he said as he dropped the bucket. "You bout shot me."

Sister shook her head. "If I wanted to shoot you, you'd be dead right now. I owe you for sending Trip and Whit after me and what the sorry bastards done to me."

"You oughta not run off," he said. He looked around. "Did they brang you back?"

She shook her head. "They didn't brang me back and they ain't comin' back cause they be dead," she said. "They done got their selves kilt."

"They be dead, both of 'em?" he said, his face showing the confusion he felt. He stared at the pistol. "Did you kill 'em?"

"I didn't kill 'em," she said, "but I sho' wanted to. I be glad they be dead."

"How come you come back if they be dead?"

"I come back to git my clothes and stuff." She pointed the pistol at him. "If'n you say one word to me I'll damn well shoot you too. You ain't nothin' but a sorry piece of trash. I be leaving when I git my stuff and if you send any more folks after me, I'll come back and shoot yo' sorry ass."

"How you gonna be goin anywhere?"

"I got Trip's boat. It be mine now." She looked at him. "The man what kilt Trip give it to me."

He picked up the bucket and walked toward her. "That be up to you. I ain't gonna bother you no more. I don't give a damn where you go or what you do. You weren't nothin' but trouble when you was here."

"I got fried chicken and sweet potatoes ready," said Gert. "You want to eat somethin'?"

Sister looked at her. "I gotta go upriver. Put me some chicken, potatoes and a piece of cornbread in a sack and I'll take it with me."

Gert nodded and ran in the kitchen.

Sister went to her room and packed her clothes in an old suitcase. She didn't have much. She picked up the suitcase, got her pillow and went to the kitchen. Her daddy and Gert were sitting at the table eating.

Gert got up and went to the stove. She handed her a sack and a fruit jar filled with tea. "I done what you wanted," she said.

"Thank you, Gert," she said. She turned and looked at her daddy. "You be lucky I didn't shoot you fir what you done to me. You ever bother me again and I will."

Her daddy looked up at her and took a bite of a chicken leg. "Don't matter to me what you do. You can go to hell for all I care."

Sister reached in her pocket, pulled out the pistol and pointed it in his face. Tightlipped, she stood staring in his eyes, her hand holding the pistol was quivering. "Say that one more time, you bastard and you be a dead man."

"Don't say nothin', Erk," said Gert. "She sho' means it."

Her daddy sat staring at her, chewing on the fried chicken.

Sister held the gun on him for a moment, then lowered it. She turned and walked out the front door. She walked to the water, loaded what she had in the boat and headed upriver.

5

F loyd was half-asleep in the chair when Virginia knocked. He jumped up and opened the door.

She looked in his face, then her eyes looked him over, down to his shoes. She smiled. "I'm impressed, you clean up good."

He stepped outside and closed the door. "Amazin' what a little soap and water can do," he said as he fell in beside her walking toward the big house.

She stopped and stared in his face. "You can go on talking like a hillbilly if you want to, Floyd. I know you're much smarter than that." She pursed her lips. "You said you knew Karen Hogan, so I called her this afternoon and asked about you. I wanted you to know that. I wanted to be honest with you."

He nodded. "You want me to leave fore supper?"

Virginia laughed. "No, Karen was nice about you. She said you were as I had thought you were. She said you were tough but honest and I could trust you. She said you could do what I'm asking you to do."

Floyd looked at her and waited. He didn't think she'd said all she was going to say.

She stared in his face. "Also, she said you have a reputation with women and you ain't housebroke."

He chuckled. "You can't believe everythang you hear, especially from a woman, but she's right about not bein' housebroke. I ain't never much liked livin' in a house."

She smiled and tucked her hand under his arm as they walked. "I think we can take care of that," she said.

He was aware of her warm hand on his arm.

When they got to the front door, she again looked in his face. "My father, as I told you, is not well. He once was a strong energetic man, but his heart attack changed him. He still has his mind so don't underestimate him as he talks. He just tires easily."

Floyd nodded that he understood.

She opened the door, led him inside and across the room to the dining room. Her daddy was already sitting at the head of a long mahogany table.

"This is my father, William Mann, Floyd," she said.

"Glad to meet you, sir" Floyd said as he shook his hand.

"Virginia and I are glad to have you in our house," he replied. He motioned for Floyd to sit on his left and Virginia sat on Mr. Mann's right.

"Virginia says you come from downriver at River Bluff."

"Yes, sir. I do.

"I met a man one time in Atlanta that owned a cotton mill in River Bluff. As I remember his name was John Gill."

Floyd nodded. "I know John well."

Mr. Mann looked at Virginia. "Let's eat supper and then we'll talk for a few minutes." He looked at Floyd. "We're having quail. I hope that suits you."

Floyd nodded. "I've been on the river for four weeks, sleeping on the riverbank. I couldn't think of anything better."

Virginia got up and walked out. In a minute two ladies brough out platters of quail, white rice and brown gravy with a platter of biscuits. The ladies poured sweet, iced tea in his glass. Floyd had never seen anything that looked so good.

They ate with little conversation. Afterward the ladies came and cleaned everything off the table.

Mr. Mann looked at Floyd. "Before I got sick, I could have handled the challenges we're dealing with, but I can't now. That responsibility has been given to Virginia. She's very capable but there are some areas she can't handle. That's where you could come in, if you're willing to do so." He looked at her. "I'm going to let her tell you what is needed and then you can decide for yourself what you want to do."

Floyd nodded and looked at Virginia.

"We have two main problems, Floyd," she said. "These times are tough here in the midst of a depression, so the farm is hard pressed to make a profit. We've had to borrow money in the past and the bank wants to foreclose on our loan and take over the land. Our neighbor that joins us is land locked. He wants to get our land, so he'd have access to the river. Both are doing their best to ruin us."

Floyd listened to what she said but he was puzzled. "How are they doin' that?"

"We farm, raise cattle and ship goods to Atlanta down the river. Recently we've had fences cut, cattle in our corn fields and cattle missing. In addition, we've had two boats sunk. All of this is not by accident."

"Don't sound like it," said Floyd. "Tell me about the folks that own the farm that's land locked."

"Charlie Hurt is the owner, he's about sixty. He has a son, Ron, he's about my age." She frowned. "Years back we dated, in fact he asked me to marry him, and I refused. He didn't like it but hasn't given up. He still calls me."

"What about the bank? I ain't never heard of a bank cuttin' fences and sinkin' boats before," said Floyd, looking at Mr. Mann.

"Never have I," said Mr. Mann, "but it is locally owned. The family that owns the bank have been ruthless in the past about foreclosing on people. Many folks are bitter about the way they were treated. They have taken over several farms in the past year."

Floyd looked back at Virginia. "You said you wanted to talk to me cause I shot two people down at Nell's place." He stared at her. "Now which of these people do you want me to shoot?"

Her face reddened. She was about to say something when Mr. Mann laughed. "He got you that time, girl."

She smiled and looked at Floyd. "It was never my intent that you shoot anybody, I'll have you know." She looked at Mr. Mann. "Daddy, I think we've talked long enough, and I don't want to wear you out. Let me talk to Floyd more and I'll let you know in the morning where we are."

"I think that's good," he replied as he looked at Floyd. "It was good to meet you, Floyd. You work everything out with Virginia."

Floyd got up. "Thank you, sir," he said. "I'll do that." He looked at Virginia.

She got up and started to the door. Floyd fell in behind her and they walked outside.

"Daddy likes you," she said, "and he's very careful about who he likes."

"I like 'im," said Floyd. "He seems like a good man."

They walked to the guest house. "It's been a long day," she said. "If you want to join me for breakfast at seven, I'll come get you."

Floyd nodded. "Suits me."

Virginia turned and went to the big house. Floyd watched her till she went inside. He went inside and went to bed. It was the first time in a month he wasn't sleeping on the ground.

She knocked on the door at seven. She looked at him as he walked out the door, her eyes again on his outfit. "You still look strange dressed like that," she said, "but at least you're clean."

He didn't comment but followed her to the big house. They ate breakfast, got in a truck and she took him over the farm. It was almost noon when they got back to the house. They ate lunch and she took him out on the patio.

"You've seen the farm," she said. She looked in his face. "What questions do you have?"

"I know you talked to Karen bout me, but you don't really know me. Karen don't really know me neither," he said. "I've done a lot in my life that I ain't real proud of. I had a woman friend named Lizzie. She grew up rough and never had much chance, but I liked her. She was my friend." He looked at her. "She ran a beer joint and a whorehouse in a swamp on the river. Some men tried to rob her one night while I was there. I kilt one of 'im and run the others off. That night the daddy of the boy I kilt come in on Lizzie. They kilt her man and hanged her naked in a tree."

"That's terrible," said Virginia, her eyes on his face.

"I found out where them folks lived. I kilt the daddy and two of his boys for what they'd done to Lizzie." He stopped and stared at Virginia. "I ain't never been a good person, Virginia. That be the kind of man I be. I wanted you to understand bout me."

She nodded. "I'm not shocked by what you just said, Floyd. Karen told me about that. She didn't sugarcoat anything about you. She also told me that you were in the army in the war."

"He nodded. "I was in France. I was in the war."

"These are hard times and when you're dealing with bad people, you have to do whatever's necessary. I don't fault you for what you've done." She patted his arm. "I want you to help me if you will."

Floyd took a deep breath. "I'll stay a week and we'll see what happens, then we'll talk again. I ain't sure about all this but I'll stay here right now."

"Fair enough," she said. "Let me take you around and introduce you to the people that work on the farm, so they'll know who you are." She cut her eyes at him. "Otherwise, somebody might shoot you thinking they gonna be scalped."

Floyd looked at her but didn't comment. He was still trying to figure out what he was doing here. He was also having a hard time figuring out Virginia. He liked her, but he always liked good-looking women.

She took him around the farm and the dock and introduced him to several people. She told them his name was Floyd, he was going to be at the farm for a while and that was all she told them. When they looked at Floyd's unsmiling face, saw how he was dressed and the pistol stuck in his belt, they didn't ask any questions. They knew the Manns had brought in a gunfighter. It wouldn't take long for the word to get out in the community that he was here.

6

After two nights sleeping in the boat Sister realized that she had problems. She wasn't prepared for living outside on the river and knew that she couldn't survive like this. She had to find a store and get supplies. All she'd brought with her other than clothes were a boiler and a coffee pot.

Later that morning she came to a bridge over the river with a few houses and a general store with a gas pump nearby. She landed, got the gas can and walked up the road. She got to the store and set the can down by the gas pump. When she turned around, she saw two young boys sitting in rocking chairs on the right side of porch. They looked to be maybe eighteen or so and they were watching her. She walked up the steps to the front door. She could feel their eyes on her. As she walked past them, one made a comment to the other and they laughed.

She had seen their kind hanging around stores before and it usually meant trouble. She glanced at them and went inside. Both were dressed in dirty ragged clothes, scraggly uncombed hair and in need of a bath.

The store layout inside was as they usually were, groceries on one side and dress goods on the other side. She talked to the owner, an old gray-haired man of unknown age. He walked with her down the aisles as she bought several items. These included a small tarp and a raincoat plus drinks and canned goods. She went out the door to the pump and filled the gas can. The two were still sitting in the rocking chairs and were watching her every move. She was aware of them as she went about her business.

She went back in the store, paid for what she bought and walked out holding two large sacks. The two young men were standing at the gas pump, one was holding her gas can.

She stopped when she saw them. "That's my can," she said.

"You can't carry all this," one of them said. "We gonna help you carry it to the river."

"I thank you, but I can get it myself."

He shook his head and looked at the other boy. "Hell, Ike, it wouldn't be right for a pretty girl like her to carry all this when we can help."

Ike laughed and shook his head in agreement

She didn't want to start trouble here at the store. It would help to get the heavy can to the boat, so she decided to let them carry it. That would keep her from making two trips. When they got to the boat, she'd handle them there. "All right," she said, "if you want to."

Ike came over and took one of the packages from her. He grinned as he took the sack and ran his hand over her arm.

They walked from the store down the road to the bridge. Sister kept them in front of her. She wanted to keep them in front where she could watch them. They walked down to the riverbank.

"That's a mighty nice boat you got there," said the one with the gas can as he put it in the boat. "I wish I had me a boat like this." He stood in the boat and grinned at her. "We helped you girl; now it's time you be nice to us. You didn't thank we done this for free?"

Ike threw down the sack he'd been carrying. "Yeah," he said, as he stepped toward her. "We ain't gonna let you get away till we have some fun. You know what we want."

Sister had her hand in her purse. She pulled out the pistol and shot Ike in the foot. He screamed, fell to the ground and grabbed his foot. She turned toward the one in the boat. "Get the hell outta my boat," she said.

He held up his hands as he looked at his partner lying on the ground holding his leg and writhing in pain. "Damn it, girl, you shot 'im."

She held the gun on him and nodded. "I shot 'im and I'm gonna shoot you too if you don' git outta my boat."

He stepped out on the bank, his eyes on her. She could see the fear in his face.

"Pick up that sack he dropped and put it in the boat," she said.

He ran over, picked up the sack and put it in the boat. He looked back at her.

She waved the pistol at him. "Git 'im up and y'all git up the bank. You better not stop."

He helped Ike up and they staggered up the bank toward the bridge.

When they got to the bridge she got in the boat, cranked up and started up the river. She felt better about everything. She was better equipped for the trip; she had dealt with her first threat, and she had a pistol. Despite all that, she knew that a woman traveling alone on the river was at risk. She would have to be careful and stay on her guard. Next time it might not be young boys after her.

Virginia Mann watched Floyd as they traveled the farm and met the people. He had a quiet confidence about him that convinced her that he was the man she needed to help her. Despite knowing he was a killer, a womanizer and probably without any morals, she liked him. Also, against her better judgement, she was drawn to him. Maybe it was the moth being attracted to the flame type of feeling but there was an attraction. So far to this point he had made no move toward her, he'd been a perfect gentleman. These thoughts she felt seemed to be hers alone.

That afternoon he came out of the guest house with a rifle. He had an empty bucket in his other hand. "I want to show you somethin'," he said as they got in the truck. "This is a 1903 Springfield 30-06 rifle. I used it in the army."

She looked at the rifle. It had a scope mounted on the top. She had seen rifles but never one like this.

When they went through a gate. he asked her to stop. He got out and put the bucket on top of a fencepost and got back in the truck. "Ride down the road a piece till I tell you to stop."

She nodded and started down the road. "Stop here," he said after they had gone several hundred yards. He looked at her. "Get out with me."

They got out. She walked around the truck to his side. "We be about 800 yards away from the bucket," he said.

She looked down the road to where the bucket was but had no idea about the distance, she'd have to take his word for it. She watched as he propped up on the truck's fender, brought the rifle to his shoulder and aimed in the direction of the bucket. He eased forward and in a moment he fired.

Virginia jumped at the report but kept her eye on the bucket as it flew off the fence post.

He looked at her.

She nodded. "That is impressive."

"I wanted you to know that I know what I'm doin'."

She smiled. "I never doubted it."

They got back in the truck. "I want to meet the folks that own the farm that might be givin' y'all the trouble," he said.

"I'll take you over there."

"I want to go with you to the bank too."

She glanced at him. "We can do that too."

"I want to know the people you be dealing with."

She nodded. "I think that would be a good idea."

They rode on back toward the farm.

"It ain't any of my business," said Floyd, "but you said that son, Ron, asked you to marry 'im and you said no."

She looked at him wondering where he was headed with this. "I told you that. Why are you asking?"

"Man asks a woman to marry 'im and she say no, that might piss a man off." He stared at her.

She stopped the truck and looked straight in his face. "It might but what is your point?"

"I thought maybe he was just getting' even with you."

"Have you ever asked a woman to marry you and she turned you down?"

Floyd shook his head. "Never have."

"So, you've never been in love and wanted to marry a woman?"

"I didn't say that" he said. "I said I didn't never ask no woman to marry me."

She took a deep breath. "That makes no sense."

"Does to me."

"Why did you ask about Ron?"

"Wondered what sort of fellow he is."

"He's nice looking and smart."

"But you didn't want to marry 'im," he said. "That strikes me as strange."

She frowned and looked at him. "Why do you think it's strange?"

"Man asks a woman to marry 'im, he probably thanks she gonna say yes."

Tightlipped, she looked at him. "What the hell are you getting at?"

Floyd saw that she was riled. "I ain't gettin' at nothin'."

"Are you saying that in some way I did something to encourage him? That I did something that made him think I would agree to marry him?"

He shook his head. "I didn't say that."

"You insinuated that I did. What do you think I did that would have done that?"

"When did I do that?"

"I'm not stupid," she said. She put the truck in gear and started off. "I'm not talking to you about this anymore." They rode back to the house in silence. She parked and got out.

He opened the door got out and looked at her.

"You be ready in the morning, and I'll take you to meet Ron. You can ask him what I did to encourage him." She turned and walked to the house.

Floyd watched her go. She seemed to be upset. He shrugged, went in the house and went to bed.

F loyd had just finished his coffee when she knocked. When he opened the door, she was already in the truck. He walked around, opened the door and got in. He glanced at her. She was staring straight ahead.

She put the truck in gear and went out the gate.

"Seems like I said somethin' last night that made you mad," he said, glancing at her.

She slammed on the brake and stopped. She stared at him. "Tell me what you think I did to make Ron think I would marry him."

"I didn't say you did nothin'."

"He did nothing more than kiss me. I didn't go to bed with him if that's what you think."

He shook his head. "I ain't never gonna say nothin' else bout 'im."

She nodded. "You make damn sure you don't." She pressed the gas and went on down the road. "We're going to see Charlie Hurt, he owns the neighboring farm. I'm going to tell him I'm concerned about the troubles we're having and ask him if he's having the same problems. You'll be with me when I talk to him. Ron may be there but maybe not. It will be best if you don't open your mouth. You have a tendency to piss people off when you talk."

He smiled as they rode on.

T hey rode up to a large farmhouse and parked. When they got out an older man came out of the house toward them. A younger man followed him. Floyd figured the younger man was Ron.

Virginia shook hands with both, then turned and looked toward Floyd. "This is Floyd Wimms, Charlie, he's with us now."

Charlie looked at Floyd, his eyes focusing on the pistol in his belt. "You always go armed, Floyd?" he asked.

Floyd nodded. "Do when I got my pants on."

Virginia cut her eyes at him. He didn't look at her.

Charlie laughed. "I ain't never thought of that but reckon that's the best time." He looked at Virginia. "What's on your mind?"

For the next few minutes, she told them about her concerns that fences were being cut and cattle were missing. She also mentioned the sinking of two boats.

During this time Floyd noticed that Ron had his eyes on him. He seemed to be especially interested in the clothes he was wearing.

Charlie listened as Virginia talked. He said that they'd had some problems, but he considered it no worse than normal. He promised that they would keep their eyes open and let her know if they saw anything.

Virginia had turned toward the car when Ron spoke up.

"I haven't seen you around here before, Floyd," he said, walking toward him. "You must be new in town. You're certainly dressed different from most folks around here."

Stone-faced, Floyd cut his eyes at him. "I dress like this when I'm workin'."

Ron looked puzzled. "And what do you do?"

"I hunt cattle rustlers and fence cutters."

"Do you have authority to arrest people in Georgia?" Ron seemed to be amused.

Floyd shook his head. "Ain't never arrested nobody."

"If that's your business, why haven't you ever caught anybody, Floyd," Ron said, looking at Virginia.

"I didn't say I hadn't never caught nobody, Ron, I said I ain't never arrested nobody."

Ron shook his head. "That makes no sense. How could that be?"

Floyd shrugged and stared in Ron's eyes. "After I caught 'im, they all ended up dead."

Ron's face reddened. He looked at Virginia and then at his daddy. "I find that hard to believe."

Floyd smiled, walked to the truck and got in the passenger's seat.

Virginia talked to Charlie and Ron for another minute, then turned toward the truck. She hadn't taken two steps when Ron called her. She walked over to him, and they talked for several minutes. Finally, they finished, and she came to the truck. She got in and looked at him. "You are a smart-ass."

She started the truck, backed out and started down the road.

"How many cattle rustlers have you killed?" she said, glancing at him.

"Ain't never kilt none."

"You said you had."

"I said I kilt all I caught. I ain't never caught none."

She shook her head.

"They don't know that, but it's in their head now."

They rode on, neither talking. She looked at him. "Ron asked me to go out with him."

Floyd didn't answer, stared straight ahead.

"Aren't you interested? You were interested last night."

"That's yo' business."

She glanced at him. "It is my business, and you remember that from now on."

They rode back to the farm in silence. They got to the house, she parked and looked at him. "After we eat, I'll take you to town. I'm going to the bank and do some business. When we get back here you can have the truck and should be able to get around on your own."

She stared at him. "No need for me to haul your smart-ass around." She got out, slammed the door and walked in the house.

Floyd went to the dining room where the hands ate their meals. When he finished eating, he came back to the house, got in the truck and waited.

Virginia came out of the house and got in. "As I said, I'll show you the way to town and let you look around. I'm going to the bank. When we come back, you can have the truck to go wherever you want."

They rode on in silence. "How far to town?" he said

"About four miles."

"What do most people do around here?"

"Farm, mostly. Other than working in town, there's not much other business here. There is one chicken farm on the other side of town."

"Lot of people havin' a hard time gettin' by," he said.

She nodded. "There's not a lot of jobs around so people are having a hard time, especially the young people."

"So, if you was lookin' for somebody to cut fences or steal cows, you wouldn't have trouble finding somebody."

She glanced at him. "Probably wouldn't."

"Where do the young people hang out?"

"There's a couple of places south of town in the next county. This county is dry, so folks go across the county line to drink."

"That was the way River Bluff was."

She looked at him. "What are you thinking?"

"People talk when they drink. Them places are a good place to find out what be goin' on."

She laughed. "They're not going to talk to you dressed like that."

"I got other clothes."

"You'd better wear them then."

He cut his eyes at her. "Maybe you would go with me?"

She shook her head. "In the first place I wouldn't go with you to a hog killing. Secondly, everybody knows me, and they wouldn't talk to you."

"Reckon I better git me another woman."

She laughed. "Good luck with that."

T hey rode into town. It looked like many small towns he had seen throughout the South. Baptist and Methodist churches on the outskirts and the main road lined with various stores and small business. The largest building was the bank in the center of town. People sat in rocking chairs in front of the general store and gossiped. He had seen all this before, just not here.

She parked in front of the bank. "Hoot Gilson is the man I'm seeing. As I said the Gilson family owns the bank. I'm going to introduce you and tell him you're working with us and if I send you in with business, he will know you."

He nodded.

She stared up at him. "Try to keep your mouth shut. You better leave your pistol in the truck. They'll think you've come to rob them." She turned and walked to the bank.

Floyd took his pistol out of his belt and laid it on the seat. He smiled as he followed her, thinking he had really stirred her up. She was really pretty when she was mad.

They went inside. She walked directly to an office at the end of the room. A fat, balding man was sitting at the desk. When he saw Virginia, he jumped up and ran to the door and shook her hand.

Floyd walked to the door. "Hoot, this is Floyd Wimms. He is working with us now and I wanted you to know him."

Hoot stared at Floyd; his brow furrowed as he looked him over. Then he thought of his manners and stuck out his hand. "Glad to meet you, Mr. Wimms," he said, as he took his handkerchief and wiped his brow. He turned to Virginia. "And what can I do for you, dear?" he said in a high-pitched voice.

Floyd didn't like him; he didn't like anything about him. He stood behind Virginia and stared at him as they talked. When they finished and she got up, he walked out and waited for her at the truck."

She came out of the bank and walked directly at him. "You about scared poor Hoot to death, standing there staring at him like you wanted to kill him. He was sweating like everything."

"Poor Hoot? Why do you say that? Ain't he givin' y'all a hard time bout yo' land?"

"Yes, he is but you need to act civil to people."

He shook his head. "Civil ain't never been my strong suit."

She nodded. "I know your strong suit; it's being a smart-ass." She walked to the truck and got in. When he got in, she wasn't finished. "And you're damn good at it." She started the car and started out of town.

He leaned over and tapped her on the shoulder. "Has anybody ever told you you're pretty when you get riled up."

"Don't speak to me. You're a terrible person."

He laughed. "I am that, but you like me."

She didn't speak all the way to the house. She parked, got out and tossed him the keys. She slammed the door and went in the house.

Floyd watched her go in and smiled.

7

Floyd ate supper and came back to the house. He'd just sat down when he heard a car drive up. He got up, walked to the window and looked out. There was a fancy red and white car sitting in front of the big house. As he watched Ron Hurt got out, walked to the front door and knocked. The door opened and he went inside.

Floyd stood at the window and waited. In a few minutes the door opened, and Ron came out with Virginia. Laughing, they walked to the car. He opened the passenger door and Virginia got in, but before she did, Floyd saw her glance his way. Ron ran around and got in, the car started, and they left.

Floyd stood at the window for a minute, then he went to the bedroom and changed clothes. He got the truck key, went outside and got in. He turned on the ignition and started toward town. He remembered she had said the joints were south of town across the county line. That was where he headed. He hadn't had a drink since he left Tub's place and he was thirsty.

There were two places in sight as he crossed the county line. One had several old trucks parked outside. The other, on the other side of the road, had some trucks but a couple of nice cars in the lot. This was Dib's Place. He pulled into the parking lot and got out.

He opened the door, stepped inside and looked around. The bar was to his right with stools in front. Several were filled. There were tables in front of the bar, about half were empty. Some had only men and two had couples. There were two waitresses standing at the end of the bar and they had their eyes on him. He walked to the far side of the room to an empty table and sat down with his back to the wall. One of the waitresses was beside him in an instant.

"What you havin', darlin'?" she said, leaning over him. Her low-cut dress showed him everything she had.

"Beer."

"You sure that's all you want, sweetie?"

"Git the beer," he said gruffly. He didn't want her bothering him half the night.

She jumped back and stared at him. When she brought the beer, he handed her a bill. "Watch me and don't let me run out," he said. "After one more beer bring me whiskey."

She looked at the bill. "You ain't gonna run outta nothin', honey," she said as she ran to the bar.

He was on his second whiskey when a man and two women walked in the door. They stood and looked around, then came across the floor and sat at a table across from him. They looked to be in their late twenties or so. It only took a couple of minutes for him to figure it was a man and his wife with another woman. Both the women were attractive. As he watched them, the other woman kept glancing toward him. Finally, they made eye contact and she didn't look away. Then she leaned over and said something to the man. He glanced at Floyd, said something to the woman and got up. He walked over to Floyd's table. "Pardon me," he said, "but you're alone and my wife's sister thought you might like to come over and talk to us?"

Floyd looked across at the sister. Her eyes were on him and didn't waver. He nodded to the man, picked up his drink and walked over to their table.

"I'm Howard," said the man, "this is my wife, Peg, and this is her sister, Rachel."

Floyd shook hands with Howard, nodded to the women and sat down.

"We haven't seen you in here before," said Peg.

"It's my first time here," said Floyd. He looked at Rachel. She was attractive and her eyes were locked on him.

"Are you passing through?" Peg was intent on finding out about him.

"I'm at the Mann farm over on the river. I just been here a few days."

"That's a nice place," said Howard. "The Manns are good people. What do you do?"

"Security."

Howard looked at him. "You with the law?"

Floyd shook his head.

Rachel leaned toward him. "How long have you been there?" she asked. He smelled her perfume. He liked it and he liked everything about her.

"Just a week," he said. He ordered drinks for everybody and told the girl to keep them coming. Howard was impressed that he was buying. They settled down and relaxed. Floyd and Rachel were talking, and Howard and Peg were doing their own thing.

"We gotta go," said Howard, about an hour later. "Peg's mother has got the kids, and she goes to bed early." He looked at Rachel.

Rachel looked at Floyd. "Well, it seems my ride is leaving."

Floyd didn't hesitate. "I'll take you home if you want me to."

She looked at Howard and then back at Floyd. She leaned closer and whispered to him. "I've just met you and don't really know you. But I've enjoyed talking to you. If you take me home, I'll get out at the door and that's it."

Floyd nodded. "That's up to you," he said, watching her face.

Rachel looked at Howard. "Floyd will take me home."

Howard nodded, shook Floyd's hand and walked out with Peg.

Floyd talked to Rachel for the next hour. He found out she taught fifth grade in the county school and was twenty- seven. He told her a little about himself but not much. Basically, he grew up downriver and came upriver. He didn't add any other details.

They went to the truck and rode into town. When they got to her house she shared with another teacher, she leaned over and kissed him. "I enjoyed meeting you and talking to you. I have the feeling that there's a lot more to you that I don't know about." She looked at him, questioning.

He looked at her but didn't comment.

"I don't normally go to Dib's Place," she said. "I just went with Howard and Peg tonight because that's where they wanted to go." She stared at him. "But I'm going to be there two nights from now. If you want to be with me, you can come. If you do come, when you bring me home, I'll ask you in. If you don't show up, I'll understand but don't say anything now." She slid over against him, this time kissed him for real, got out and ran in the house.

He sat there for a full minute before he drove off.

When Floyd came back from breakfast the next morning, a man that worked on the docks was waiting for him at the house. He told him that he had been in one of the joints in the next county the night before and he overheard three men talking about a job they had tonight at the Mann farm. He wasn't sure exactly what all was said but he was sure it had something to do with the Mann farm. They'd been drinking and were bragging about the money they were making. When they noticed him listening, they stopped talking.

Floyd talked with the man for several minutes, going over exactly what he'd heard. Then he took the man to one of the men that looked after the cattle, and they talked. Based on the bit he'd heard; it seemed the men were planning to steal cattle from a field and drive them to another location. There they would be loaded on trucks and hauled away. The man involved with the livestock said one of the fields downriver was the only field where such a move would be possible. That field was adjacent to a field that they didn't own, and somebody could bring in a truck.

Floyd thanked the man from the docks for his help. He and the other man got in the truck and went downriver to the field in question. Floyd wanted to see the land in daylight and come up with a plan, if indeed the men showed up. The field was fenced with barbed wire and there was a large herd feeding there.

He came back to the house, dressed and got his rifle. He went by the kitchen and got a jug of tea and some ham biscuits. He went to the dock, got in his boat and headed downriver. He landed upriver from the field and walked in. He set up on high ground where he could see the entire field and waited. He was thankful there would be a full moon.

He was eating a biscuit when he sensed a change in the cattle. They were restless and moving about; the noise level in the field changed. Then he realized there were men in the field and the cattle were being slowly herded to the far side toward the fence. He jumped up and headed along the edge of the trees in the direction they were moving. The fence had been cut and the cattle were moving through the opening. He saw lights as a large truck came into the other field and stopped. The cattle were being herded in that direction. Men got out of the truck with flashlights. Floyd figured the truck was about six hundred yards away from his position.

He set up and aimed through the scope. The rifle held five rounds, and he had several extra clips. The bright headlights made it easy to spot the truck. There was a man in front of the truck with a light. Floyd aimed at him and fired. The light went out. He then aimed at the truck's headlights and emptied the clip. The next clip he fired one at a time into the engine and the cab of the truck.

The noise of his firing and men yelling stampeded the cattle and they scattered in all directions. Suddenly the cab of the truck burst into flames and this added to the noise and confusion. Floyd stopped firing and watched.

In a few minutes it was obvious that the men had all left the field. He had no idea if he had hit anybody or not and didn't care one way or the other. There was nothing else for him to do here so he went to the boat and headed back to the dock. He went by the bunkhouse and told the man in charge of the cattle that they had a roundup to do. He went back to the house and went to bed.

∼

He was up early the next morning. He ate a bite of breakfast, got in his boat and went downriver to the field where he'd been last night. He landed and walked in. Several men were in the field with the burned-out truck rounding the cattle back through the fence. He saw two police cars parked near the truck.

He saw the man in charge of the cattle and walked over to him. The man smiled when he saw Floyd coming. "I didn't know what you planned to do about these people when we talked, but you damn well stopped them."

Floyd looked at the police cars. "I see the law is here."

The man nodded. "Sheriff's deputies. I called them."

"What did they say about the truck?" said Floyd

"They checked and said it was stollen in Atlanta yesterday."

Floyd nodded. "Did you tell them what happened?"

"I didn't say nothin' bout last night. I didn't say a word about you."

"What else did they say?"

"They said the truck was full of bullet holes and they asked did we hear shooting last night?" He looked at Floyd. "I said we heard the truck explode and that's when we come down, but we didn't know what happened."

"That's good," said Floyd.

"They knew I was lying but they didn't care. They're glad somebody done somethin' about these people stealing."

"Y'all was the first people here this morning. Did you find anybody shot?"

He shook his head. "If anybody got shot, they must have carried 'im off, cause we didn't find nobody."

"It was dark, and I couldn't tell if I hit anybody or not," said Floyd

He laughed. "If you didn't hit 'em, you sho' scared the livin' hell outta 'em."

"That's what I wanted to do," said Floyd. "Let me know if anythin' else comes up." He turned and went to his boat.

He parked at the dock and walked to the house. He was surprised to see Virgina standing by the truck waiting for him. 'Well," she said as he walked up, "seems you put on quite a show last night. Everybody's talking about you this morning."

He walked up and stared in her face. "So?"

"Do you even know if you killed anybody with all that shooting?"

"They didn't find no bodies, so I reckon I didn't." He shrugged. "Didn't make a damn to me if I did anyway."

"That's terrible," she said. "What are people going to think of us?"

"I hope they'll think they oughta kept their ass outta y'all's pasture if they don't want to get shot." He stared at her. "What was I supposed to do, let 'em steal yo' cows?"

She stared back at him, not knowing how to reply.

He smiled. "You and Ron have a good time last night?"

Her face changed; she didn't appreciate his comment. "It's not any of your business but yes, I had a good time. He's a nice person, unlike some people." She patted the truck. "I noticed the truck was gone when I came home."

"I went honky tonkin'," he said, watching her face. "I went to Dib's Place. Met some nice people."

She stared at him and shook her head. "Nice people don't hang out at Dib's. But you probably like the kind of women that do."

He smiled. "They were sho' friendly. I liked 'em." He grinned. "I'll tell you one thing. If you'd been with me, you'd of had more fun than you did with Ron."

"I don't want to talk to you anymore," she said as she turned around. "You're despicable."

He watched as she walked across the road. *Damn, that's a good-looking woman, he thought.*

8

Floyd didn't see Virginia anymore that afternoon. Later he got in the truck and rode to town. He didn't bother changing out of his buckskins and had his pistol stuck in his belt. He rode south out of town and crossed the county line. He parked at the joint across the road from Dib's Place, got out and went in. It was dark and smoky inside and it took him a minute for his eyes to adjust.

There were several men sitting at tables and one man on a stool at the end of the bar. Floyd walked to the bar. Every eye in the house was on him. Being dressed like a injun always got attention wherever he went.

The bartender, a slim man with a beard walked over and looked at him. "What you want?" he said. He kept his head down. "I know who you be," he whispered.

"Beer," said Floyd as he looked over the men in the room. He didn't recognize any of them.

The bartender brought the beer and sat it in front of him. He had a towel and wiped the bar. "I ain't got nothin' fir 'em folks what steal another man's cows," he said in a low voice as he kept wiping the bar.

Floyd took a drink of the beer. He didn't look at him.

"Word is you hit one of them folks last night what was in that truck."

Floyd drank and kept his head down. The man seemed to want to talk.

"Hit 'im in the leg, you did. The doctor came to his house and treated 'im."

"Do you know his name?"

"Don't know that but he lives downriver at the ferry crossing." He kept wiping. "They say he's got a brother lookin' fir you."

"You know 'im?"

"Don't know 'im but they say he's real tall with black hair. The word is he be bad."

Floyd drained the beer and put a bill on the table. "I'll be back tomorrow night. Find out what you can."

The bartender picked up the bill, looked at it and smiled. "Sho' will," he said.

Floyd went out to the truck and went back to the farm.

He was up early the next morning. He ate breakfast, then went to find the man in charge of the cattle, whose name was Wash. He told him what he had found out. He got in the boat and headed downriver. When he got to the ferry the old man was sitting on the west bank. He watched as Floyd landed and got out.

"I'm looking for a man," said Floyd, "about doing some work. I don't know his name but they say he lives around the ferry. He's black-headed and real tall."

The old man studied for a moment. "That must be Woody Sharpe, he be the tallest man round here. He lives with his brother up at the end of the street in that white house."

Floyd thanked him, got in his boat and went back upriver.

The old man watched him go and scratched his head.

Floyd got to the Mann's dock, landed and went to find Wash. He told him what he had found out and asked him to call the sheriff's office and tell them.

Wash called, talked for several minutes and hung up. He looked at Floyd. "They say them folks at the ferry live in the next county, they don't have any proof he was involved and they ain't gonna fool with it."

Floyd nodded, thanked him for trying and walked out. It was obvious he would have to handle this problem himself.

As he walked back to the house, he remembered that Rachel had told him she would be at Dib's tonight. She had made it clear by what she'd said that she would be waiting for him. She had no other reason to be there.

He realized that the shooting last night had changed the rules of the game. He now had at least one man, or more, looking for him and they didn't want to talk. He felt he had to talk to Mr. Mann.

He walked over to the big house and knocked on the door. He heard someone walking inside, the door opened, and he was looking at Virginia,

"What do you want?" Her tone wasn't friendly.

"I need to talk to yo' daddy."

She took a deep breath as she looked in his face. "He's on the patio. Come with me." She started walking away and he followed. She went out the side door to the patio.

Mr. Mann was sitting in a chair the shade. He looked up as they came out the door. "Well, Floyd, I'm told you went to work last night," he said. "I expect some people were surprised by what happened."

"Yes, sir, I did." He then told him what the bartender had told him. He also told him about his trip to the ferry, the call to the sheriff and their refusal to do anything.

"The sheriff's reaction doesn't surprise me," said Mr. Mann. "He's under of lot of pressure from other folks and is trying to avoid taking sides."

"I wanted to tell you that I ain't never let folks that are after me pick the time and place to fight. I'll do that myself. I'll take care of this fellow at the ferry, but it might not be pretty. I wanted you to know that."

Mr. Mann nodded. "I leave that up to you, Floyd. It seems you go straight at a problem."

"I don't want none of yo' folks to get hurt so I'll get it settled right away."

"You do what you have to, Floyd," said Mr. Mann.

"Thank you, sir." Floyd turned and looked at Virginia. She started toward the door and Floyd followed her out. She stopped at the front door. "What do you intend to do?"

"I'm gonna clean this up."

Her lips tightened. "What are you going to do, shoot this man?"

"If I have to."

She stared in his face. "You intend to kill him?"

"If I have to."

"That doesn't bother you?"

He shook his head and watched her face. "This is what I do, Virginia. You were lookin' for me because I shot two people. What the hell did you thank I was going to do? Kiss 'em?"

"You're right," she said. "You are what you are, and I knew it." She opened the door and walked outside.

He stepped out and closed the door.

She turned to him. "How are you going to do this?" she said calmly.

"I've got to find out where he hangs out and go get 'im."

"I expect you've done this before?"

"I have."

"When are you going?"

"Right now."

She looked out across the river and then her eyes swung back to him. "When you get back tonight, let me know you're all right."

"It might be late and there ain't no need of you waiting up," he said. He wondered about this sudden interest in his welfare.

She looked at him. "We asked you to do this so promise me you'll let me know."

He nodded. "All right but there ain't no sense in it."

"Be careful," she said as she turned and went in the house."

He went in his house, got his pistol and headed toward town. He got to town and drove south across the county line. He stopped at the joint across from Dib's, got out and went in. He stopped and let his eyes adjust. The same bartender was on duty.

Floyd walked over, sat on a stool and waited for him to walk over. He laid a bill on the bar. "Where does he hang out?"

The bartender picked up the bill and put it in his pocket. "There's a place on the road to the ferry called Tub's."

Floyd nodded. "I know where Tub's be."

"They say he be there most every night. He probably won't be by his self."

"Don't make no difference to me," said Floyd. He got up, walked out and got in the truck. He drove across the street to Dib's.

When he walked in, he saw Rachel sitting at the same table where they had sat before. She was watching the door and saw him immediately. She smiled but then he saw her expression change when she saw how he was dressed, and the pistol stuck in his belt. He walked straight to the table and sat down by her.

Her eyes were on his face. "Before you say anything, Rachel, let me explain," he said.

She frowned but nodded. "All right."

"I can't stay with you tonight because I have to go somewhere else. But I stopped by to let you know that I wanted to be with you." He shook his head. "I can't tonight, but I'd like to another time."

She pursed her lips. "Howard told me you were involved in a shooting last night and people are saying you are a killer. I didn't believe it and wanted to talk to you. But now I see you and I don't know what to believe."

"Men was stealing the Mann's cattle last night and I ran them off. I did shoot at 'em, but nobody was killed."

"Howard said the sheriff checked on you and you killed some men somewhere downriver."

Floyd nodded. "I did but that's a long story." He stared at her, trying to say the right words. "Rachel, you're a nice, sweet girl. You ain't got no business with me. You need to find you a good young man and marry him and have kids, but that's not me. I ain't the marrying kind. I'm tellin you right now."

She frowned as she listened to him. "Let me decide that."

He shook his head. "You don't know me. I would go to bed with you and use you and then one day I'd be gone. You don't want that."

"Where are you going now?"

"I'm looking for a man from last night."

"What are you going to do if you find him?"

He shrugged. "Depends on what he does."

She sighed. "You don't want to be with me?"

"It ain't that, Rachel. You don't need to be with me. I done told you how I am." He smiled. "I ain't never been a man what people call honorable but walkin' away from you would be honorable on my part."

She reached over and took his hand. "I'll be here Saturday night waiting for you like I was tonight. I hear what you've said, and I appreciate your concern. You let me worry about what I do."

He stood up and looked down at her. "Damn it, girl, you make it awfully hard to do the right thang." He turned and headed for the door.

Rachel watched him go and smiled.

Tub's joint was where he remembered it being. Floyd rode past it to where he could see the white house where the man at the ferry had said Woody Sharpe lived. He pulled over to the side of the road and backed up in some bushes. He had a good view of the white house. He sat back and waited.

He'd been there for an hour when a very tall, dark-haired man came out of the house and got in a truck. He figured that was Woody Sharpe. The truck backed out and headed down the road. Floyd followed him.

The truck went into the parking lot and stopped. Woody got out and walked inside. Floyd pulled up behind him, waited a few minutes and then went inside. Like all these places, it was dark and smoky inside. Floyd stopped inside the door, let his eyes adjust and looked around. The bar was to the right, with two bartenders, both women. Three men were on stools at the bar. Woody was sitting on a stool at the far end of the bar facing him. His eyes were on Floyd.

Floyd walked to the bar. The bartender came over and asked what he wanted. "Whiskey," he said. His eyes never lost contact with Woody. He took the glass and walked in front of the bar toward him. He had his hand on his pistol as he walked. He stopped, eased onto the stool in front of Woody and put the glass on the bar.

"I hear you be lookin' fir me," he said.

Woody frowned and shrugged. "Why would I be lookin' for you?"

"How' yo' brother?"

"What do you care?"

Floyd shook his head. "I don't, but I heard he's been shot, and I was wonderin' how that happened?"

Woody looked at him and shook his head. "You be bout stupid comin' in here by yo' self. You be in my place. How come you thank you gonna get outta here?"

Floyd nodded. "I know it be yo' place but I don't thank you want to die right now. If anybody starts anything, I'll kill you first. I can do it and I thank you know it." Floyd watched his eyes and knew he was right.

"Why are you here?"

"I don't give a damn bout you," said Floyd, "but I want to know who hired you. Tell me that and I won't say another word to you."

Woody laughed. "Are you stupid? I ain't gonna do that."

"How much did they pay you? I'll pay you more."

Woody shook his head and his expression changed. Floyd saw in his eyes that he was about to make a move

Suddenly, Woody started standing up and Floyd saw the pistol in his hand. He jumped up and threw the whiskey in Woody's face, drawing his pistol at the same time. The whiskey blinded Woody for an instant. He yelled and fell back, trying to clear his eyes where he could see Floyd.

Floyd was on him. His right hand came up and he hit him on the side of the head with the pistol. He grabbed the stunned and blinded

Woody by the arm and fired the pistol toward the ceiling. People at the tables hit the floor. Floyd pushed Woody behind the bar, grabbed him by the arm and headed toward the door. He shoved the bartenders out of the way as he ran. He came around the end of the bar, shoved Woody out the door in front of him and ran toward his truck as he looked back. Two men came out the door and fired at them, but they ducked back inside when Floyd fired back. He pushed Woody in the truck, jumped in, started the engine and went out of the parking lot. He didn't stop until he was a mile down the road.

Woody was getting his senses back by this time. "What you gonna do with me?" he said, looking at Floyd.

"I oughta just shoot yo' dumb ass," said Floyd. "You want to tell me who hired you?"

"I don't know who he was. He was from Atlanta, and he had the truck. I didn't never see him but that one time."

"Have you heard from him since then?

Woody shook his head.

"If you hear from him again, you let me know. I won't say nothin' bout you if you do."

Woody looked at him. "You gonna let me go?"

Floyd nodded. "Next time I won't."

Woody opened the door and looked back at him. "If I find out about'em and tell you, you'll pay me?"

Floyd nodded. "According to what you have."

"They ain't nothin' to me, I ain't got no use fir 'em" said Woody. "I'll let you know." He got out of the truck.

Floyd drove off, leaving Woody standing beside the road.

He got to the farm and parked in front of the house. He was getting out of the truck when Virginia came out of the big house. She walked straight toward him, her eyes on him. "What happened?" she said as she walked up to him.

He looked down at her. "I got rid of the problem."

"Did you kill him?"

"No, I didn't kill 'im."

"You didn't shoot him?"

He shook his head. He didn't see any sense in going into the details.

"It don't bother you to kill a man?"

He stared at her. "We done been over this."

She nodded. "Yes, we have."

He started toward the guest house.

"Have you eaten?" she asked as she walked beside him.

Surprised by her question, he looked down at her and shook his head. "Didn't never thank bout it."

She took his hand and pulled him back. "Come with me. I'll fix you something."

She held his hand as they went across the parking lot and in the big house. She led him to the kitchen and told him to sit down at the table.

"How do you like your eggs?" she asked.

"Scrambled," he said, still uncertain as to what was going on here.

For the next few minutes, he watched as she cooked. He was impressed. She brought two plates of eggs, bacon and toast to the table. She poured coffee and sat across from him as they ate.

"This is good," he said.

"Did you think I couldn't cook?"

He laughed. "I thought you just walked around and looked pretty."

She smiled and nodded, her eyes on him. "That's the first compliment

I've ever gotten from you. I'll remember that."

He got up. "I thank you for feeding me."

She smiled. "Glad to do it."

As they walked out, she took his hand and walked beside him. He stopped and looked down at her.

"What are you doing?"

"I'm walking you to your house. You don't want me to?"

"I just want to make sure you know what you're doing."

Virginia smiled. "I'm a big girl, Floyd. I know what I'm doing."

He reached down, put his arm around her waist and pulled her against him. He leaned over and kissed her. She returned his kiss."

She looked in his eyes. "When we get to your door, I'll say goodnight. This is enough for tonight."

They walked to the door, he kissed her again and watched her run across the road to her house.

9

Sister was tired and hungry. Living on the river, sleeping on the ground and traveling in the sun or rain every day had worn her out. She would give anything for a warm meal of fried chicken, butterbeans and corn with a pitcher of sweet tea. Her decision to follow the injun was beginning to seem right stupid.

She got up that morning and decided she had to find a place where she could stay for a day or two and recover. She had no idea where that might be because she had no idea what lay ahead. Surely there would be a settlement somewhere on up the river. She still had money so she could pay if she could find a place.

The sun was straight overhead when she rounded a bend and saw a house on the right side of the river. There was a cornfield between the house and the river, so she knew there had to be people there. She pulled over to the bank and landed. When she got out, she saw a clothesline in the yard beside the house with clothes, including a dress, hanging on it. There had to be a woman here and that was a good sign.

She walked around a corner of the house and an older woman was standing on the back porch. She saw Sister about the same time.

She walked to the end of the porch and stared at her. "Where in the world did you come from, honey?" she said.

"I come up the river," Sister said.

"You be by yo' self?" the woman asked, looking back toward the river.

"It just be me," sister said as she stepped up on the porch. "I be by myself."

"Lordy" said the woman, "how come you be on that river all by yo' self?"

"I be lookin for my man."

"Yo' husband? How come he left you all by yo' self?"

"He ain't my husband but he be my man."

The back door opened, and an older man walked out. He was surprised to see Sister and looked at the woman. "Who that be, Maude?" he asked staring at Sister.

For the next few minutes Sister explained her situation to Maude and Luther, that was the man's name. They had a hard time understanding why she was on the river and who she was looking for.

"You would know 'im if you saw 'im," said Sister. He sorta be dressed like a injun with beads and leather."

"We done seen 'im," said Luther. "He come by here over a week ago. He didn't say nothin' bout leavin' no woman and you be lookin' for 'im."

Sister didn't comment anymore about looking for her man. They didn't seem to understand what she was saying and neither did she. She didn't even know his name, so it was best to keep quiet about it.

Maude took her in the kitchen and fed her the first good meal she'd had in days. Then she took a bath in a tub and washed her hair. She felt like a new woman. Maude gave her a nightgown and put her to bed. Sister slept all that night and most of the next day.

Maude and Luther were glad to have someone to talk to and they couldn't do enough for her. They said their children had all moved away and they got lonely. Their nearest neighbor was over a mile away.

By the end of the second day Sister was feeling much better. She was well enough to continue her trip, and felt she was getting further behind staying here. Both Maude and Luther told her she was foolish to go on.

"Yo' man is way over a week ahead of you," said Luther. "There ain't no way you can catch him lest he stops for several days."

Sister knew what he said was right, but she decided she would go on till the river ran out. She knew if she didn't find him before then, she'd have no other choice but to stop. There was no way she could walk to the Cherokees, wherever they were.

She left the next morning. She gave Maude and Luther more money than they had seen in a year. They didn't want to take it, but she insisted. They both told her that if she gave up, she could come back and live with them. Sister thanked them for everything, got in the boat and headed upriver.

Sister had never been one for prayer, but she was about ready to start. Luther had been right; she had little chance of catching the injun unless he stopped. "Tell 'im to stop and wait fir me," she yelled out as she forged ahead. She wasn't sure who she was talking to, if anybody, but she felt better for having said it.

When Floyd walked back from breakfast the next morning, he saw a Sheriff's car parked in front of the big house. He wasn't surprised, he'd figured somebody would want to talk to him about last night. He went inside his house and waited. It wasn't long before there was a knock on his door.

Virginia was at the door. She looked at him. "Sheriff White would like to talk to you. He's inside with Daddy."

Floyd nodded and walked out behind her. He followed her across the road and into the house. Mr. Mann and the sheriff were on the patio as they walked out. Mr. Mann was sitting in a chair.

"I'm Sheriff White, I'd like to ask you some questions," was the way the sheriff started the conversation.

Floyd nodded. He figured the less he said, the better.

"The sheriff in the next county called me and said you fired at some people at Tub's place last night and attacked one of their customers."

Stone-faced, Floyd stared at the sheriff.

Mr. Mann spoke up. "Floyd, Sheriff White is our friend, has been for years. He's not trying to trap you with these questions. He's just doing what he has to."

"Were you at Tub's last night?"

Floyd nodded. "I was there. I went to talk to Woody Sharpe about his brother what got shot."

"What happened at Tub's?"

"I walked in; he was sittin' at the bar. I walked toward 'im and he pulled a gun. I hit 'im with my pistol."

"The witnesses say he didn't have a gun."

Floyd nodded. "They was all his people."

"You're right, they were," said the sheriff. He looked at Floyd. "You knew when you went in that place there would be trouble."

Floyd nodded.

"But you went anyway?"

"I was afraid he was gonna hurt some of our folks. He needed to be stopped."

"The sheriff in the next county don't care a bit about Woody Sharpe gettin' hurt. He and his whole family ain't never been nothin' but trouble," said the sheriff. "They're just fillin' out paperwork like I am. Won't nothin' come of it."

"That's good," said Floyd.

The sheriff stared at him. "I did check up on you with the places downriver and it seems this ain't the first time you've been involved in a shootin'."

"You be right," said Floyd.

"If I was you, I'd stay away from folks at Tub's and around the ferry for a while. You might not get out next time."

Floyd chuckled. "I ain't plannin' to go back no time soon."

The sheriff looked at Mr. Mann. "I thank you for your time, sir."

"You're welcome any time, Tim. The door is always open to you."

"Come with me, Sheriff," said Virginia. "I'll see you out."

Mr. Mann looked at Floyd after they left. "I appreciate your concern about things, Floyd. I know you were reacting to what has gone on and I commend you for it. But it would be good if we could quiet it down some." He stared at him. "You know what I'm saying."

"Yes, sir, I know what you mean."

Virginia walked back in the room. She looked at her daddy and at Floyd.

"We're through," said Mr. Mann. "You can show Floyd the way out."

She nodded, looked at Floyd and walked out. Floyd followed her. He was wondering how she was going to act after last night.

When they got outside, she stopped and turned to him. "You hit him with your pistol but didn't kill him."

"I did."

"Sheriff said you'd been involved in shootings downriver."

He looked at her and shook his head. "You knew about that, Virginia. I told you about Lizzie getting' killed and me killin' the men what did it. I ain't never kept it from you."

"I know you told me but hearing it from the sheriff made it more real."

"I am who I am, Virginia, you oughta know that by now."

She nodded. "I know that." Her eyes looked in his face. "What about last night?"

He turned and looked across the river, then back at her. "I did what you wanted me to do. You know that."

She pursed her lips and looked at him, waiting for him to say more.

"You're a good-lookin' woman and you know it. I'm a man and you can move me if you want to and last night you wanted to." He leaned over and looked in her face. "If you want me to bed you, I will, but then when I get ready to leave, I'll be gone. I ain't never gonna make no promises. That's the way I am."

She took a step back. "Damn, you're a hard man, Floyd. You

would use me and then, without any thought, you would throw me away."

"That ain't the truth. I've been with women I didn't remember the next day but that wouldn't be the same with you. I like you and have regard for you." He frowned, "I ain't never had much regard for many people."

She smiled. "Somehow, that seems to be a compliment, but it doesn't exactly sound like a compliment. From what you've said, if I go in the house with you right now, you'll go to bed with me but that's it. There's nothing more."

"Let me thank on that for a minute," said Floyd. He nodded. "If you go in the house with me right now, I'll go to bed with you, but I won't promise nothin'."

Virginia leaned over, put her face in her hands and laughed. Still leaning over, she looked up at him. "You have to be the most honest and the sorriest son of a bitch I've ever met." She turned and ran to the big house. She opened the door, went inside and ran to her room.

She picked up the phone and called. "Ron," she said, "could you do me a big favor and take me out right now." She listened. "Thirty minutes? That's fine. I'll be waiting."

Floyd was in his house when he heard a car drive up. He looked out the window as Ron Hurt got out of the car and went to the door. Virginia opened the door, came out and laughing, took his arm. He opened her door, ran around to the other side and got in. The car started and they drove off.

He watched until the car was out of sight and went to bed.

10

The next morning Floyd ate breakfast and when he walked outside, he saw Virginia at the dock talking to one of the workers. He watched her for a minute, then walked down the hill and stopped behind her. She finished talking and when she turned around, she saw him. She didn't look pleased to see him.

"What are you doing sneaking up on me?" she said. She walked past him and started up the hill.

Floyd followed her. "I just walked down to speak to you," he said.

She kept walking. "I told you last night what I thought of you." She looked back at him. "I haven't changed my mind one bit. I really don't like you."

He was walking behind her. "Go out with me tonight?"

She stopped and stood with her back toward him. "Why would I do that?"

"Because you want to."

She didn't turn around. "You are a conceited ass."

"We won't go in town, that'd cause too much talk. We'd ride north toward the mountains."

She turned and looked at him, her eyes searching his face. "You're serious?"

He nodded. "I know a place to eat. You'll like it."

"You've been there?"

He nodded. "It's a ways off. You need to git ready and go right away."

She frowned. "This is so sudden. I don't know what to say."

He stared at her. "Yes, you do."

"You're going right now?"

"As soon as you git yo' self in the truck."

"I have to dress," she said as she ran toward the big house.

He went inside, changed clothes and was sitting in the truck when she came out and got in.

"You look nice," he said.

"Thank you," she said as she stared at him, her face uncertain as to what she was doing. She wasn't accustomed to him talking and acting this way.

He drove through town and onto the main highway north. She had relaxed some as they rode and talked. After a few miles she relaxed and was enjoying being with him. Soon they were in the foothills and climbing. The scenery was beautiful. After another hour they came into a small village. He pulled into a lot and parked. "You like trout?" he asked.

"Yes, I do."

"It's good here."

She stared at him. "You are full of surprises."

"I was here when I worked in the gold mine."

Her eyes widened. "You worked in a gold mine?"

"It wasn't a big mine, but I did well with it."

"You lived around here?"

He nodded. "Here and farther up north with the Cherokees." He got out, came around and opened her door.

He took her hand and helped her out. They walked in the restaurant, got a table and sat down. The place was very nice, and she was impressed.

"You have completely fooled me, Floyd. I never expected this."

He smiled. "Ain't no need to let no woman know everything bout you."

"I'm not paying any attention to you anymore," she said as she took his hand and smiled.

The waitress came, they ordered and talked until the food came. They ate until they were stuffed.

"This was delicious," she said

"Told you you'd like it."

They went outside, got in the truck and started down the mountain. She slid over against him. "I've had a good time," she said. She put her head on his shoulder.

"I'm glad. Me too." He put his arm around her and held her all the way to the farm. He parked, pulled her to him and kissed her. She kissed him back. They stayed in the truck getting to know each other until she pushed him away.

"Not in the truck," she said. "Let's go in the house."

He looked at her. "You sure?"

She nodded, opened the door and took his hand. They jumped out and went inside. He led her to the bedroom, both shedding clothes as they went. They got in the bed, she wrapped her arms around him and stared in his face. "No promises," she said.

He laughed. "I ain't asked you for any," he said as he pulled her to him and kissed her.

Later she rolled away from him. "I've got to be in the house before daylight." She got up, gathered her clothes, kissed him and went out the door.

Floyd got up early. He wondered about Virginia and looked for her while walking to breakfast but didn't see her. He wondered what she thought about last night and how she felt this morning. He was also wondering the same thing about himself and hadn't come to any conclusion. Asking her to go with him to the mountains had been a spur of the minute decision. Prior to asking her, he'd not thought about such a move. But everything had turned out well, at least he thought so. She'd seemed to be pleased also.

Ending up in bed with her when they got back was also unplanned, certainly on his part. He thought it was for her too. He would have to talk to her and see her reaction to really know how she felt about it. While in bed she didn't seem to be questioning what she was doing, but in the light of day she might feel different.

He ate and came back to the house. He had told her that he would stay a week and then they'd talk but he'd decided he'd be here longer. He wanted to see the job finished for one thing, but he now had Virginia on his mind. That certainly had not been planned, but he would have to deal with it.

If he was planning to stay longer, there were things he had to do. He got in the truck and headed to town. He parked in front of the bank, put his pistol on the seat and went inside. Hoot Gilson was at his desk at the far end of the room and Floyd headed straight for him.

When Hoot looked up and saw him coming the color drained out of his face. He jumped up, came around the desk and stuck out his hand. "Morning, Floyd," he said as Floyd shook his hand. "How can I help you?" He pointed to a chair, went around to the desk and sat down.

Floyd sat down. "I want to open a account with yo' bank," he said as he handed Hoot a check. "This is my personal check."

Hoot took the check from him, leaned back in his chair and looked at it. Floyd saw the surprise in his face. Hoot leaned forward and looked at Floyd. "This is quite a large amount of money," he said, "I'll have to verify it."

Floyd looked at him. "The check's good."

Hoot shook his head. "Oh, I'm sure it is. I wasn't questioning that, it's just bank policy." He took out his handkerchief and wiped his face. He jumped up. "I'll be back in a minute," he said as he hurried toward the back of the room.

In a few minutes he was back. "Everything's fine, Floyd. I hope you weren't thinking I was questioning you."

Floyd didn't answer; he just stared at Hoot.

Hoot wiped his face. "Is there anything else I can do for you?"

Floyd shook his head. "Some folks stole a truck in Atlanta and tried to steal the Mann's cattle this week. We stopped them and we intend to find out who's behind this stealing."

Hoot nodded. "That's good. There's too much of that going on." He cut his eyes at Floyd. "I heard you had an altercation at one of the beer joints the other night."

Floyd nodded. "Yeah, with Woody Sharpe. He and his brother was part of the folks tryin' to steal the cows. His brother got shot. Woody told me they was there."

Hoot's eyes widened. "He told you that. You talked to him?"

"I was either gonna talk to 'im or kill 'im. He decided to talk."

Hoot wiped his face. "What did he say?"

'He said enough," said Floyd. He got up. "I need some checks," he said.

"I'll have some out to you tomorrow, Floyd," said Hoot.

Floyd nodded, turned and walked out. He got in the truck and went back to the farm. When he parked, he saw Virginia walking out of the big house. He got out and waited for her. Her eyes were on him.

She walked around the front of the truck to where he was standing. "I want you to know that you are a sly bastard if there ever was one," she said, her eyes on his face. "You fooled me, acting like a perfect gentleman all night." She shook her head. "I knew what you were, you'd already told me, but I forgot. And then like a fool, I climbed in the bed with you." She pursed her lips and looked at him.

Floyd looked down at her. "You done what you wanted to do, little girl and I did what I wanted to do. Didn't nobody fool nobody."

She looked up at him and smiled. "You're right but I'd swore I wasn't going to let you bed me, but I did. You fooled me and caught me at a weak moment."

He laughed. "You knowed the first time you saw me you was gonna bed me. You know that's the truth."

"Damn, you're despicable," she said as she turned and walked away.

He watched her and smiled.

11

S ister pulled into the right side of the river and landed on a small
sandbar. She needed a break. She pulled the boat up out of the
water and started taking off her clothes. The sun was straight
overhead, it was a warm day and she decided to take a bath. The
sandbar was a perfect place. It had been four days since she'd left
Maude and Luther and she'd seen no sign of the injun.

She put her clothes in the boat, got a bar of soap and a rag and
waded out into the waist-deep water. She was soaping her arms and
upper body when she heard a man's voice.

"Now you're about the prettiest thing I've seen on this river in a
long time."

She whirled about and there was a young man sitting in a canoe
at the end of the sandbar. He was staring at her and smiling.

She put her arms and the washrag over her breasts. "Where the
hell did you come from?" She saw he was nice-looking and dressed
nice. He looked like somebody you'd see in town and not on the river.

"I could ask you the same thing. You seem to be here alone."

"I be by myself, if it be any of yo' business."

"You're right, it's not my business. I didn't mean to sneak up on
you, but I came around the bend and there you were. Since I'm

already here, you go ahead and finish bathing. It won't bother me." He was smiling as he looked at her.

"You gonna sit there and watch me?"

"I'd like to but if you wish, I'll turn around."

She thought back to her experience with the men at Nell's place. If she'd ever been shy, she'd lost it there. When she bent over and let them look down her dress and let them touch and fondle her, she got a lot more business.

She didn't care if he looked as long as he didn't try to hurt her. She wasn't worried about that anyway; she had her pistol. She shrugged and looked at him. "I reckon you done seen most of me, so it don't make much difference. I want you to know I've got a pistol right here in the boat and I can use it."

He laughed. "I don't doubt that, but I have no intention of bothering you. I'm enjoying looking at you too much."

She stared at him. "You sho' are sassy."

He laughed. "And you sho' are pretty. My name is Brooks, by the way."

"Don't matter to me bout yo' name. Soon as I wash off, I'll be gone and won't never see you again."

He shook his head. "I wouldn't want that to happen. I have a cabin about a mile up the river. I want you to come eat supper with me. You probably need a good meal."

"I ain't goin' to no cabin or nowhere else with you. I don't know you one bit."

"I assure you I mean no harm. What is your name?"

"I be Sister."

"Glad to meet you, Sister," he said, smiling at her. He was enjoying himself.

"You gonna sit there and stare at me or turn around and let me finish washin'?"

"Do you want me to turn around? I'm enjoying looking at you. I haven't seen a woman in a while, certainly not one like you."

Sister shrugged. "Don't matter to me," she said. "You done seen most of me noway." She started bathing off again, then waded toward the sandbar to where the water was ankle deep. She faced him, washed her legs and lower body and looked at him. "You done seen enough?"

Brooks laughed. "You're the best I've ever seen. Now come and have supper with me."

"Where yo' cabin be?"

"About a mile up the river. You get dressed and I'll paddle on up and get things ready." He turned the canoe and started up the river.

Sister stood in the water and watched him leave. She rinsed off and started putting her clothes on. She reached in her bag and found the bottle of lotion Nell had given her. She'd never put any of it on before. She decided she would put some on now because Nell had said the men liked it and it would make her smell good.

She wasn't concerned about going to Brook's cabin with him. He didn't look like a man that would harm her, unlike some of the men in Nell's place. Besides, she had her pistol. She finished dressing, got in the boat and started up the river.

It didn't take her long to reach the cabin. It looked good sitting back in the woods, better than any river cabin she'd ever seen. She saw the canoe on the bank as she landed. Brooks walked out of the cabin and came to the boat.

"I didn't know if you would stop or not," he said. "I'm glad you did."

She got out and walked up to him. He was taller than she'd thought when he was in the canoe.

"You smell good," he said as they walked to the cabin.

They went inside. She looked around. She'd never seen a cabin on the river decorated as nicely as this one was. "You live here?" she asked.

"No, I live on my farm," he said. "I just come here sometimes."

"I ain't never seen no cabin so fancy as this."

"I like to be comfortable when I'm here," he said.

She laughed. "I spect this sho is."

He smiled. "Where did you come from, Sister, and where are you going?"

"I lived on a farm downriver. My mama died and my daddy be mean to me, so I left."

He nodded. "And where are you going?"

Sister stared at him. She had decided to never tell anybody she was looking for her man because that was too confusing. "I be lookin' for my brother. He went up the river and I be tryin' to find him."

"He's on the river ahead of you then?"

"He be bout a week ahead. You might have seen 'im? He be dressed like a injun sorta."

Brooks nodded. "I saw him several days ago. He was dressed somewhat like an Indian, with leather and beads."

"That be 'im."

"Where is he going?"

"He say he be gonna winter with the Cherokees like he done before."

"I hate to say this, Sister, but you can't go in that boat much longer, the river will play out. You better catch him before then."

Sister nodded. "I figured that. If he don't stop, I won't never catch 'im."

"What will you do if you don't find him?"

Sister shook her head. "I don't know. Go back downriver, I spect."

"You're welcome to stay here tonight in a comfortable bed. I have some steaks I'll cook. After we eat you can rest and get an early start in the morning if you want."

She looked at him. "Where we be sleepin', if'in I was to stay here?"

He smiled. "I have two bedrooms. You'll be by yourself."

"How come you're bein' so nice to me?"

"I like you and want to help you. I assure you I like women but only if the liking is mutual."

She stared at him. "I ain't sure what that means."

He smiled. "I would only be with a woman if she wanted me to."

She pursed her lips. "I like you; you've been good to me. But I don't know you good enough yet to be with you."

"That's what I thought too," he said. He got up. "I'll fix supper."

She watched him as he cooked and got supper ready. She'd never been around anybody like him in her life. All the men she'd known had treated her badly and wanted something from her. That was the reason she'd responded to the injun. He had saved her and wanted nothing from her. Brooks was helping her, and he didn't demand anything of her either.

They ate and talked. He listened as she talked about running away from home and the men catching her and treating her badly. She left out about the injun saving her; she just said she got away.

Brooks listened intently. Her story touched him deeply and he felt for her. But if she was going to leave to find her brother, he couldn't help her.

When they finished eating, he showed her the bedroom where she could sleep. He left her and walked back in the kitchen. In a minute he heard her moving about. He looked around as she came out of the bedroom. Her eyes were on him.

"What's the matter, Sister?" he asked.

She stared at him. He could tell she was grappling with wanting to ask him a question.

He walked over to her. "What's the matter?"

"Could I sleep with you in yo' bed?" she said, her eyes looking deep in his. "Not nothin' else, just sleep with you. I'd like to talk to you. I been by myself for a long while and I would like to be close to somebody."

Brooks nodded. "If that's what you want."

"That's what I be wantin'."

They walked in the bedroom. He gave her one of his pajama shirts. She put it on, and they got in bed. They lay quietly for several minutes, then she eased over with her back against him. He put his arm around her and held her close. Her body was warm against him, she smelled good, and he was stirred. But she had asked him to only hold her, so he did as she asked. Sometime later they went to sleep.

It was daylight when he eased out of the bed and prepared breakfast. He didn't wake her but let her sleep. It was two hours later when she came into the kitchen.

"I done sho' slept late," she said.

He walked over and hugged her. "That's fine, you were tired."

She looked at him. She'd never been hugged by a man when she liked it. It was a new feeling for her. She looked at the table. "You done got up and cooked?"

"I thought you'd be hungry when you got up."

She stared at him. She was totally confused about everything. She'd been on the river all this time chasing a man whose name she didn't even know. The last time she'd seen him he told her he didn't want anything to do with her. *"Why am I doing this?" she thought.*

"I gotta git dressed," she said.

He walked over and stared in her eyes. "It's been good to have you with me."

She nodded. "You sho' been good to me. I thank you."

He laughed. "In my entire life I've never met anybody like you, Sister. I hate to see you go. I'll miss you."

She looked at him, then went in the bedroom and dressed. When she came out, he was at the kitchen table. She walked over, put her arms around him and hugged him. "I be goin' but I wanted to tell you I sho thank you fir everthang," she said, looking up at him.

He looked down at her face inches away and smiled. Then he pulled her to him and kissed her.

Surprised by his move, she hesitated for a moment, then kissed him back.

He held her close and continued to kiss her, and she responded. She was having feelings and tingling she'd never felt before. She pressed her body against him even more. His hand slid down on her rear and pulled her lower body tighter against him.

Finally, she pushed back from him and stared in his face. "How come you done that? You done got me all stirred up," she said. "You be makin' me have feelings I ain't never had before."

"You got me all stirred up too, Sister," he said looking down at her. "I didn't want you to forget me."

She shook her head. "I don't thank I'll ever forget you now."

He laughed. "Let me tell you this. Upriver a ways is a ferry that carries people across the river. Then on past the ferry a ways on the right side of the river is a large storage building with docks in front of it. If you get there and you haven't found your brother, I don't think you'll ever catch him." He looked in her eyes. "It'll take you several days to get there. If you haven't found him, come back to see me and we'll decide what to do."

Tightlipped, she stared at him. "What you be thankin' bout me doin' if'in I was to come back to you?" As she stared at him. The feelings she'd had while he was kissing her were still bothering her.

"We'll talk about that when you come back." He smiled. "Promise me you'll come back."

"You gonna be here at the cabin?"

"I'll come every day and wait for you."

She nodded, turned and walked away. As she headed for the boat a part of her wanted to turn around and go to him. She kept going, got in the boat and looked back toward the cabin. He was standing on the porch. He waved.

She waved, cranked the motor and started up the river. All the way to the first bend she fought the urge to turn around and go back to him.

12

It was Saturday and as Floyd ate breakfast, he had Rachel on his mind. She'd said she would be waiting for him at Dib's Saturday night, and he hadn't decided what to do about it. He knew the best thing he could do was not show up. But Rachel was a sweet girl and he hated to do that and hurt her. On the other side, if he did show up and she expected to be with him, he was going to hurt her anyway. Based on what had happened with Virginia, there was no way he could be seen with Rachel.

He was in the midst of this dilemma when he saw one of the men from the dock come in and walk toward him.

"Floyd," he said as he got to the table, "there's a man at the dock that wants to talk to you."

Floyd took a drink of coffee and looked up at him. "Who is he?"

The man shook his head. "I ain't never seen 'im before. He come up in a boat from downriver and asked for you. He asked me to find you but not say nothin' about 'im being here to nobody else. He seemed sorta nervous."

Floyd got up. "Take me to 'im." He followed the man outside.

They walked past the warehouse and down to the end of the dock.

"He's in the boat down by the trees," said the man.

"Thanks," said Floyd and walked on down past the end of the dock. As he walked around the last post, he was surprised to see Woody Sharpe sitting in the boat looking at him. He walked on to the boat. "What you doin' here, Woody?"

"Come to see you," he said. "Them folks from Atlanta come to see me and I thought you oughta know bout it."

Floyd laughed. "I know you ain't doin' this outta the goodness of yo' heart. What you want?"

Woody shrugged. "Money. I want money. I figured tellin' you bout this oughta be worth somethin'."

Floyd nodded. "Could be, pendin' on how it comes out."

"They know who you be," said Woody. "They say you be Floyd Wimms and they say you come from a downriver town called River Bluff."

Floyd looked at him. He was surprised that they had found this out about him. "What else did they say?"

"They say you killed some folks downriver. They say you be sho'nuff bad and they be worried bout you."

Floyd stared at him and waited. He knew Woody had something else to say.

"They say they gonna kill you fore they have another try at them cows. They scared you'd mess 'em up again."

"Who are these people?" said Floyd.

"Two men be all I seen. I don't know 'em, but I know they be from Atlanta."

"When did you see 'em?"

"They come to the house this mornin' early. They say they gonna git you fore next Saturday and then git the cows.

"What did they look like?"

Woody shook his head. "They look like regular folks but they ain't from here. They talk funny, not like us." He thought for a minute. "One has a mustache and long black hair. He done all the talkin' bout you. The other man didn't say much."

"Did they say when they gonna see you again?"

"They said fore next Saturday."

"If you hear from them, you let me know," said Floyd. He took some bills out of his pocket and handed them to him.

Woody took the money, pushed the boat away from the bank and headed down the river.

Floyd figured that what Woody said was the truth because there was no way he could have found out his name. These people, whoever they were, were after him for sure. He walked back to the dock and then to the guest house.

Virginia stood at the window in her bedroom and watched Floyd walking back from the dock. She wondered what he'd been doing down there. She wondered about a lot of things having to do with him. She knew that he was what the old folks called a scalawag, a rascal. He had admitted as much to her; but he was much more than that. The trip to the mountains the other night with her had shown her that.

She had seen that he could be charming. In fact, despite all her intentions to the contrary, he had charmed her into his bed. Being in bed with him was the first time for her since her senior year in college with Rex Fox. She'd thought that he was the man she'd spend the rest of her life with, but she'd been wrong. Since then, she'd stayed away from any serious involvement with any man.

She'd been drawn to Floyd since she met him that first day. She couldn't explain it, but the attraction was there. All she knew about him at that time was that he'd killed two men downriver at Nell's place. He had supposedly protected a woman they were harming when he killed the men, so that was in his favor. But other than that, she knew nothing about him. Hardly enough to feel she wanted to bed him right off.

He'd told her what a cad he was; he was open and honest about that. He didn't lie and keep things back from her, at least as far as she knew. He'd said he'd bed her and then walk away, and she believed he'd do exactly that. Despite knowing that, she was still drawn to him.

But there was something else. Since she'd first talked to Floyd and asked him to help her, he'd never said one word about what he'd be paid. He'd never mentioned money a single time. She had wondered about that but hadn't said anything to him about it. Then yesterday she was at the bank on business. Hoot had run over to her, and she could tell he had something on his mind.

"Morning, Virginia," he said. "I hope you're doing well."

She nodded. "I'm well, Hoot." She knew he was leading up to something else, he always did.

"Your man Floyd was in the bank yesterday," he said. "When you introduced him to me, I thought he was just a hired hand for y'all."

She looked at him. "He is just a hired hand. What are you getting at, Hoot?"

"For a hired hand he must do very well," he said smugly as he cut his eyes at her. "He opened an account here with a personal check for a large sum of money." He stared at her. "I was surprised at the amount. Of course, according to bank policy I had to verify the check. The check was valid." He waited for her reply.

Virginia stared at him as if she wondered why he was telling her this. There was no way she was going to give him the satisfaction of having surprised her. She shrugged. "You wouldn't have been surprised if you'd known that he'd done well in the gold mines north of here. He told me all about that." She looked at him. "Did you have anything else you wanted to talk to me about?"

Hoot was crestfallen. He'd thought for sure that he would surprise her. "No, I don't have anything else." He turned and walked back to his desk.

Virginia thought of that conversation as she watched Floyd go in his house. She turned, went downstairs and out the front door. She walked across the street and knocked on his door. The door opened and she was looking at him.

"Mornin'," he said. He stood there wondering what this early visit was about.

"Don't try that sweet talking with me," she said as she walked past him into the house.

He turned and looked at her. He'd never expected her to come inside with him alone. By what she'd said so far, she had something on her mind, and it didn't seem to be good. "What's the matter with you?" he said, walking over to her. "What are you talkin' about?"

"It seemed strange to me that since you've been here, you've never said a word about what you'd be paid for helping us." She stared at him. "You've never mentioned money one time. I thought that was strange."

He frowned. "I hadn't really thought about it," he said as he looked in her eyes. He didn't know why she had started this conversation and what was the point.

"Most people aren't rich enough to not think about money when they're working," she said. She was watching his face. "Are you rich and you don't worry about money?"

"I git by," he said, still puzzled as to what she was talking about.

She shook her head. "That's bullshit and you know it," she said, and her tone changed to confrontational. "I talked to Hoot yesterday at the bank. He said you opened an account at the bank and deposited a great deal of money. That sounds like you do more than get by."

"Hoot has got a big mouth," Floyd said, "and I ain't real sure why we be talkin' bout this. The money was mine."

She shook her head. "We're not talking about Hoot; we're talking about you."

"What are you so stirred up about?" he said. "I told you I was in the goldmine and done well. I told you that."

"You mentioned it, that was all." She walked over and opened the door. "Leave this door open. I don't want people to see me go in this house and start talk."

He walked over and looked down at her. "Why don't you go in the back with me, and we'll give them somethin' to talk about."

She stared up at him; her lips tightened. She pushed him aside and walked to the door. She stopped and looked back. "Is that all you think about?"

He walked over to her. "What do you want me to tell you?"

"Why did you open that account at the bank?"

"I might need some money and that makes it easier to git it quick."

"Why would you do that really?" She looked at him, her eyes searching his face. "You said you'd be moving on in a bit."

"I might be movin' on or I might not." He stared at her. "We done talked bout that. I done told you how I do."

She frowned. "What the hell does that mean?"

"It depends on what happens."

She stared up at him. "What does it depend on? What keeps you here?" She watched his face.

Floyd knew she was trying to get him to say more than he wanted to say. He shrugged. "It depends on when I catch them rustlers. That's what you asked me to do."

Her lips tightened and she took a deep breath. "You are a bastard," she said as she slammed the door and walked away.

Floyd smiled.

That afternoon Floyd got in the truck and went to town. In town he turned south toward the county line. He crossed the line and pulled into the joint across the road from Dib's. The bartender here had told him where to find Woody, so he was informed about what was going on. Floyd walked in and saw the same bartender working behind the bar. He walked over and sat on a stool. The bartender saw him and came over.

"What you want?"

Floyd put a bill on the bar. "There be some out-of-town people lookin' for me. I want to know when they git in town and where they are."

The bartender nodded. "I heard that. If they come in town, they'll probably be at Tub's place where Woody hangs out. I doubt they'd come in here, but they might."

"You let me know when you hear anythang. I'll come back and check with you."

"The bartender picked up the bill and nodded. "I hear they be bad people. Folks say it's good to stay away from 'em."

Floyd shrugged. "They just be thankin' they be bad. They ain't run up on nobody as bad as me."

The bartender smiled as he watched Floyd walk out.

F loyd went outside, got in the truck and went back to the farm. He was inside trying to decide what to do about Rachel when he heard a car drive up. He walked to the window and saw it was Ron Hurt's car. Ron got out, went to the door and knocked. The door opened and he went inside. In a few minutes Virginia came out of the house with him. He had his arm around her, and they were laughing as they went to the car,

Floyd saw her look his way as Ron opened the door for her. She got in, he shut the door, ran around to the other side and got in. They drove off toward town.

Floyd stood at the window for a minute, then went to the bathroom, took a bath and dressed. Virginia's actions had made up his mind for him. He went out, got in the truck and headed to town. All his honorable intentions were gone, Virginia had killed them. Two could play this game. He got to Dib's, parked and went inside. Rachel was sitting at the same table where she had been before. She smiled when she saw him walking toward her. He noticed that several other people had their eyes on him too.

She got up and hugged him. "I was afraid you wouldn't come."

He hugged her and they sat down. She leaned over against him. The waitress came over and they ordered drinks.

"I heard you got into a fight the other night at Tub's," she said.

"I told you I was goin' lookin' for a man, and I found 'im."

She nodded. "You're all right now?"

"I'm good."

"I'm glad you came tonight. I was hoping you would."

"Rachel," he said, looking in her eyes. "I tried to tell you the other night what kind of person I am. You're a schoolteacher here in town and a nice, sweet girl. You bein' seen with me tonight ain't gonna do nothin' good for yo' reputation."

She smiled. "That's sweet, Floyd. You let me worry about what I do." She took his hand. "You're here and I'm here. If you don't want to be with me as I am, you can leave. But, if you stay, then let me do what I want to and I want to be with you."

He nodded. "It's up to you."

"Howard brought me out here to wait for you. If you want to go, he'll come get me." She stared at him. "If not, you can take me home."

He got up and held out his hand. She took his hand and got up. They walked out of the club, got in the truck and started toward town. She slid over against him. He put his arm around her. She directed him to her house. They pulled into the drive, parked and he turned off the motor. He pulled her to him and kissed her. She returned his kiss with passion. They stayed in the truck for several minutes getting to know each other. She was responsive in every way and held nothing back.

Finally, she drew away. "Let's go inside," she said. "We're steaming up the car." She smiled at him. "Steaming me up too. I've got a bed inside." She jumped out and he followed her.

She unlocked the door, and they went inside. She reached up and kissed him. "I'll be back in a minute," she said and ran in the bathroom. She came out shortly, took his hand and led him to the bedroom.

He undressed and then watched her slowly take off her clothes. Her eyes were on his face as she removed each piece.

"Damn," he said. "You're a good-lookin' woman, Rachel.

She came over to him, wrapped her arms around him and kissed him. He picked her up, put her on the bed and lay down beside her.

. . .

When he woke up the sun was well up; it was mid-morning. She was lying on the pillow looking at him. "It's Sunday," she said, "can you stay all day with me?"

"I don't know bout that," he said. "What do you want to do?"

She rolled over against him and kissed him. "Staying right here suits me fine for now. I'll get up and fix something to eat after a while."

He laughed. "Girl, I sure had you figured wrong."

She laughed and kissed him again.

The sun was almost down when he parked at his house. He got out and went inside. He was in the bathroom when he heard a knock on the door. He walked to the front and opened it. Virginia was standing there staring at him.

"You been out tom catting all this time?" she said. "I saw that you didn't come home at all last night."

He stared at her. "I saw you go out last night with Ron and I figured I could do the same." He frowned. "I forget thangs sometimes. Did I promise you I'd just be with you? I sho' don't remember doin' that."

Her face reddened. "You didn't promise me a damn thing, nor did I." She pursed her lips. "It was my mistake to think you were anything but what you are."

He grunted. "I done told you that more than once. Anyway, twice now when you got mad with me about somethin', you run off with Ron. Don't thank I'm gonna sit here when you do that."

She nodded. "You've proven that for sure."

"You knocked on my door, I didn't call you. What did you want?"

She shook her head. "I've forgotten," she said. She turned, walked across the road and went in the big house.

Floyd watched her go and closed the door.

~

S ister had been on the river for two days since she'd left Brooks. Every hour she had to talk herself out of turning around and going back to him. The feelings she'd had when he kissed her were still with her.

She'd decided that she would go to the ferry he'd told her about and then to the warehouse. If she didn't see the injun by then, she was going back downriver. She rounded a bend, and the ferry was right in front of her. It was on the right bank and an old man was sitting in a chair watching her as she approached.

She rode the boat to the ferry, cut off the motor and grabbed a rope. She looked at the old man. He was staring at her intently.

"Hardly ever see no woman in a boat on the river by herself," he said. He spat a wad of tobacco into the water beside him.

"I be lookin' for my brother," she said. "He be in a boat ahead of me."

"Seed lots of people on the river in boats," said the old man.

"He be a big man, wears leather and beads sorta like a injun."

He nodded. "I seed 'im, back some days ago. He asked me about a tall man what lives here. I told 'im it was most likely Woody Sharpe; he be the tallest man round here. He lives up the road in that white house."

"What did the man in the boat do after he talked to you?"

The old man shook his head. "Didn't do nothin'. I told him bout Woody and he cranked up and went back up the river. Damndest thang I bout ever saw. I still ain't figured out why he come down here."

"You seen 'im since then?"

The old man shook his head. "I ain't seed him no more. He ain't gone downriver cause I woulda sho'seed 'im go by."

Sister looked up the road toward the houses. "Y'all got a store here?"

He chuckled. "Got one but it ain't much. Better than nothin', I reckon." He pointed behind him. "Right up the road there."

She beached the boat, tied to a willow tree and walked toward what town was there. The man had said the injun had come down to the ferry and asked about a tall man. That must have meant he had been staying close but why would he be looking for a man? That all sounded strange.

She saw the general store and as she approached, a man came out the door and stood on the porch. She stopped and stared. He was taller than any man she'd seen in a while. She wondered if he was the man the injun was looking for. There couldn't be many men taller than he was.

He was standing on the porch staring at her when she walked up. She didn't like the way he was looking at her. She put her hand in her purse and grabbed the pistol.

"Hey, Missy," he said, grinning as he looked at her. "You sho' be bout a good-lookin' thang. I just might want to go out with you."

She took the pistol out of the purse and held it in front of her chest where he could see it. She looked up at him. "You take one step toward me, and I'll be done shot yo' stupid ass."

He laughed and held up his hands. "Damn, I believe you would sho' do it." He looked toward the river. "I ain't gonna bother you. Where did you come from?"

"I come up the river looking for my brother. Maybe you done seen "im. He's a big man, dressed sorta like a injun." She saw his facial expression change and knew he had seen him.

He stared down at her. "You talkin' bout Floyd Wimms? Floyd be yo' brother?"

She nodded. *So that was his name, Floyd Wimms.* "You seen 'im?"

"I seen 'im. He be up at the Mann place up the river."

"Where that be?"

"Not far. There's a big warehouse and docks there. He lives in a house there."

That puzzled her. "He lives in a house?"

He nodded. "He works up there." He grinned at her. "It's gonna git dark fore long and you can't git there fore dark. I got a house right across the road. You can stay with me and sleep in a real bed tonight. I got supper too."

She shook her head. "You must thank I be stupid if you thank I be goin' off with you."

He laughed. "When you see Floyd, you tell 'im you talked to Woody Sharpe. Tell 'im I told you where to find 'im."

She didn't answer him. She turned around and went back to the ferry.

The old man looked at her as she walked up. "You didn't buy nothin'?"

She shook her head. "I met that Woody at the store, and he say my brother be at a warehouse up the river."

The old man nodded. "That would be the Mann place," he said. "That be the only warehouse upriver. That be where you goin'?"

"If that be where he be, that be where I goin'." She got in the boat, pushed away from the ferry and went upriver. It was almost dark when she stopped and set up camp. She planned to be on the river at daylight. She was close to finding the injun and didn't want to waste any time. But when she thought about that, it didn't excite her as it had in the past. Her mind kept going back to her time with Brooks. That injun done said he didn't want her. Brooks told her to come back cause he sho' wanted her.

~

Virginia was beside herself. She knew Floyd had been out all Saturday night and then until late Sunday afternoon. It bothered her, especially since she had no idea what he had done. She had no idea where he had been or who he might have been with. She didn't think he knew any women here, but that didn't necessarily mean he wasn't with a woman. She'd discovered that Floyd was full of surprises. She'd already seen that part of him.

Then, when she'd faced him about being out all night and all day, he'd thrown it in her face that she'd gone out with Ron. She'd had no defense for his charge; she was guilty. She'd thought her going off with Ron would make him jealous but that hadn't been his reaction at all. Like he'd said, he wasn't going to sit and mope, and he hadn't.

The next move was hers; he wasn't going to give in. It wasn't just that she liked him; she was taken with him more than she'd been with a man in years. She knew she had to keep him here; he was her only hope to stop the rustling and their other problems. She made her decision. She went downstairs, across the street to his house and knocked on his door.

Floyd was about to go down to eat supper when he heard a knock on the door. He walked over, opened it and was surprised to see Virginia looking at him. Before he said a word she walked in the room and closed the door behind her.

She looked at him. "All right, you win. I have no shame. I want peace."

He stared at her. "Peace? What are you talking about?"

"I know you don't make agreements or promises, but maybe we can come to an understanding."

He nodded as he looked in her face. "About what? You ain't said what we be talkin' about."

"I've decided that I won't go out with Ron anymore; I'll just be with you." She watched his face. "And you'll just be with me. *Like the folks say, I'll be yo' woman.*"

He frowned and pursed his lips. His brow furrowed as he stared at her.

She saw he didn't understand. "I'll be with you whenever you want me. I'll be in your bed every night if you want me. You just tell me what you want."

He cocked his head and looked at her. "Are you talkin' 'bout us gettin' married?"

She laughed. "No, silly. I'm saying I'll be with you whenever you want me, and you won't be with other women."

He was still frowning. "Why you be sayin' this?"

"Despite not wanting to, I like you," she said. "I want to be with you out in the open. I want everybody to know we're together."

"You plannin' on livin' over here in this house with me?" He was looking in her eyes, his brow still furrowed.

"No, not exactly," she said, shaking her head. "Daddy wouldn't ever go for that. But I'd come over at night when you wanted me to."

He shrugged. "You can come over at night now if you want to. I ain't never said you couldn't, but you ain't come 'cept for that one time."

She took a deep breath. "I want us to date and be together like we did when we went to the mountains. I want to let everybody know we're a couple."

"What did yo' daddy say about this?"

"I haven't discussed it with him, but I know Daddy likes you."

"I'll go out with you anytime you want me to," he said. "You can be in my bed whenever you want to." He paused. "But what you be sayin' sounds like me bein' tied down." He shook his head. "I ain't never been tied down with no woman fir long."

"Then you don't have any special feeling for me?" She watched his face as she talked.

He nodded. "Sho' I do. I like to be with you like the other night and I like to go to bed with you."

Virginia was tight lipped as she stared at him. "That's all you feel about me?"

He was puzzled. "What else do you want?"

She shook her head, walked to the door, opened it and looked back at him. "I don't want a damn thing from you." She started across the street, stopped and came back to the door. "Damn, I'm stupid. I don't know why I wasted my time talking to you." She went across the street and went in the big house.

He watched her until the door across the street slammed. He shrugged and shut the door.

H e went inside, changed clothes and went to town. He drove to Rachel's house, parked and walked to the door. Suddenly the door opened, and Rachel ran out and hugged him. He kissed her and they went back inside.

He was in the bed with Rachel lying beside him and thought about the meeting with Virginia. He liked to be with her, and it seemed she liked to be with him too. He looked down at Rachel. He liked her too. He wasn't sure exactly what Virginia had been asking him to do but it sounded like he'd have to stop seeing Rachel if he agreed. Why would he ever do that? It didn't make sense.

13

Sister camped on the river above the ferry. She watched behind her for that man that called his self Woody. She had been afraid he would follow her, but she didn't see any sign of him.

Woody had said that the injun's name was Floyd Wimms and he was living at that big warehouse up the river. She couldn't figure out how he had done that but if he was there, she was about to find him. However, she had mixed feelings about finding him. Doubt had crept into her thinking.

When he'd left her at Nell's, he'd said to her face that he didn't want her with him. In fact, he'd said it more than once. She'd tried to convince him to let her go with him. She told him she could cook for him but that didn't make no difference to him. Since then, she'd thought a lot about that and figured out she'd offered him the wrong thing.

She'd decided that when she caught him, this time she would offer to go to bed with him. She was sure that would change his mind. She knew men wanted to bed her, all the men at Nell's had wanted to. Every day they even offered her money to do it. Men just seemed to be that way around her. But then it wasn't just her.

She knew Tillie and her sister didn't look as good as she did, but men still paid money to bed them. They went to the backroom most every night with men. Most of the time they weren't gone long and sometimes they went more than once. Tillie bragged about how much money she made.

All this was in her mind as she broke camp and loaded the boat. But now, since she'd met Brooks, the plan to find the injun, bed him and stay with him wasn't as clear in her mind. In the last few days, she'd thought more about going back down the river.

Regardless of what had happened, she intended to find the injun. She had trouble thinking of him and calling him Floyd Wimms. When she found him, she'd see how he acted toward her and then she'd decide what to do. It had always been in her head that he had saved her, and she owed it to him to be his woman. She wasn't sure why she thought that, maybe somebody had told her that was the way it was.

As she rode up the river, she decided that when she got to the warehouse, she'd tell whoever she saw that she was looking for her man. She wasn't going to fool with saying he was her brother. His name was Floyd Wimms and he looked sorta like a injun. She'd just come right out and say it.

The sun was straight overhead when she came around a bend and saw the warehouse and docks on the right bank as the ferry man had said. There were several big boats tied up and men were loading bales of hay on them.

She turned into the bank and landed. She got out, tied the boat up and walked toward the dock. She saw a woman standing on the dock staring down at her. The woman was young and pretty and continued to stare at her as she approached.

Virginia felt like a fool and fools do stupid things. She certainly had. She had gone to Floyd and offered herself to him like a common slut. She'd been so upset and hurt that he'd been out all-night Saturday night and all-day Sunday that she reacted stupidly. What made it worse was she didn't know where he'd been or what he'd done while he was gone. Without any evidence she'd decided he was with a woman. As far as she knew, he didn't know any women here.

Why had she acted as she did was the question in her mind. She'd never done anything like that in the past, certainly not about any man. But Floyd was different from any man she'd ever met. She had been attracted to him when she met him for the first time. She'd been attracted to other men but not in the way she was to Floyd. And that attraction had increased each time she was with him until she ended up in his bed.

After then she'd thought there was a mutual attraction, and they would build on that. That hadn't happened. Since that night in his bed, he'd treated her like a whore, a woman he'd paid to be with him. When she'd given him an opening to say he had feelings toward her, he'd said nothing. His attitude infuriated her.

Then she'd really acted the fool. She'd gone to him and offered herself to him without any commitment on his part in return. She would come to him and do his bidding when he called. The more she thought about what she'd done, the more she felt like a complete idiot. Or maybe she was a common whore.

She swore that she'd never have anything to do with him in the future. As soon as he got the problems with the rustlers handled, she was going to tell him to leave and never come back. She'd try to tolerate him until then.

Virginia walked down to the dock. They were shipping hay downriver today and she had to make sure all the paperwork was in order. She was standing on the dock when she heard a boat coming up the river. She looked as it came around the bend and could see the lone driver in the boat. When it got closer, she was surprised that the driver was a woman; she looked to be young. That was strange, she never remembered seeing a woman on the river in a boat alone. The boat landed below the docks, the woman got out and started walking up the bank. She was right, the woman was young, and very attractive, even though her hair was uncombed, and she was dressed rough. Virginia walked to the edge of the dock and waited. "Good morning," she said as the woman came up the bank toward the dock.

"Morning," the woman said. She was staring at Virginia, her face questioning.

"Can I help you?" As she looked closer at the woman, it was evident she had something on her mind.

"I be lookin' fir my man," she said, watching Virginia's face as she spoke. "A man downriver told me he be here."

"You're lookin' for your man, and you think he's here? Is that right?" said Virginia. "And what is your name?"

"I be Sister."

Virginia nodded. "And what is your husband's name?"

Sister shook her head. "He ain't my husband, he just be my man. His name be Floyd Wimms, he sorta looks like a injun."

The color drained from Virginia's face, and she felt dizzy. She stared at Sister as she tried to get control of her feelings. "His name is Floyd Wimms and he's your man but he's not your husband? Is that what you said?"

Sister nodded. "That be right."

"What happened? Did he leave you and go off?" Virginia looked in her eyes as she spoke.

Sister nodded. "I told him I would go with 'im but he didn't wait for me."

Virginia nodded. "That's just like a sorry-ass man. Does he know you're looking for him?"

Sister frowned. "I ain't sure bout that."

"Why not? Didn't you tell him you were going to come with him?"

Sister had grown tired of all these questions. "I done told you all that. Is he here? Do you know 'im?"

Virginia smiled. "He's here and yes, I know him." She chuckled. "Come with me and I'll take you to him. I bet he will be surprised to see you."

Sister didn't say anything, but she also thought he would be surprised.

Virginia started walking away from the dock and Sister fell in beside her.

"Have you been with Floyd long?"

Sister shook her head. "Not long."

"Do you have children?"

Sister stared at her. "Ain't had no time for that."

Virginia was having a hard time understanding Sister. What she said didn't make sense. "We're going to Floyd's house. I saw him go in not long ago." She stopped and looked at Sister. "I bet he'll be glad to see you."

Sister frowned. She wasn't too sure about that.

Floyd had come back to the house after eating lunch and was about to go to town and see if the bartender had any news for him. He was changing shirts when he heard a knock on the door. He walked over, opened it and was surprised to see Virginia standing there. After last night he didn't know if she'd ever speak to him again. She was smiling and that surprised him even more.

"Good news, Floyd" she said. "Your woman has finally found you."

His brow furrowed as he stared at her. *"What the hell is she talking about?"* he thought? *"Is she talking about herself?"*

Then she turned and pointed.

He looked where she was pointing and saw Sister. He stared at her; she was the last person he'd ever expected to see again.

"She said she had followed her man all the way up the river. Now, ya'll can be together." Virginia stepped back and looked at Floyd's shocked face. She was enjoying every minute of this.

"Sister," he said, "where the hell did you come from?"

"I told you I was gonna be yo' woman. I come to find you."

Virginia was standing to the side, and she saw the hurt in Sister's face. She knew something about what was going on here wasn't right.

She looked at Floyd. "Why are you talking so mean to her? Don't you see you're hurting her?"

Floyd wheeled about and stared in her face. His movement was so sudden that she thought he was going to hit her. She stepped back.

"You stay the hell outta this, Virginia. You don't know what the hell is going on here." He walked over and faced Sister. "I told you I didn't want you to come with me. Just because I killed them men didn't mean a damn thang about savin' you. I don't give a damn about you and you sho' ain't stayin' with me."

Virginia walked up behind him. "Who is she, Floyd?"

He cut his eyes at her. "She'd the girl that them two men at Nell's had. I kilt 'em and she thanks I saved her life so she oughta stay with me and be my woman. She's crazy as hell."

Virginia looked at him and shook her head. "You are one mean bastard, Floyd," she said as she walked over and put her arm around Sister. "Is that why you came, Sister?" she said. "He saved your life, so you think you should stay with him?"

Tears flowed down Sister's face as she looked at Virginia. "That seemed to be the right thang to do. I'd been told that."

Virginia smiled and shook her head. "That's not true, Sister. You can be grateful for him saving you, but you don't owe him anything for doing it. You certainly don't have to be his woman."

"That's what I told 'er," said Floyd.

Virginia turned and stared in his face. "You shut the hell up, Floyd. Don't be a worse bastard than you already are." She looked at Sister. "It's obvious he don't want you, so you come with me."

Sister shook her head. "I ain't gonna stay here. I done come all the way up the river cause of 'im. I done seen 'im. Now I'll be goin' back down the river."

"That's not a good idea, Sister," said Virginia. "It's late and it will be dark soon. Stay with me, have a good meal and a good night's sleep. If you still want to leave in the morning, you can eat breakfast and we'll give you food to take with you. That makes more sense."

"You got a place for me to stay?"

Virginia smiled. "You'll have a bedroom to yourself. We'll treat you like a princess." She looked at Floyd. "Damn it, Floyd. Can't you see what this girl did because of you. Maybe she was wrong in her thinking, but I know she's been through hell getting here." Tightlipped, she stared at him. "Surely there's at least a smidgen of decency in you."

He stared at both of them. Then he slowly walked over to Sister. "I be sorry bout all this, Sister. I didn't mean for you to do all this and come after me. I be sorry I talked mean to you."

Sister pursed her lips and stared at him. "I was gonna be yo' woman cause you saved me. I can cook and I would let you bed me if I stayed with you. All the men at Nell's wanted to bed me. They even offered me money."

Virginia put her arm around her. "Don't tell him that, Sister. He'll be all over you in a minute if you say that. Floyd would take a goat to bed, if he couldn't find a woman." She stared at Floyd. "Damn, you are a sorry man." She led Sister toward the big house.

Floyd stood in the street and watched them. He got in the truck and headed to town. He didn't want to talk to any more women right now.

Virginia took Sister into the house and up the stairs. She showed her a bedroom and bath that would be hers as long as she stayed here. Sister had never been in a house like this and was amazed.

Virginia took her into her bedroom and showed her the closet. "I'm larger than you are," she said to Sister, "but I have some nice clothes that I've outgrown, and you can have them." She started pulling out clothes nicer that anything Sister had ever seen and stacking them up. "We will put these in boxes when you go, and you'll have plenty to wear from now on." Sister couldn't believe that Virginia was giving her all of these clothes and she thanked her over and over.

Virginia smiled. "You should get something out of the trip you've made for that worthless Floyd. What do you think you'll do now?"

Sister looked at her. She'd never had anyone treat her like Virginia and she trusted her. "I be going back downriver," she said. "I met a man and he asked me to come back to 'im. He said he would be waiting for me."

"Is he a good man and did you like him?"

For the next hour Sister told her all she knew about Brooks. Virginia was impressed. "You slept in the bed with him, and he never touched you?"

Sister nodded.

"Sounds like he's a good man," said Virginia. "You wouldn't ever do that with Floyd. He has the morals of a tom cat or maybe worse."

Sister stared at her. "Have you been with 'im?"

"I'm sorry to say I have," said Virginia. "I made a mistake." She looked at Sister. "Let's change the subject. Tell me about him saving you and killing those two men."

"He sho' kilt 'em," said sister and she launched into the entire story.

"So, you felt that since he'd saved you, you should go with him?"

Sister nodded. "I didn't have no other place to go but I stayed with Nell."

"What did you do while you were with Nell?"

Sister smiled. "I served the men drinks." Then she told her about the men touching her as they gave her tips. "They wanted to pay me to go in the backroom with 'em. But I didn't never do it like Tillie and her sister did."

Virginia shook her head. "I couldn't ever do that. It's hard to imagine all you've been through, Sister." She looked at her. "You're welcome to stay here with me as long as you want to."

Sister pursed her lips and thought. "If you don't mind I 'spect I'll stay till I rest up."

Virginia smiled. "Just stay away from Floyd while you're here. I told you that he has no morals."

Sister frowned. "What do that mean?"

"It means that he'll take advantage of any woman and never think twice about it. He wouldn't think any more about getting you in his bed than he would a goat."

Sister stared at her. "It sho' sounds like you be in love with 'im."

Virginia shook her head. "That's crazy, Sister. I can't stand him." She jumped up. "Let's go downstairs and I'll introduce you to my daddy."

14

F loyd parked and went in the joint across the street from Dib's. His bartender was on duty. Floyd sat on a stool and waited until he came over. As usual Floyd put a bill on the table and took his beer.

The bartender started wiping the bar. "Word on the street is them folks in Atlanta done brought in two men to come git you. They supposed to be sho'nuff bad people. They gonna be at Tub's tomorrow night with Woody, so people say." He picked up the bill and walked away.

Floyd glanced over the people at the tables. Several had been looking at him but quickly looked away. He drank his beer and then walked out.

W hen he got back and parked at the farm, he saw Sister walk out of the big house and start toward the dock. He got out and walked behind her. "Where you be goin', Sister?"

She stopped and looked back at him. "I be goin' to the river and git my thangs." She stared at him. "I ain't gonna talk to you."

He walked up to her. "I'll go with you and help you."

She stared at him. "Why you be doin' that?"

"I thought you might need help."

"Virginia say I oughta stay away from you."

"Why did she say that?"

She looked in his eyes. "She say can't no woman trust you. She say you ain't got no morals."

He laughed. "She's probably right but I ain't gonna bother you."

She frowned and stared at him. "You ain't? Don't you thank I be pretty?"

He walked over to her, looked down in her face and put his arm around her. "You sho' be pretty. You want to go to the house with me?"

She stared up at him. "I ain't feared of you."

He bent over and kissed her on the forehead. "Let's go git yo' stuff before I talk myself into something".

Sister smiled and looked in his face. "I seen it in yo' eyes. You be joshin' me but you want to take me to yo' house. I thank I be in yo' house fore I leave here."

He shook his head. "You need to hush, Sister. I be tryin' to do the right thang here and you be makin' it mighty hard fir me."

She smiled and followed him to her boat. They got her belongings and walked back to the big house.

He set what he had carried at the door. "I ain't goin' in. Virginia might shoot me."

Sister walked over to him. "I done come all this way to find you. I ain't leaving till I be with you. Then we be even for you savin' me."

He stared at her. "Best you don't do that little girl." He smiled. "If you come around me, what happens ain't my fault."

She grinned. "Won't be mine neither, but I be comin'." She turned and walked in the house.

Woody Sharpe grew up in the small settlement on the riverbank at the ferry. In addition to the ferry, there were a few houses, the small general store and Tub's, a beer joint. Most of

Tub's business came from across the river. The county on that side was dry so people came across the ferry to get alcohol. Without the business at Tub's the town would have died long ago.

The surrounding area was poor with no industry and few jobs, especially during the depression that had every area hurting. There was some farming and good fishing on the river but little else. People in the town had little hope that things would get better, so they just existed day to day.

Woody had a younger brother, Sol. Their daddy was a drunk and their mother wasn't right in the head, she'd always been that way. Without any guidance from his parents, Woody was on his own from his early years. Surprisingly, despite his parents being as they were, he was intelligent. He used his intelligence to get money however he could and survive. Stealing and other petty crimes was the easiest way to get by.

He was smart enough not to steal from his neighbors, he did that in the surrounding area. He was good at it and prospered. By the time he was twenty he had developed a relationship with people In Atlanta that bought stolen goods and asked no questions. The local law enforcement knew his name, they suspected that he was involved in robberies, but he'd never been arrested. The people at the ferry protected him for two reasons, he brought in money, and they were afraid of him.

In time he branched out into other crime areas which was how he came to be involved with the cattle rustling. The people in Atlanta were looking for someone that knew the area and he was perfect for the job. He felt he had arrived now; he was big-time. He was carrying a pistol.

But that changed the night he met Floyd Wimms. He was sitting in Tub's drinking and savoring the moment when Floyd came in and walked over to where he was sitting. When Floyd started talking to him, he felt threatened and started to draw his pistol. That was his first mistake. Floyd grabbed him, pulled out his own weapon and pistol whipped him till he was near unconscious. When he was dragged out of Tub's that night like a sack of potatoes, he thought he was a dead man.

He was relieved when it turned out Floyd had no interest in him but was after whoever was behind the rustling. He wanted information. To stay alive, Woody would give him whatever he wanted.

After Floyd turned him loose that night, Woody not only feared him, but he also admired him. It seemed to him that Floyd was more in charge than the people in Atlanta and he didn't want to end up on the wrong side of whatever was going to happen. That was the reason he'd gone to Floyd and told him the men in Atlanta had put out a contract on him. He had no regard or loyalty to the Atlanta people. When Sol got shot, they did nothing to help them. He realized then that he was hired help and regarded as expendable.

Now the men from Atlanta were back. They were after Floyd and intended to kill him. He knew he was walking a dangerous path talking to Floyd. If the Atlanta people found out, they wouldn't hesitate to kill him. Despite knowing that, the fact that Floyd had let him go when he could have killed him swayed him. He went to the river, got his boat and headed upstream.

F loyd walked out of the house and was headed to his truck when he saw one of the men from the dock coming toward him. He stopped and waited.

"That fellow is back at the dock and wants to see you," said the man.

"Same one from the other day?"

The man nodded. "Same one."

Floyd thanked him and headed toward the dock. He walked to the end of the warehouse and down to the river. He saw Woody sitting in the boat waiting for him. He figured Woody was going to tell him what the bartender had already told him. He walked up to the boat. "What you got, Woody?"

"Them Atlanta people will be at Tub's tomorrow night. They want me to meet 'em there." Woody stared at him. "They want me to find out where you are this week, and they say they gonna kill you."

"How many will they be at Tub's?"

"I thank just two, but they say there be more coming. They sho' want you bad."

Floyd nodded. He knew Woody was right. "Does Tub's have a back door?"

Woody nodded. "It at the far end of the bar. It goes in a room where they store stuff. There's another door from that room to outside."

Floyd looked at him. "Git a table next to that door. When I come in, I want to go out that back door."

Woody frowned. "What you be plannin' on doin'?"

"I don't want to git in no gunfight with 'em," said Floyd. "Fore they have time to git up I might have to kill one of 'em. I want to take one of 'em alive if I can. I gotta find out who these people be and who hired 'em." He stared at Woody. "You better be tellin' me the truth bout all this."

"Everthang I told you be the truth," said Woody. "I ain't got nothin' fir 'em. They ain't done nothin' for Sol since he be shot."

"If they thank you helped me, they gonna be after you."

Woody nodded. "That be the truth. I sho' know that."

"Best you stay out of the way when the shooting starts," said Floyd.

"I plan to," Woody said. "If the same two guys are here, the one in the mustache is the one you oughta shoot first. He acts like he's sho'nuff bad. The other guy just does what he says."

Floyd nodded. "That be good to know."

Woody pushed the boat away from the boat, cranked the motor and started downriver.

F loyd left Woody and walked back toward his house. As he came around the end of the warehouse, he saw Virginia and Sister come out of the big house and start walking toward him. When they saw him, they stopped, looked at each other, then stared at him as he approached.

"*I ain't never seen two better looking women,*" he thought as he walked up to them. "What y'all be up to?" he said.

"What we do is not any of your business, Floyd," said Virginia. "We're not having anything to do with you."

He looked at Sister. "Virginia is mighty hard on me; I'm trying to help 'er, Sister. What do you think?"

She smiled. "I done told you what I think. You know what I'm gonna do."

Floyd cut his eyes at her. "I done told you what I thought of what you said, little girl. I ain't gonna tell you again." He walked past them, went to his house and went inside.

Virginia stared at Sister. "I've never seen anybody shut Floyd up like you just did. What in the world did you tell him?"

"I told 'im I done come all this way to find 'im cause he saved me from them men. I be in his debt, and I have to settle with 'im cause I owe 'im," said Sister. "I said I would be his woman. I would cook fir 'im and git in his bed, but he wouldn't do it."

Virginia was relieved. "Well, you're lucky there. He would have used you till he tired of you and then he would have been gone. That's the kind of man he is." She looked at her, her brow furrowed. "But you said something else while ago and he didn't like it. I've never seen him walk away like that. What you said bothered him. What was that about?"

"I told 'im last night that I still owed 'im for savin' me. I told 'im fore I leave I be gonna go in his house and bed 'im. Then we be even."

Virginia stepped back. Wide-eyed she stared at Sister. "You told him that?"

Sister nodded. "Sho' did."

"But you were joking with him?"

Sister shook her head. "I weren't jokin'. That be the fair thang to do and then we be even. I don't owe 'im nothin' no more."

Virginia frowned. "You can't do that, Sister. That's not right. You don't have to do that."

"It be right," said Sister. "I done told 'im."

Virginia walked over and put her arms around her. "You come with me," she said. "I need to talk to you about this."

F loyd was in bed and almost asleep when he heard a knock on the door. He wondered what was going on as he staggered out of the bed. He went to the front room and opened the door. Sister was standing there in her nightgown.

"Sister," he said, "what the hell are you doing here?"

"I told you I was comin'," she said as she walked past him into the room. "I be leavin' tomorrow, so I come to you."

"I done told you not to do this," he said. "You don't owe me nothin'."

Sister reached down and pulled the nightgown over her head and stood naked before him. "It don't matter what you say. I be ready. Virginia don't know I be over here."

He stared at her. "Damn it, girl, I ain't never done the right thang about any woman in my whole life. But I be tryin' to do the right thang here." He shook his head. "You sho are makin' it hard to do right."

She reached over and took his hand. "Where be yo' bedroom?" she said as she led him down the hall. They walked into the bedroom. She led him to the bed, put both her arms around him and hugged him. She raised on her tip toes and kissed him.

He pulled her to him and kissed her. He looked in her eyes, shook his head and pushed her back on the bed.

L ater she rolled off his arm and kissed him. "I got to git back to the house."

He kissed her and pulled her over against him. "Why don't you stay a little longer?"

She kissed him and smiled. "That be what I hoped you say."

. . .

I t was almost daylight when she jumped up, ran out the door and across the road to the big house.

~

I t was almost noon the next morning before all of Sister's boxes and packages were taken to the dock and loaded in her boat. She'd never had so many nice clothes.

She and Virginia were walking back to the dock from the house.

"Are you settled with this thing about getting even with Floyd?" Virginia said. "He was nice to help us get your packages to the boat. After our talk last night, I hope you understand how foolish your thinking was about owing him for saving you? Getting in his bed wasn't called for."

Sister nodded. "All that be settled now."

"I'm glad," said Virginia. "That really bothered me."

Sister nodded. "It bothered me too but now it don't."

Floyd was waiting for them on the bank at the boat when they walked up. Sister walked over to him, hugged him and kissed him.

"I thank you fir helpin' me," she said, smiling up at him.

"I was glad to help." He leaned over. "If you want me to help you again, stay another night."

She laughed and walked away. She hugged and thanked Virginia one last time and got in the boat. They watched as she started the motor and headed down the river. She turned, waved and went around the bend.

V irginia walked over to Floyd. "I hate to see her go. I liked her." Floyd nodded. "I liked her too."

"She was determined she was going to get in your bed until I had a long talk with her. Then she understood how foolish her thinking about that was."

"That was good you got her straight on that," said Floyd. "I ain't seen no woman wanting to go to bed with me like that in a long time."

She frowned and looked at him.

He smiled. "I thank you be the last one that knocked on my door and crawled in my bed."

Her lips tightened. "You are truly a bastard," she said as she walked off toward the big house.

15

Floyd finished seeing Sister off. He'd fussed with Virginia as usual, then went to his house. He had several hours before he was to go to Tub's and confront the men from Atlanta. He hoped that Woody's information was correct about their visit.

He put several short pieces of rope in the truck. If he took one of the men alive as he planned, he would tie him up and bring him back to the farm for questioning. He knew that might be easier said than done. He could plan it in his mind but when it started, there was no telling what might happen. He had been in enough of these encounters to know that was true. They never went as planned.

All these thoughts were in his mind when he walked down to eat at noon. As he walked outside the house, he saw Virginia come out of the big house. Surprisingly she walked toward him, and her face was friendly

"I'm glad to catch you," she said. "Daddy asked me to find you and see if you'd eat with us."

"I was on my way to eat so that will work," he said.

"I'm sorry I was so rude," she said, staring at him. "Why do you always rub me the wrong way?" She started walking toward the house.

He hurried and caught up with her. "For the same reason you come over and got in my bed," he said, putting his arm around her waist. "You like me, and you know it."

She stopped and looked up at him. "See, that's what happens when I'm trying to have a serious conversation with you. You say something like that." She didn't move his hand nor move away.

"I am serious," he said.

"Daddy is waiting for us," she said as she walked over and opened the door.

M r. Mann was on the patio. Their meal was already on the table. "It's good to see you, Floyd," he said. "Have a seat and bring me up to date on anything going on."

Floyd sat down. "I have a man that lives down at the ferry giving me information. He's the man I dragged out of Tub's that they complained about. He was involved the night of the rustling and his brother was shot. He told me the Atlanta people are after me for burning their truck."

Virginia interrupted. "What does that mean, they're after you?"

He looked straight in her face. "They want me out of the way."

She looked at her father and then back at Floyd. "That's terrible. They'll try to harm you?"

"Do you want me to get the sheriff involved?" asked Mr. Mann.

Floyd shook his head. "Not right now. Two men are meeting tonight at Tub's with the man from the ferry. I plan to see what happens there." He looked at Mr. Mann. "There could be trouble and you might hear about it."

"Are you going to meet these men?" asked Virginia.

Mr. Mann looked at her. "I think Floyd knows what he's doing, Virginia. Sometimes it's best we don't know all that's going on." He looked around at Floyd. "Let's eat and no more talk. If you need the sheriff involved, you let me know."

When they finished eating Mr. Mann asked Virginia to show Floyd out. When they were outside Virginia grabbed his arm and looked at him. "These men are going to try to harm you?"

"They want me gone."

"You will see them tonight?"

He nodded.

"When you get back, let me know what happened."

"It'll probably be a late night. I'll talk to you tomorrow."

"Be careful."

He smiled. "I told you that you liked me." he turned and walked away.

She nodded as she watched him leave. She did like him.

There was a large crowd at Tub's when Floyd drove by. He went down to the ferry, turned around and came back. He parked on the side of the road, sat and watched for several minutes. There was one newer car in the parking lot that looked out of place among the older trucks. He figured that belonged to the men from Atlanta. He didn't notice anything suspicious going on, so he pulled his truck around back and parked near the back door.

He got out and walked around to the front. He opened the door and stepped inside, taking care to stay to the side where it was darker. The room was filled with smoke and there were few lights. He scanned the room. He saw Woody at a table in the back past the end of the bar. There were two men at the table with him. That was as he had expected and what he had planned for.

Floyd stood and watched them. Woody was sitting with his back to the wall, the man with the mustache was sitting to his left. The other man was to Woody's right. Floyd took the pistol from his belt and held it by his side. A waitress came out from behind the bar with drinks and started toward Woody's table. He fell in behind her, using her for cover as she walked. He was almost to the table when the mustached man saw him and started getting up. Floyd stepped around the waitress and hit him in the head with the pistol. The solid blow knocked him out of his chair onto the floor where he lay still and didn't move again.

The other man was getting up when Floyd stuck his pistol in his face. He raised his hands, his eyes on Floyd's face. Floyd grabbed his arm and started pulling him toward the back door. Woody came up beside him. "I gotta go with you," he screamed in Floyd's ear. "I can't stay here now."

Floyd nodded and dragged the stumbling man toward the door. Woody grabbed the man's other arm and they hustled him out the door, through the storeroom and outside. "Throw him in the back of the truck." said Floyd. They picked him up and tossed him in the back. Floyd opened the door, reached in the truck and got several pieces of rope. He handed them to Woody. "Get in back with him and tie him up. I'm gonna git us out of here."

Woody jumped in the back, turned the man over and started tying his hands and feet. Floyd jumped behind the wheel, started the truck and came out on the road. He headed for the farm.

He went through the gate at the farm, went past the houses and on down to the docks. He got out and walked to the back of the truck. The man was sitting up looking at him. He stared at Floyd.

"You're a stupid bastard," he said. "They gonna be after yo' ass."

Floyd ignored him. "What's yo' name?" he said as he climbed in the back of the truck. He knelt on one knee in front of him and stared in his face.

The man shook his head. "Go to hell," he growled. "You gonna be a dead man."

Floyd slapped him on the side of his face as hard as he could. The man's head snapped to the side. He shook his head trying to get it to stop spinning. Floyd looked at him. "I ask you again, what's yo name?"

The man started to say something but stopped. "Gus."

Floyd nodded. "That's better, Gus. I'm going to ask you some questions. I expect you to answer them or I will git mad, and you damn well won't like me being mad. You understand?"

Gus shook his head. "I ain't telling you shit. They'd kill me if I told you anything."

Floyd smiled. "Listen, stupid. They ain't gonna kill you cause if you don't tell me what I want, I'll kill you. I ain't got no problem with killin' you. We ain't tryin' to make a deal here." He punched him in the chest. "You answer my questions, or I'll hurt you. You ain't gonna enjoy any of it."

"Don't matter," said Gus. "You can beat me all you want, I ain't gonna talk."

"It be up to you, but you ain't got no idea what's about to happen to you." Floyd said. He turned to Woody. "Untie his feet and bring him up on the dock." Floyd got out of the truck and walked up on the dock. Woody followed with Gus.

On the dock was a large metal boom the workers used to load goods onto the boats. It would rotate from the dock out over the water. Then the end of a rope wound on a winch was tied to the box or bale. When the winch was turned, it would lower or raise the goods onto or off the boat. It could be used to both load and unload.

Gus looked around. "What are you doing?"

"What do you care?" said Floyd. "Who do you work for?"

Gus stared at him but didn't answer. He didn't know what was about to happen, but he didn't feel good about it.

Floyd looked at Woody. "Tie his feet." When Woody finished, Floyd tied the rope from the boom under his arms and around Gus's body. He cranked him up and shoved the boom out over the water. Gus looked down; he was hanging six feet above the river.

"What the hell are you doing?'" he yelled at Floyd. He didn't understand what was going on, but he knew it wasn't good.

Floyd unloosed the winch and Gus splashed into the water. With his arms and legs tied, he quickly sank. Floyd watched him for several seconds and cranked him up until his head was out of the water.

Gus came up spitting and coughing and cursing. He looked up at Floyd.

"You ready to talk to me?" said Floyd.

When Gus didn't answer, Floyd dropped him again. After the third try, Floyd hoisted him up and let him hang there for a minute.

"The only reason you be alive, Gus is that you have information I want. If I decide you ain't gonna talk, I'm gonna drown you and give you to the river. The fish and the turtles will eat you as you go downstream. It be yo' choice." He dropped him again and let him stay longer this time. Air bubbles were coming to the surface when Floyd finally hoisted him up.

Gus gagged and coughed and threw up. Now he was scared; he'd thought he was going to drown this last time. He stared up at Floyd standing on the dock.

Floyd could see the fear in his face and knew he was breaking. "Who do you work for?"

Gus was still hanging out over the water. He spat and sputtered trying to breathe. "His name is Doc. That's all I know. Gil always talked to 'im."

"Who is Gil?"

"You hit 'im back at Tub's."

"You been to where Doc stays?"

He nodded. "I been there."

"How many folk work for 'im?"

Gus shook his head. "I don't know fir sure, but I seen eight or ten there." He looked at Floyd. "I be answering yo' questions. I can't hardly breathe. Put me on the ground."

"If I brang you over here," said Floyd, "and you don't keep answering my questions, I'll dunk you again."

Gus nodded. "I'll tell you what you want to know. I don't want that again."

Floyd pulled the boom around and lowered Gus onto the dock.

Gus's eyes were on Floyd. "What you gonna do with me? I gonna answer yo' questions."

"I don't give a damn bout you, Gus. You do what I tell you to, and I'll let you go when I git through." He leaned over and stared in his eyes. "You try anythin' and I'll cut yo' throat."

Gus nodded. "I ain't gonna be no trouble. Just don't dunk me again."

Floyd looked at Woody. "I thank you fir helpin' me back there. You know them people gonna be after you now."

Woody shrugged. "Don't matter to me. We'll see what happens."

"I ain't gonna wait fir 'em to come after me," said Floyd. "I be goin' after this Doc, if he be the head man.

Woody nodded. "Suits me. Them folks ain't never done nothin' fir me."

"I want Gus to show me where this Doc's place is," said Floyd. "I'm gonna figure out a way to kill 'im. We gotta keep Gus locked up till we git through with 'im."

He untied Gus's feet and said to him. "I'm gonna lock you in a room till mornin', I'll come back then and get you somethin' to eat. You know what'll happen if you try anythin'."

Gus stared at him but didn't reply.

Floyd looked at Woody. "There's a room in the warehouse where they keep valuable stuff. I'm gonn lock 'im up there till mornin'. Right outside the room is a place the night watch sleeps sometimes. You can stay there till I come back and git you."

Woody nodded that he understood.

They walked in the warehouse, put Gus in the room and locked the door. "I'll be back in the mornin'," said Floyd to Woody. Then he walked to his house.

He opened the door and went inside. He went to the bathroom, took a bath and then walked to the bedroom. He stopped in the doorway. Virginia, fully clothed was asleep on his bed. He walked over and sat on the bed beside her. He leaned over and kissed her on the cheek.

Her eyes opened and she stared up at him. "You got back."

"I did," he said. "What are you doin' here?"

"I was worried about you."

"I told you I'd be back."

She raised up "You're all right?"

"I'm all right." He got up and looked down at her. "You better git home."

Her lips pouted. "Can I stay with you?"

He shook his head. "I got thangs to do early in the mornin' and if you stay I won't git no sleep." He leaned over and kissed her. "Maybe tomorrow night."

She rolled off the bed. "I keep offering myself to you and you keep refusing me. One day I will stop. Then you'll be sorry."

He smiled and put his arm around her waist as they walked to the door. "No, you won't." He kissed her, opened the door and patted her on the rear as she walked out.

~

The sun was just up when Floyd left the house. He went to the warehouse, woke Woody up and unlocked the door to the storage room. Gus came to the door. He looked like hell.

You're going to eat breakfast with us," Floyd said to Gus. "If you act up, I'll dunk you again."

Gus cut his eyes at him but didn't reply.

They went to the mess hall, ate and walked to the truck. "I want you to show me where Doc hangs out," Floyd said to Gus. "You tell me where to go."

They got in the truck and headed toward town. In the middle of town, they turned south. An hour later they were in the outskirts of a small town.

"Turn right at the next road," said Gus. "It's like a big two-story house on the right side of the road."

When Floyd saw the house, he pulled over to the side of the road. There were several cars and two trucks parked outside the building. The house was surrounded by large fields.

"What does Doc look like?"

"Big man," said Gus, "with a big stomach. He always smokes a big cigar."

"Do you know where he lives?"

Gus shook his head. "I ain't never seen 'im 'cept right here."

"Which car is his?"

"That big one on the end."

Floyd backed up and they headed back to the farm.

~

Doc was irate as he looked at the four men sitting in front of the desk. "He dragged Gus away and y'all ain't killed 'im yet? What the hell have y'all been doin'?" He puffed on his cigar. "You know Gus is gonna tell 'im everthang he knows about us, and the bastard is gonna be down here after us. According to the folks there, Woody was helping 'im," said one of the men. "He was in the truck when they left."

Doc sneered. "Never did trust Woody. His kind will sell out to the highest bidder." He shook his head. "Y'all can't just sit here and wait for 'im to move. You gottta kill Gus and Woody too when you kill that Floyd guy."

The four men got up and walked out.

16

Sister left the Mann's landing and headed downriver. She was sad to leave becauseVirginia and the people there had been good to her. She'd never met people like them before. The folks she'd grown up with had treated her badly, but they treated everybody badly. It'd been good to be around people that were so different.

She thought about Floyd Wimms as she rode. She came here in her search for him, however misguided that search had been. It had possessed her for all those weeks on the river, and they were hard weeks. But she'd persevered and despite the hardship, she'd found him. She'd known from the beginning that if she found him, it would probably not work out as she hoped. And it hadn't. He'd told her from the start that he didn't want her with him. She'd known in her heart that she was destined for failure, but regardless she'd gone on.

Despite all that she was glad she'd found him. Now she could go on with her life and not worry that she owed him for saving her. Her relationship with Floyd had been strange from the beginning. She'd been physically attracted to him that first day, even before he'd saved her. There was just something about him that drew her, although she didn't understand it at the time. After the shooting, the attraction she'd felt gave her a reason to pursue him.

Virginia obviously felt the same way about Floyd, although she claimed that she didn't. She was in love with him; she also claimed that wasn't true. She admitted she'd gone to bed with him but continued to claim there was nothing to it. She wanted Floyd to treat her as a normal man treated a woman, but he didn't. He wasn't a normal man in that way and that drove Virginia crazy.

Sister knew that if Floyd had allowed her to stay with him, she would have stayed. She would have done whatever he asked her to do and would have been happy to do it. That one night in bed with him had convinced her that she'd have stayed with him. But he didn't want her to stay, so she'd left. She was going to Brooks; He'd said he wanted her to come back to him.

Late that afternoon she passed the ferry. Soon afterward she stopped and set up camp on the riverbank. She planned for this to be her last night to sleep on the ground, tomorrow night she'd be with Brooks.

She thought about that and what it might hold for her. He'd asked her to come back to him, but they didn't discuss what that might involve. The last thing he'd said was that they'd talk.

She remembered the feelings she'd had when Brooks kissed her and held her close. Those feelings had been new for her. She'd never had those feelings before with a man. Those same feelings came over her when she was in the bed with Floyd. When Trip had thrown her down and used her, disgust was what she felt. She was excited and looking forward to being with Brooks.

She was up early the next morning and on the river. Her mind was on Brooks and getting to him. He'd said he would be waiting at the cabin every day looking for her to return. She expected him to be there.

She rounded a bend and saw the cabin on the left bank. She landed in front of the cabin, tied the boat up, got out and looked around. There wasn't any sign of Brooks. She called out, ran up on the porch and pushed on the door. It was locked. She walked over and peeped in the window but there was nobody inside.

She sat in a chair on the porch, feeling sure he would be here before night; he'd promised he would. As the sun went down behind the trees on the other side of the river and darkness crept in, doubt filled her mind. She went to the boat, got her tarp and set up camp in front of the cabin. Soon it was completely dark. She crawled under her quilts and went to sleep.

~

Floyd got back to the farm and parked in front of his house. He looked at Gus. "I can't keep you here. I'm gonna call the sheriff to come get you and lock you up. You'll be safe till we git all this settled down."

"You gonna let me go then?"

Floyd nodded.

Gus shook his head. "I gotta git out of town. I know Doc is gonna be lookin' fir me."

Floyd laughed. "I spect he will be." He looked at Woody. "Keep 'im here till I git back." He got out, walked to the big house and knocked on the door.

In a minute Virginia opened the door. She glared at him. "What do you want?"

"I got this man here that I want the sheriff to lock up. Could you ask yo' daddy to call 'im?"

"Who is he?"

"He's been givin' me information. He needs to be locked up. The folks he works for will be lookin' fir 'im."

She looked at him. "You come tell Daddy. He's sitting right in here."

Floyd followed her in the next room where Mr. Mann was sitting. Floyd quickly explained the situation and Mr. Mann called the sheriff.

He hung up the phone and looked at Floyd. "He'll be here in a few minutes."

Floyd thanked him and followed Virginia to the door. She opened the door and looked at him. "I thought you'd have apologized by now."

Floyd frowned and looked at her. "Fir what?"

"For how you talked to me."

"Cause I wouldn't let you stay last night?"

"I was worried about you."

"I thank you fir that, but I gotta get this mess cleaned up first."

"I might not answer the next time you call me," she said.

He smiled. "Yes, you will." He walked out the door.

She slammed the door behind him. He walked across the street smiling.

T he sheriff and a deputy came, Floyd explained the situation to him, and he took Gus away.

Floyd walked over to the truck where Woody was standing. "What do you want to do?" Floyd asked.

"I can't go home," said Woody. "They sho' gonna be watching for me there."

"I spect they will," said Floyd. "We got rooms down at the dock for guys when they have to work over. I can get you set up down there. It be best you stay here for a while."

Woody agreed that was the smart thing to do. Floyd went with him to the dock, got him a room and set him up to eat in the mess hall.

"Let me ask you something,'" said Floyd as they walked outside. "When you was talking to them Atlanta people, did they ever say anything about anybody from around here? I'm talkin' bout somebody paying them to steal the cattle and do other stuff?"

Woody shook his head. "They didn't ever say any name that I heard of. But somebody was telling them what to do. That night you caught us, none of them Atlanta people had ever been here, but they knew what fences to cut, and they told us."

"So, somebody up here was telling them where to go?"

Woody nodded. "I don't know who it was, but somebody did."

"Damn it," said Floyd. "I should have asked Gus about that before he left. You stay here. I'm going' to the jail and talk to 'im." He walked to the truck and headed to town.

He got to the jail, parked and went in. He told the deputy what he wanted, and he led him back to Gus's cell. Gus was surprised to see him so soon.

"I forgot to ask you, Gus, but did them Atlanta folks ever say who was payin' 'em to steal the cows?" said Floyd.

"I didn't never hear no name," said Gus, "but they was doin' it for somebody. I know because Gil talked to somebody about it. Somebody told him what to do."

"Who was Gil?"

"I was with him at Tub's when you got me," said Gus.

"He was the one with the mustache?"

Gus nodded.

"If you thank of anything else 'bout it, you let me know." said Floyd as he walked out.

He went to the truck, got in and pulled out of the parking lot. He had just turned on the road to the farm when a car came up behind him moving fast. Suddenly the car pulled out to pass him. He glanced at the car as it came alongside. The man in the passenger seat was staring at him and had a gun pointed at him. He fired and glass in the side window and the windshield shattered. Floyd felt pain in his left shoulder and his arm. He jerked the steering wheel to the right to keep the other car from ramming him. His truck went into the ditch and turned over.

Virginia was in the bedroom when the phone rang. "Hello," she said as she answered.

"Virginia, this is Sheriff White. Floyd Wimms has been shot. He's in the hospital right now and I thought you'd want to know. He's alive but right now that's all I can tell you. I don't know any more about his condition."

"Thank you for calling me, Sheriff. I'll come to the hospital right now." She hung up the phone, ran downstairs and told her father about the call. She ran outside, got in her car and headed to town.

She parked at the hospital and ran inside. The sheriff was waiting for her.

"He's in surgery right now, Virginia," he said. "He got a bullet in his left arm and in his shoulder, but they say he'll live. He was lucky he didn't get hit in the head. Them people was right on 'im when they shot 'im."

"It was the people from Atlanta," she said. "The man you have in the jail was one of them."

"I've talked to him," said the sheriff. "He told me he'd told Floyd all he knew about the Atlanta people. He's nervous as a cat since Floyd was shot because he thinks they'll be after him too."

"What are you going to do with him?"

"I was holding him because yo' daddy asked me too. I have nothing to charge him with so unless you know of somethin', I'll have to let 'im go."

Virginia shook her head. "Floyd didn't tell me anything so I can't say what to do."

"I'd as soon get him out of town and rid of 'im," said the sheriff. "I don't want any more trouble out of this. I don't want them people coming up here looking for 'im."

"I guess all we can do is wait until the surgery is over," said Virginia. "I guess he is lucky to be alive." She walked across the waiting room and sat down. There was nothing she could do but wait and pray.

I t seemed like hours before a doctor came out, saw her and walked over to where she was.

I'm Dr. Ricks," he said. "Are you Mr. Wimms' wife?"

Virginia shook her head. "I'm not his wife. I'm Virginia Mann. He works on our farm. He has no family here."

He nodded. "I did the surgery and Mr. Wimms is a lucky man. He had three bullets hit him but none of them hit anything vital. One went through his arm, and I dug out the other two from his shoulder and back."

"But he'll be all right." she asked.

"In time he will," he said. "Mr. Wimms is in good physical shape; he will be sore for a while, but he'll recover. He'll stay here for two or three days and then he can go home." He looked at her. "Mr. Wimms has another scar in his side that looks like he'd been shot before. Do you know anything about that?"

She shook her head. "I've only known him for a short time. I do know he was in the army and fought in France."

"That may have been where he got it," said the doctor.

"When can I see him?"

"He's in recovery and will be groggy for a while. The nurse will come get you when you can go back." He turned and walked away.

Virginia was relieved. She walked over to a chair and sat down.

Sometime later a nurse came out, told her he was awake and led her to his room. When she walked in, he was asleep.

"He'll probably sleep most of the night. We'll check on him."

She sat in a chair by his bed. Minutes turned into hours, and she dozed off. When she woke up and looked toward him, his eyes were on her.

"What are you doin' here?" he said.

She stared at him. "I'm looking after a damn fool that got himself shot."

"You be right," he said. "I was careless."

"You're lucky to be alive, Floyd."

"That's what the doctor told me."

"You said they wanted to get rid of you and they did."

He shook his head. "I ain't dead yet. They just done made me mad."

"You have to recover first, Floyd, before you think of anything else." She smiled. "I'll help you."

His eyes were on her face. "Best thang you can do for me is sleep with me ever night. I thank that would do me good."

Her lips tightened and she glared at him. "This is serious, Floyd. I know you don't ever have much sense, but sometimes you're really stupid."

"Does that mean you won't sleep with me?"

She shook her head. "You need to go back to sleep."

He smiled, his eyes closed, and he went to sleep. In a minute his breathing was regular and even.

She sat in the chair and looked at him. *"Damn you," she thought, "I don't want to love you."*

The nurse came in and gave him a shot. "He's going to sleep all night now, that's what he needs to do. If I was you, I'd go home and come back in the morning? There's nothing you can do tonight but he'll probably need you tomorrow."

Virginia knew that was the smart thing to do. She got up, went to her car and headed to the farm.

She had a restless night, was up early and headed back to the hospital. When she walked in his room, he was still asleep. She had just sat down when he moved and groaned. The look on his face showed that he was hurting. For the next hour he was like that, moving and groaning.

Then he woke up and looked at her. "You been here all the time?"

She shook her head. "I went home." She reached over and touched his hand. "You've been hurting and moving around. Are you all right?"

He nodded. "Kinda sore."

"The doctor said you would be."

"What else did he say?"

"You'll be here a couple of days and then you can go home."

"You gonna look after me?"

"Why should I do that?"

He laughed and when he moved the pain hit him. She saw his face grimace. He waited until the pain faded. "Cause you like me."

"We've already been through all that," she said. "You don't try to be a likable person."

He gritted his teeth, took a deep breath and turned away. In a minute he was asleep. It was like this for several hours, sleeping and then pain for a bit. She held his hand, sometimes wincing in pain when he squeezed her too tightly. It was late in the afternoon when he seemed to feel better and talked to her.

"I thank you for lookin' after me," he said.

She smiled. "Somebody needs to."

He laughed and grimaced. "Don't make me laugh. It hurts."

She leaned over and kissed his forehead. "You go back to sleep. I'll be back in the morning."

"Tomorrow night you can get in the bed with me."

She shook her head. "I'll see you in the morning," she said as she walked out.

W hen she walked in the room the next morning, he was awake and looking at her. She walked over to the bed and kissed him. "You look better than when I left you."

"The doctor come in and said I could go home later today, if I didn't have no more problems." said Floyd. "He said I would be as good at home as here in the hospital."

"That's good," Virginia said. She looked in his face. "You know you have to do right and not try to do too much right away. You have stitches and if you tear them, you'll have real problems."

He pursed his lips. "I know that, but you know I ain't gonna wait long. Them folks tried to kill me and they ain't gonna git by with that."

She shook her head. "I know what you're thinking but you have to heal first. You're not able to do anything yet." She took his hand. "Maybe we should let the sheriff handle all this."

"I done started this and I aim to finish it." He looked up. "You know I ain't gonna let it go."

She sat down in the chair. "I know that, and it bothers me. You've got to wait until you're well."

He laid his head back on the pillow. "I gonna git well quick."

She stared at him. She knew he meant that and when he decided to go, she wouldn't be able to stop him.

The doctor came in later and told them that Floyd could go home as soon as all the paperwork was done. They would carry him in the ambulance so he wouldn't have to be moved around so much. He cautioned Floyd about what he could and couldn't do. He said he would come out in a week and check on him.

Virginia was in the chair beside the bed when she heard the door open. She looked around and saw a young attractive woman standing in the door. Virginia had never seen her before and thought she must be in the wrong room. The woman looked at Virginia and then her eyes shifted to Floyd lying in the bed. She walked quickly across the room to his bedside.

"Floyd," she said, staring down at him. "I just heard you'd been shot and was in the hospital. I had to come see about you."

Virginia was surprised by the woman barging into the room, but she was more surprised by what she said to Floyd. Virginia stood up. She might not know who the woman was, but it seemed that the woman knew Floyd and he knew her. She stepped to the bed, glanced at Floyd and then turned and stared at the woman.

Floyd saw Virginia's face and knew he was in trouble. "Rachel" he said to the woman, "this is Virginia."

Rachel stopped and looked at Virginia. "I'm sorry for barging in like this," she said. "I'm Floyd's friend."

Virginia looked in her eyes and she knew immediately that Rachel was more than a friend. Her women's intuition told her that. She didn't know who Rachel was or where she came from, but she knew that her relationship with Floyd was much more than friendly.

"I'm sorry, Rachel," she said, her tone icy, "but I don't believe I've ever seen you before. Who are you and how do you know Floyd?

Rachel looked in Virginia's face and she knew by her expression and her eyes that Virginia was much more than a friend with Floyd. She had barged into a situation that she didn't want to be in. "I'm sorry, Virginia. I'm Rachel Ware and I met Floyd at Dib's recently. He and I had talked some, and I heard he was in the hospital. I was concerned about him."

Virginia cut her eyes at Floyd and then looked back at Rachel. "That's good of you to be concerned but he's being taken well care of. I'm taking him home this afternoon and he will be looked after. I will look after him."

Floyd lay in the bed watching this exchange and he knew that all this didn't bode well for him. He was going to go home with Virginia, he was virtually helpless in the bed right now and Virginia knew that Rachel was more than a friend.

Rachel understood what Virginia was saying to her. She had made it clear that Floyd was her man and was telling her to get her ass out of the room and away from Floyd. She looked at Floyd. "I'm sorry about your troubles, Floyd," she said. "I hope you get along well." She stepped back and looked at Virginia. "It was nice to meet you, Virginia. If there's anything I can do let me know." She turned and fled from the room.

Virginia turned her eyes on Floyd. She leaned over the bed and looked in his face. "You are one sorry bastard," she said. "Tell me about Rachel right now. You better tell me the truth, or I will walk out of here and leave you in this hospital by yourself. I will never speak to you again. And if you dare try to come to the farm, I will shoot you myself." She stared at him and waited.

Floyd knew she meant what she said. "Rachel teaches school here. Like she said I met her at Dib's. She was with her sister and her husband, and they asked me to have a drink with them. I had a drink and talked to Rachel.

"That's not all?" she said, her eyes boring in him.

"The night we argued at my house, and you went off with Ron, I went to Dib's. Rachel was there. We talked and I went home with her."

"And went to bed with her?"

Floyd nodded.

"And then?"

"I was with her one other time. That's it." He looked at her. "I ain't never made you no promises bout how I'd act, Virginia. I told you I didn't never make no promises."

She nodded. "You're right, Floyd but you didn't ever tell me you would sleep with every woman you could find. It's my fault, I should have realized how you were." She got up and walked out of the room.

Floyd watched her close the door. If she didn't come back, he knew he had a serious problem. He had no place to go if he couldn't go to the farm. If he was alone and the Atlanta people knew where he was, they'd kill him. There was nothing else he could do but wait and see what she did. Sometimes he regretted not having better sense about women.

17

Sister woke up early. She heard thundering to the west, and it was cloudy. The last thing she wanted today was to get caught in a thunderstorm. Then she thought about Brooks. He hadn't come. She was disappointed that he hadn't been here when she arrived. He'd said he would be here every day and she had believed him.

She lay under the tarp and thought. What if he didn't come? What if he came and he didn't want to be with her? The fact that he hadn't been waiting for her had triggered all these thoughts in her mind. She'd never had these doubts about him before now.

If he didn't come, she would go back upriver. That was really her only other choice, there was nothing for her downriver. Virginia was upriver and she had no doubt she would take her in. That was what she would do if Brooks didn't come.

She took down the tarp and gathered up all her belongings and put them in the boat. She went on the porch and sat down in a chair. Then the rains came, and lightning lit up the sky. She wrapped up in a quilt and waited.

She was half asleep when some noise woke her. She was trying to clear her head when she realized it was a truck driving up. She ran to the end of the porch and looked up the road as the truck pulled up and stopped. She saw Brooks get out of the truck and he saw her at the same time.

He ran around the end of the cabin, jumped onto the porch and grabbed her. He pulled her to him and kissed her. She wrapped her arms around him, held on and kissed him back.

He looked in her face. "You came back. I'm so glad you did."

"I come back yesterday," she said. "You weren't here. I thought you done forgot bout me."

He kissed her again. "I had to go see about business in town." He looked at her. "But I'm with you now." He took her arm and led her to the door. "Let's get inside. It's cold out here in the rain."

He opened the door, and they went in. He ran over and lit a fire in the wood stove. "Are you hungry?" he said looking at her. "I haven't eaten this morning I've been so busy. I'll fix us somethin'."

Sister stood and looked at him. "You said for me to come back and here I be. I come back to be yo' woman."

He walked back to her and looked down. "I wanted you to come back to me, Sister. I want you to be more than my woman, I want you to be my wife."

She stared up at him. "You don't know me much yet, Brooks."

"I know you as much as you know me. Will you be my wife?"

"You mean with the papers signed and ever thang?"

He laughed. "Yes, with the papers signed and ever thang." He kissed her. "We'll go to town tomorrow and see the preacher."

"I got some pretty dresses to wear. They be in the boat."

"I'll get your stuff and bring it in," he said. "I want you to go and see the farm. That's where we'll live."

"It be all yo' farm?"

"Yes, it's been mine and now it'll be ours. You gonna be my wife."

She frowned and looked at him. "You got any folks?"

He shook his head. "My parents are dead. I'm by myself."

"Then I be with you, and you won't be by yo'self no more."

He laughed. "That's true. That's what I want, to be with you. I want to have children so when I get old, I'll have someone to help on the farm. I'll have someone to leave the farm to."

She thought on what he said. "You want me to have yo' chillun?"

"Yes, that's what I want."

"I gonna be yo' wife tomorrow?"

He nodded. "That's what I said."

"We stay here tonight?"

"Yes, if you want to."

She took his hand, kissed him and led him into the bedroom. "Ain't no reason to wait," she said as she pulled her dress over her head.

Brooks stared at her standing before him. He shook his head. In all his dreams he'd never thought he'd have a woman like this. He wrapped his arms around her and pulled her to him.

It had been two hours and Floyd had heard nothing from Virginia. Suddenly the door opened, and she walked in. Tight lipped she stared at him. "The doctor said that they're coming to get you and take you to the farm." She walked over and looked down at him. "I'll help you get well, that's the Christian thing to do since you're hurt." Her eyes bored into him. "When you get well enough to travel, you get your sorry ass in your boat, and you leave. I don't give a damn where or what direction you go, so long as you go. They'll be to get you in a minute," she said as she walked out.

The nurses came in, put him on a stretcher and carried him outside to the ambulance. Virginia talked to them. "Y'all follow me and when we get to the farm, I'll show you where to take him." She walked to the car and got in.

The road to the farm was rough and every time the ambulance hit a bump; Floyd groaned. He was glad when they got to the farm. When they opened the doors and pulled him out, Virginia was standing there. "Y'all follow me," she said and started walking toward the big house.

This surprised Floyd. "Where are you takin' me?" he asked.

She stopped and looked at him. "I'm putting you in the bedroom next to me. That will be easier. I'll have the maids help look after you over here. I'm not running across to your house every time you groan."

Floyd lay back and didn't say anything else. They took him upstairs, put him in the guest room bed and left.

Virginia walked over to the bed and stared down at him. "Don't you think that since you're close to my bedroom, it would be easy for me to come in here and be with you. That is not going to happen."

Floyd frowned. "I ain't never thought of that."

She sneered. "You're a liar. That's on your mind all the time." She nodded. "Maybe we can get Rachel to come over and tend to your needs. I damn well ain't." She wheeled about and walked out.

Floyd watched her go, thinking that woman is sho' mad.

Sister woke up, rolled over and kissed Brooks. The sun was well up and they had slept later than usual. He kissed her back and hugged her. "Good morning, Sister," he said, staring in her eyes.

She nodded and smiled. "I thank I be pregnant," she said.

He laughed. "You can't know this quick."

"If I ain't, it sho' missed a good chance."

"That's true," said Brooks. "I've never been with a woman like you, and I took advantage of it."

She kissed him. "We can go one more time if you want to."

Brooks jumped out of the bed. "You done tuckered me out, girl. Maybe later."

They both fixed breakfast, ate and he loaded all of her packages in the truck. He locked the cabin and they headed to his farm.

Sister looked at everything as they rode. It was all new to her and she was excited.

Brooks pointed to fenced pasture on the right side of the road. "This is where the farm starts. This is our land."

Sister looked at him. She never owned anything in her life, and she couldn't believe her good fortune. She moved over against Brooks and held on to him. They went past cornfields and then she saw two big red barns. Past the barns was a farmhouse painted white with flowers all around.

"This be yo' house?" she asked, marveling at how neat it was. She'd never seen such a house.

"This is our house, Sister."

"How did you git all this?" she said. "I ain't never seen such in all my life."

"My grandaddy had it and then my daddy had it. Then he gave it to me like I want to give it to our children."

She hugged him. "That be good. We gonna have chillun."

He stopped the truck in the yard, and they got out. He unloaded her packages and brought them inside. Sister walked slowly through each room in the house. She had never been in such a house and was amazed. She still couldn't believe this was hers.

"I called the Baptist preacher and he said he'd be waiting for us this afternoon to marry us," said Brooks. He looked at her. "I go to the Baptist church, Sister. I go every Sunday. I'm a Christian and I want you to go to church with me."

She nodded. "I ain't never been to no church," she said. "But if you want me to go with you, I sho' will."

Brooks walked over and hugged her. "As soon as you're ready, we'll go see the preacher."

She went upstairs and put on one of the dresses Virginia had given her. When she walked downstairs Brooks stared at her. "Lord, Sister, you are a beautiful woman."

She walked over and kissed him. "I thank you for saying that" she said. "I be yo' woman."

He hugged her, they got in the truck and headed to town. The preacher and his wife had been surprised when Brooks called and said he wanted to get married. He was older and they had never known him to have a girlfriend and thought he would end up a life-long bachelor. They were even more surprised when he walked in with a beautiful young girl wearing a nice dress. They'd never heard of her and wondered how he'd met her.

The preacher's wife came over, smiled and shook hands with Sister. "I don't believe I've ever met you, Sister. Brooks is a lucky man to get you. He had never mentioned that he had a girlfriend, and I was wondering how he met you?"

Sister looked at her. "I was takin' a bath naked in the river. He come up on me in his boat and seen me. He weren't tryin' to hurt me or nothin', so I let him look while I washed. Then he asked me to come to his cabin and eat with 'im." Sister stared at her. "That be how we met.

The preacher's wife smiled somewhat. "That's interesting. I've not heard of a meeting quite like that."

"He say he wants me to have chillun so they can help on the farm."

"That's good," said the wife. "A couple should have children."

Sister nodded. "We started last night getting' me pregnant. I sho' like tryin'."

The wife blanched and walked away, suddenly having a coughing spell.

The preacher saw that his wife was having more than she could deal with, so he came over. "We're going to have the ceremony now if you're ready."

They all gathered in front of the preacher. The message and vows were short, and Brooks and Sister were married. The preacher signed the papers, and it was official.

The preacher's wife congratulated Sister. "I hope you'll be happy," she said.

Sister thanked her. "Do you and the preacher have chillun?"

The preacher saw that his wife didn't want to get into this subject again with Sister, so he came over, put his arm around her and looked at Sister. "You're a married woman now, Sister. You can try to get pregnant all you want." He paused. "Some married women don't try to do it as much as they could."

His wife cut her eyes at him, moved his arm off her and walked away.

. . .

Brooks and Sister left the preacher's house, got in the truck and headed back to the farm. She slid over against him. "You don't know me much," she said, "but I can cook, I can milk cows and I know bout chickens."

Brooks hugged her. "That's good, Sister. You can help me, and we'll do good."

"You don't never have to thank about needin' another woman. I gonna be all you need. I gonna see to that."

Brooks smiled. "I have no doubts about that, Sister. You've already shown me that."

18

A week had passed. Floyd was getting stronger and was walking around the room trying to get his energy back. He was sore. The doctor had come to see him and had taken out the stitches but movement hurt, especially in his shoulder.

He had seen little of Virginia. The maid had brought him his meals each day. Virginia did come in at night and check on him, but to this point had not been friendly. He was surprised when she came in the room earlier than usual.

"The doctor said that you were well enough to go downstairs and have supper with me and Daddy if you want to," she said.

"I'd sho like that," he said. A week locked up in the room had about done him in.

She walked over to the bed and took his arm as he got out of the bed.

"I thank you for helpin' me git well, Virginia," he said. She held his arm as they walked to the stairs.

She didn't look at him. "I'd do as much for a hurt dog," she said, in the sarcastic voice she'd used since they left the hospital.

They started down the stairs. After she said the hurt dog comment, he put his hand on her shoulder and leaned on her more than was necessary. He liked the feel of her body against him. She didn't comment but didn't move away.

"It's good to see you up, Floyd," said Mr. Mann as they walked in the dining room and sat down at the table.

"Thank you, sir," said Floyd as he sat down. "All your people have been mighty nice to me."

They talked as they ate. Virginia was quiet, letting her father and Floyd do the talking. She watched him the entire time.

"What are your thoughts when you get well?" asked Mr. Mann.

Floyd thought for a moment. "Woody say them Atlanta people are sho' mad cause they didn't kill me. They still gonna be after me. I gotta go get 'em."

"I can understand you feeling that way, Floyd, after they tried to kill you," said Mr. Mann. "But maybe you should let the law handle it."

Floyd shook his head. "I ain't never let the law handle nothin' what was my place to handle."

Mr. Mann laughed. "I don't doubt that is true, but you're up against an organized gang this time."

"That be true, but I can't not do what I got to do." He looked at Mr. Mann. "I done found out somebody up here is payin' them Atlanta folks to cause y'all trouble."

"Are you sure of that?"

Floyd nodded. "I be sure. Woody and Gus told me them Atlanta folks told 'em where to brang the truck that night and what fences to cut."

'You're right," said Mr. Mann. "They wouldn't know that unless somebody told them where to go. Otherwise, they wouldn't have any idea."

"It's got to be farm people to know what to do about fences and such," said Floyd.

Mr. Mann nodded. "That makes sense."

Virginia looked at Floyd. "You don't think somebody we know is doing this to us? We know all the farmers in this area. I can't believe anyone we know would do that."

Mr. Mann looked at her. "Don't be naive, Virginia. People will do all sort of things for money."

She shook her head. "I still can't believe it."

"We're tiring Floyd out, Virginia," said Mr. Mann. "You better take him back upstairs."

Floyd thanked him for the supper, Virginia took his arm, and they went to the stairs. When they got to the first step, Virginia stopped and looked at him. "I'm not stupid, Floyd. I know that when we came down the stairs you were draped all over me and that wasn't necessary. You try that again and I'll shove you down them myself."

He looked at her. "I be weaker than I thought."

Her lips tightened. "The only place you're weak is between your ears, Floyd. I'm not going to fool with you." She took his arm and they started up the stairs. They got to his room, and she helped him get into bed.

"The doctor brought some cream to be rubbed into your shoulder. He said to do it every night. I'll go get it and rub it in for you." She walked out of the room.

Floyd laid back in the bed and waited.

In a few minutes she came back in with the cream. He noticed she had changed clothes and was now wearing a night gown.

She came around behind him. "Slide up some in the bed and let me sit on the bed behind you so I can get to your shoulder. You'll have to take your shirt off."

He took off his shirt and moved up in the bed.

She slid in the bed behind him. She was warm where she was touching him.

"You have another scar on your side," she said. "The doctor asked me if you'd been shot there?"

"I got shot in France," he said.

She cut her eyes at him. "By a woman or an irate husband?"

He glanced back at her. "In the war," he said.

She started rubbing the cream on his shoulder. It felt soothing and he enjoyed her touching him. "That feels good. I thank you for helpin' me."

She didn't reply.

As she reached down his shoulder, she would lean her body against him, and he was getting aroused. He didn't say anything but pushed back against her even more. In a few minutes she had him about to explode.

"Virginia," he said, "I be sorry bout Rachel, but I didn't never promise you I would just be with you."

"I know that" she said. "You already told me that. Why are you bringing it up now?"

"I was just goin' to say that I ain't never promised somethin' like that to a woman. But if I did promise that I sho' wouldn't never touch another woman."

"Well, that is certainly a noble thought, Floyd," she said. "Why in the hell are you telling me this?"

"I'm just sayin' that if I asked you to be with me and you wanted to, I would promise you that I would never be with another woman. I'd just be with you."

She smiled but didn't let him see her smile. "That sounds like you're asking me to marry you, Floyd."

His head snapped around and he stared in her face. "That ain't what I said. I be just talkin' bout bein' together."

"So, you'll make me that promise if I want to be with you?" She leaned over against him as she massaged his shoulder.

He could feel her breasts against his back and her warm breath on his neck. She had him stirred up out of his mind.

"I tell you what," she said as she got up out of the bed. "Let me think about that until tomorrow. I need to study on what you said and see if I believe you'll keep that promise." She smiled at him and walked to her room.

He was so frustrated when he fell back on the bed.

He was up early the next morning. He walked in the room for a while. When he hadn't seen Virginia by the middle of the day he went downstairs and walked outside. It felt good to out in the air. He needed to build up his strength. He walked across to his house and went inside. He had decided that there was no need for him to be in the big house so he would move. As soon as he saw Virginia, he would tell her. He went back to the big house and upstairs.

He was resting on the bed when the door to Virginia's room opened, and she walked in.

He watched her as she walked over to him. "I thought you'd done left," he said, watching her face.

"I was thinking about what you said last night," she said. "Take off your shirt and I'll rub your shoulder."

He took off his shirt and moved up in the bed. She sat on the bed behind him and started rubbing his shoulder. "I thought about it, and I think you'd stay away from other women as long as you're laid up, but when you got out, you'd do what you've always done."

He turned and looked at her. "I wouldn't if I promised you that I wouldn't."

She nodded. "I'm sure you mean that right now, but old habits are hard to break. You've been that way all your life."

"That be true," he said, "but I ain't never had a woman I wanted to make that promise to." He turned and looked at her face.

"So," she said, as she rubbed his shoulder and pressed her body against his back, "you feel differently now?"

He was aware of everywhere she was touching him. He was aroused and his mind was telling him to turn around and take her. He knew that wasn't a smart thing to do. "You be doing yo' best to git me all stirred up," he said.

She shook her head. "I don't know what you're talking about," she said as she smiled. She knew exactly what she was doing. She got up and looked down at him. "If you don't want me to rub your shoulder, then I won't. The doctor said it would be good for you."

"I 'spect it be good for me," he said. "But rubbin' yo'self all over me be drivn' me crazy." He looked up at her. "You know what you be doin'."

She smiled. "You could have had me many times, but you turned me down. You had your chance." She started walking toward her room.

"I be ready to move back to my house," he said.

She stopped and looked back at him. "If that's what you want to do, then go. You can eat at the mess hall." She turned, opened the door to her room and went in.

He lay there for a minute, got up and gathered his belongings. He went downstairs, opened the door and went across the street to his house.

Floyd knew that he had to forget about women and anything else right now and focus on the Atlanta people. He also knew that he wasn't completely healed. The little moving around he'd done had made him sore and his shoulder ached. He still had a ways to go before he was at full strength.

He had almost been killed before and they might not miss the next time. He was also sure that since he had survived, they were still looking for him. He couldn't sit and wait for them to make the next move; he had to go after them.

He knew where Doc's place was, the problem would be to get there without them knowing about it. He left the house and walked to the dock to find Woody. He found him in his room. Woody hadn't been off the farm since the shooting, so he had no idea what was going on in town or elsewhere.

"What you gonna do?" Woody asked as Floyd walked in his room.

"I gotta kill Doc and I want to find out who hired him," said Floyd. "Somebody from a farm around here is telling them what to do. I thank I know who it is but right now I can't prove it."

"It's sho' gonna be hard to get to Doc cause you know they gonna be watching us," said Woody.

Floyd nodded. "You be right but we can't hide all the time." He looked at Woody. "I'm going to that joint across from Dib's and talk to the bartender there. He seems to know what's goin' on. Get yo' pistol and go with me so we can watch each other's back."

Woody nodded. He went to the nightstand, opened the drawer, got his pistol and stuck it in his belt. He followed Floyd out, walked to the truck and got in. Floyd started the truck and headed toward town.

"When we get to the joint," said Floyd. "I'm goin' to let you out fore we get there. You walk up and stay in the dark. I don't want 'em to know there be two of us if they be there. I'll go in and talk to the bartender. I'll come out, get in the truck and leave. You watch and see if anybody comes out after me and follows me. I'll ride around and come back and get you."

Floyd drove to within sight of the joint across from Dib's, stopped and let Woody out. Woody walked on up the road to the edge of the parking lot. Floyd pulled in and parked. He got out, looked at Woody across the lot and went inside.

The room was half-filled and as usual was loud and smoky. He stayed out of the light and walked to the end of the bar. There were two men on stools at the other end of the bar. He scanned the people at the tables but didn't see anybody that looked suspicious.

He put a bill on the bar. The bartender saw him, walked over and stared at him. "Damn," he said as he picked up the bill, "you got balls walkin' in here. Them people be lookin' fir you."

"Any in here now?"

The bartender shook his head. "One come in last night. He wanted to know if we'd seen you. I told 'im you usually went to Dib's." He frowned. "That one wouldn't be hard to spot. Had long blond hair down on his shoulders like a woman. You might look over at Dib's."

Floyd thanked him and walked out. He got in the truck, pulled out of the parking lot and drove into town. He drove slowly and watched behind him. He didn't see anybody following him. He drove around the courthouse and back to the parking lot. Woody ran out and jumped in the passenger's seat.

"Didn't nobody come out after you left," he said.

Floyd nodded. "Nobody followed me." He told Woody what the bartender had said.

"What you gonna do?" said Woody, his eyes on Floyd's face.

"I'm goin' in Dib's and see if he's there."

"What you want me to do?"

"Go in with me and be ready if any thang happens. You stay at the door and watch."

Woody looked at him. "Stayin' round you sho' be dangerous."

"You be right bout that," said Floyd as he pulled in and parked. They got out and walked to the front door. Floyd had his pistol in his hand at his side. Woody did the same. Floyd opened the door and stepped in with Woody right behind him. They both moved away from the door out of the light. Floyd looked over the crowd at the tables.

The longhaired man was at a table on the far side of the room with his back to the wall. He looked like the bartender had described him. He was alone at the table. A full drink sat on the table in front of him. As Floyd watched he lit a cigarette and took a swallow of the drink, then sat the drink down. He took the drink with his left hand. His right hand was out of sight under the table.

There were two men and two women at the table in front of the man. They finished their drinks and got up. The women were getting their purses and milling around. They blocked Floyd's view and he knew the man he was watching couldn't see him either. He started across the room.

One of the women at the table glanced up and saw him coming toward them. Then she saw the gun in his hand and screamed. One of the men followed her eyes, saw Floyd and started toward him. Floyd shoved him out of the way into the other woman and she fell over a chair to the floor.

The longhaired man reacted quickly. He pushed his chair back and started to get up. He saw Floyd as his right hand came out from under the table holding a pistol. As he squeezed the trigger and fired, Floyd shot him in the chest. The longhaired man's bullet hit one of the men at the next table in the back and knocked him to the floor. There was panic in the room as all the people started running toward the front door.

The longhaired man staggered back and as he was trying to fire at Floyd again, the second bullet killed him. He collapsed.

Floyd headed toward the back door, shoved it open and burst out into the night. He ran around the end of the building toward the parking lot that was in chaos. People were still streaming from inside the building and others were in their cars trying to get out of the lot. He ran to the far end of the lot where he had parked. Woody was standing at the truck and got in as Floyd came up. In a minute they were on the road headed to the farm.

"I couldn't see," said Woody. "Did you git 'Im?"

Floyd nodded. They got to the farm, parked and got out. Floyd looked at Woody. "I speck I'll hear bout this in the mornin'," he said to Woody. "I don't thank they saw you, so you don't say nothin' bout it."

"I ain't plannin' on sayin' nothin'," said Woody. He headed toward the dock.

Floyd went inside his house, sat down and waited.

He had dozed off when someone knocked on the door. He got up, went to the door and opened it. A tightlipped Virginia was standing there staring at him. "You bastard, I've been trying to get you well and you go to town and kill a man." She shook her head. "What kind of man are you?"

"It was self-defense," said Floyd. "He had a gun."

"I don't give a damn what he had. They say you came in and rushed at that man with a gun. That's what started it all. In the shooting an innocent man got shot and it was all your fault."

"How do you know this?"

"Sheriff White called and said the sheriff in the next county called about it." She looked at him. "He called me because he didn't want to bother daddy. Sheriff White said the other sheriff said if he catches you in his county, he'll arrest you. He don't care that the other man had a gun."

"The man was from them Atlanta people," said Floyd.

Virginia stared at him. "I don't care who he was. You can't keep doing this."

"What do you want me to do?"

"I don't know," she said. Then her face softened. "How's your shoulder?"

"It don't bother me none."

"He was from the Atlanta people?"

"He was."

"So, they're still after you."

"They are."

"You plan to kill all of them?"

"All I can."

She looked up and held her hands in the air. "And to think I liked you and went to bed with you. How could I have done that?"

He walked to her and looked down. "I fixin' to go to bed. You want to stay with me?"

She looked up at him, turned and walked away.

He laughed and went back in the house.

19

The next afternoon Floyd went to the dock and found Woody. "Come with me," he said. He walked to the end of the dock, down the steps and to where he had his boat landed. Woody followed.

"Tonight, Woody," he said, "this is what I want you to do. You remember the field where y'all cut the fence and the truck burned?"

Woody nodded. "I spect I won't never forgit it."

"On the other side of that field is a pasture that belongs to Charlie and Ron Hurt," said Floyd. "They got a good many cows in that pasture. They got a big cornfield on the other side of the pasture and they ain't picked it yet. Tonight, I want you go and cut the wire at the pasture and drive the cows into the cornfield."

Woody looked at him. "How come you doin' that? Them cows gonna tear up that corn."

"That's what I want," said Floyd. "I thank some farmer here is with them Atlanta people and I thank it be that Ron Hurt. I want to send 'im a message."

"How he gonna know it be you what done it?"

"He won't but I want 'im to be worried bout what be happenin.'"

Woody shook his head. "I reckon you know what you be doin'. It don't make much sense to me."

"It be the same as me killin' that man last night at Dib's," said Floyd. "I sent 'em a message that they be foolin' with the wrong man."

Woody looked at him. "Don't you reckon killin' that man really pissed 'em off more?"

Floyd nodded. "I wanted to git 'em sho'nuff mad cause mad folks make mistakes. When they make a mistake, I be gonna git 'em myself."

Woody shrugged. "I reckon you know what you be doin'. When do you want me to do it?"

"About midnight," said Floyd. "I want them cows to have plenty of time in that cornfield."

"You stay in yo' room tomorrow and don't come see me," said Floyd. "No matter what anybody says tomorrow, you don't know nothing about no wires bein' cut."

He nodded. "I gotta go git me some wire cutters," he said as he walked back toward the dock.

Floyd went back to his house. He hadn't seen Virginia all day and wondered where she was.

V irginia was standing at her bedroom window and saw Floyd as he came from the dock. He glanced toward her house, and she stepped away from the window, she didn't want him to see her watching him.

He was the most infuriating man she had ever known. She'd dealt with men all her life and she had always felt she was in control. That wasn't true with Floyd, he was always one step ahead of her and it was frustrating.

She knew she was pretty and attractive and that gave her an advantage when she met a man. All attractive women had that advantage. Men were hunters, they'll prowl looking for prey. An attractive woman had the right bait to interest them. She had never had to do much to get their attention. She'd easily gotten Floyd's attention; that hadn't been difficult at all. But holding his attention was a different matter.

In the past when she gave a man her full attention and indicated she would give that attention to only him, the man had done the same. Not Floyd, he didn't do that. He took what she offered and went looking for more. It seemed he had found that with Rachel.

She thought back to Sister. That poor girl followed him up the river wanting to be his woman. She said it was because he saved her but there seemed to be more to it than that. She was attracted to him and offered herself to him on several occasions, but he refused her. She felt she was in his debt and wouldn't rest until she paid that debt. The last day Sister was here, it still bothered her. They talked and she told Sister that her feeling like that was foolish. She'd thought her talk did some good.

Then she thought about the day Sister left. She went to the dock with her; Floyd had been there too. They all said their goodbyes. She remembered Sister walking over to Floyd and kissing him. It wasn't just a peck on the cheek, but a real kiss. Afterward Sister was smiling. She didn't say one word about owing Floyd anything.

Then it came to her. Sister had spent the night in the bedroom next to her, but she hadn't checked on her until morning. As she thought about all this, she knew that Sister slipped out of the house and paid her debt to Floyd. There was no doubt in her mind that he had accepted her payment that night.

She looked out the window. Floyd was nearing his house. She ran out the door, down the stairs and out the front door. He was at his front door and looked around as he heard her slam the door.

She walked across the street toward him. "You are one sorry bastard," she said as she walked up to him and stared in his face.

He was startled at her attack and looked down at her. "Well," he said "good mornin' to you. What's got you stirred up?"

"Tell me you didn't sleep with Sister?" She stared in his eyes.

He frowned. "Did Sister tell you that?"

"No, she didn't tell me that, but I know you did. She owed you for saving her and she wouldn't have left unless she paid you."

"None of that was any of yo' business, Virginia. That was between me and Sister. I ain't never made you no promises. Not about Sister or nobody else." He turned to open the door and then looked back at her. "I offered to be with just you and you wouldn't do it." He stared at her.

Virginia shook her head. "I couldn't trust you. You might stay with me for a while but then one day you'd be gone. I know that's what you would do."

He nodded. "You probably be right. I ain't never been tied down in one place fir long. I told you that when I got here, I was gonna winter with the Cherokees, and you asked me to stay for a while. I've already done that."

She had no answer for what he'd said. She knew he was right, but it didn't lessen the hurt she felt. She wanted to be with him and all she did was fuss at him about the way he was. Her fussing hadn't changed him one bit. He had told her how it would be with him if she was with him. He wasn't going to marry her.

She took a deep breath and looked in his face. "You told me the other day that you would promise to only be with me if I was just with you. Is that right?"

He nodded. "That be what I said."

"Would you still do that?"

"If you want to be with me," he said, "I'll just be with you. We ain't gonna talk about nothin' what happened before."

She smiled, took his hand and kissed him. "You promise?"

"I done said I would."

She opened the door and pulled him inside.

Later he looked at her lying beside him. He had made a promise to her, and he intended to keep it. Only time would tell how all this ended up.

His mind also thought about Woody. He hoped he would do what he had asked. Then they would see what the Hurts' reaction to that was.

. . .

S he rolled over at daylight. "I'm going to the house. Starting tomorrow I will be here with you if that's all right.
"That be up to you."
She kissed him, jumped out of bed and went out the door.

~

F loyd got up, dressed and was about to go outside the next morning when he heard a car drive up. He looked out the window and recognized Ron Hurt's car. Ron parked, got out and went to the front door. He knocked and stood waiting, his hands on his hips.

In a minute Virginia opened the door. When she saw Ron, she closed the door behind her and stepped outside. Floyd could see her talking to him but couldn't hear what she was saying.

Ron then replied to whatever she had said, and he was loud and seemingly agitated. As he talked loudly, he was waving his arms and gesturing about.

Floyd cracked the door a bit and listened. He couldn't understand everything Ron was saying, but he heard enough to know that Woody had done what he'd asked him to do. Floyd opened the door, stepped outside and walked across the street to where Ron and Virginia were.

Ron's back was to him, but Virginia saw him coming and looked at him. "Ron says that somebody cut their pasture fence last night and the cows got in their cornfield and tore it up"

Ron spun around when she spoke and looked at Floyd. His face wasn't friendly. "They cut the fence and all the cows got out into the cornfield. They torn it all to hell."

Floyd nodded. "They cut our fences too. We told you about that."

Ron's face was red. "They didn't try to steal the cows, they just let them out into the corn. Who the hell would do that?"

"They've cut our fences and sunk our boats and other things," said Virginia.

"I know that." said Ron. "Why would they do it to us?"

"Why would you be different?" said Floyd, "Y'all's place is next to the Mann's land."

"Floyd says it's the people from Atlanta doing all this," said Virginia.

Ron looked at Floyd. "Why do you say that? We don't know anybody from Atlanta."

Floyd stared at his face. "I know it because I caught one of 'em Atlanta people. He told me it was 'em. Their boss is a man named Doc and I know where he lives." Floyd was watching Ron's eyes when he said this, and he saw the change and the fear all over his face. He now knew that Ron was the culprit as he had suspected.

Virginia was watching Ron's face also and she too saw his expression change. She knew something wasn't right.

Ron caught himself and tried to correct his mistake. "Well, that might be true about y'all having problems with some people in Atlanta, but we certainly don't. I've never heard of this man you say is named Doc." He looked at Virginia and then back at Floyd. "You seem to be the one that causes problems all the time, going around shooting and killing people. We don't know who the hell you are and where you came from. Maybe we need to look into that?"

He looked at Virginia. "I'm sorry Virginia. I'm not going to stand here and have this conversation with a man I have no use for." He turned, got in his car and drove off.

Virginia watched the car head toward the gate and turned to Floyd. "Did you do this?"

Floyd shook his head. "I was with you all night."

She shook her head, keeping her eyes on his face. "Let me explain something to you, Floyd. I am with you now, you agreed to that last night. That means I'm in your bed and with you in every other way. Whatever you do, I'm with you. Do you understand what I'm saying?

Floyd stared at her.

She nodded. "We're not married but as Sister would say, *"I'm yo' woman."* And as long as you keep our agreement, I'll be with you, regardless of what you do." She stared in his eyes. "I'm going to ask you again. Did you do this?"

"I had Woody do it last night."

"For what reason?"

"For what happened just now," said Floyd. "Did you see his face when I told him about Doc?"

She nodded. "I saw his face. He's hiding something."

"That's what I figure."

She looked at him. "What are you going to do now? Should we tell Daddy?"

"I wouldn't," said Floyd. "Let me do some more lookin' around and see what happens fore you do anything. You know about Ron, so if anything happens to me, you go to your daddy and the sheriff."

She shook her head. "Don't say that. Don't you let anything happen to you." She walked over and hugged him. "I just have got you to act like you have good sense."

He laughed and hugged her. "I've got to go find Woody. I'll let you know before we do anything else."

"You better," she said as Floyd turned and started toward the dock.

W oody was in his room when Floyd got there. "Looks like you done a good job last night. Ron Hurt was here raisin' hell about the cows tearin' up his cornfield."

"It was easy," said Woody. "What do you want me to do tonight?"

"Nothin' else right now, they'll be watchin'." He looked at Woody. "You been to Doc's house before, so you know it good. How far is it from his house to the river?"

Woody frowned. "I ain't never thought bout that. I ain't never been from his house to the river but it can't be far, cause they keep a boat back there. They use it sometimes to go to Atlanta."

"Do the woods come up close to the back of the house?"

"Not real close," said Woody. "Maybe like a hundred yards."

"I remember big fields on both sides of the house."

"That be right," said Woody. "It be a long ways from the house to the trees. Be too far to shoot from the trees to the house,"

Floyd smiled. "Not for the rifle I got." He got up. "I'll let you know what we're going to do."

Floyd walked out of Woody's room and went to the dock. He found the man in charge of the boats. "Could you take me down the river to a place, put me out on the bank and come back to get me later?

The man nodded. "If Virginia tells me to, I can."

"All right," said Floyd. "I'll tell her to talk to you when I want to go." He walked out and started toward the house. He saw Virginia come out of the big house, look at him and wait. It was obvious that she wanted to talk to him.

"Charlie Hurt called Daddy and told him about the wire cutting and cornfield," said Virginia. "Daddy asked me about it, and I told him Ron was out here and told me. He asked me if you knew about it, and I told him you did. He wants to see you."

He followed her into the house and into the den. Mr. Mann was sitting in a chair when they walked in. "Virginia told me that you heard Ron Hurt talk about someone cutting their fence and letting the cows in their cornfield."

"Yes, sir, I heard him."

Mr. Mann stared at him. "Tell me what you know about it." His eyes were on Floyd's face.

"I had Woody Starke cut the fence and turn the cows in the cornfield," said Floyd.

"Why did you do that?"

"I suspected Ron was behind them folks from Atlanta and I wanted to see how he took it."

"And what did you learn?" Mr. Mann was watching Floyd's face intently.

"When I told 'im that I caught one of the Atlanta men and the man told me the name of the boss was Doc, I seen it in his eyes. He knows 'em Atlanta people."

Mr. Mann looked at Virginia. "You were there. What did you think?"

Virginia nodded. "I saw Ron's face. Floyd is right about it."

"That's bad, if that's true and I don't doubt what you're saying. Charlie Hurt and I have been neighbors for fifty years and never had any trouble." Mr. Mann looked at Virginia. "I think Ron had hoped to marry you and get control of our farm. I never did trust him." He looked at Floyd. "What do you plan to do now?"

"I ain't really sure," said Floyd. "I ain't never been one to tippy-toe round no problem. I like to go right at it."

Mr. Mann smiled. "I think we've all found that out by now." He looked at Virginia. "I worry about Charlie if Ron is tangled up in this. We need more proof about his involvement before we say anything." He picked up the phone. "I have an idea." He called Sheriff White. After telling him who he was and going through the pleasantries, he asked if there had been a report from the Hurt farm about their fences being cut. He hung up the phone and looked at Floyd. "They haven't reported anything."

Floyd stood up. "Virginia will tell you what I'm doin', sir."

Mr. Mann nodded. "That'll be good."

Floyd and Virginia walked out of the house. She looked at him. "You be sure and tell me before you do anything."

Floyd smiled at her, turned and walked toward the dock.

Rachel was in love and she was miserable. She had made a fool of herself at the hospital by going to see Floyd Wimms. Without knowing one thing about his personal life and certainly not knowing he had a woman she had rushed into his room. She had thought he would be alone, but he wasn't. When she turned and saw Virginia's face staring at her, she immediately knew she had trespassed into another woman's territory. Virginia didn't have to tell her that Floyd was her man and she was going to take care of him.

The look on her face had already told her that. But she told her anyway in no uncertain terms that he was hers.

Rachel was left with no choice but to tuck her tail, apologize and try to get out of the room as gracefully as possible. Humiliated, her self-respect gone, she had run out the door.

She remembered that Floyd had warned her repeatedly when they met that she should stay away from him. "You are a sweet girl," he'd said, "and you don't need to be with me. You are a schoolteacher, and this won't help yo' reputation." He'd also told her he would use her and leave her and that was what he did. Everything that had happened was her fault but knowing that didn't lessen the pain and hurt she felt.

All this started the night she'd been at Dib's with her sister and her husband, Harold, and Floyd had walked in. She was immediately attracted to him. She asked Harold to go over and ask him to have a drink with them. Harold took one look at Floyd and told her that she didn't have any business getting involved with him. Ignoring Harold's warning, she again told him to go ask him. Meanwhile, she had stared at Floyd with her best *come and get me look*. It worked because when Harold asked him, he got up and came over. From that moment on she was his. She would do anything he asked her to do. There were no limits.

Her actions were contrary to her upbringing and how she'd acted in the past. Except for a brief fling during her freshman year in college, she'd never had a serious involvement with a man. Her parents were both schoolteachers and had taught her by example how a person should act. She had always done as they taught her.

But she forgot all that when Floyd sat down at the table beside her. From that point on she may as well have been holding up a sign that said, *Here I am, Take me.* From that point on she did everything she could to take him home and get him in her bed. Finally, he went home with her, and she succeeded.

He also came to see her another time and stayed with her. That visit had fueled her fire. When she'd heard he'd been shot and was in the hospital, she'd reacted without thinking. She rushed to the hospital and was a complete fool.

D ays later she talked to the bartender at Dib's, and he'd told her Floyd was from a town downriver called River Bluff. He'd killed several men down there in some family feud and left town with several people wanting to kill him. His last time leaving town had something to do with his involvement with some man's wife. He had come upriver and ended up at the Mann's farm. Since he'd arrived, he'd killed one man, beat up at least one other and burned a truck. Trouble seemed to follow him wherever he went. Now he'd been shot but that didn't satisfy the people hunting for him. They wanted him dead.

Rachel knew all this, but she didn't care. She didn't care that he'd killed people and she didn't care that he had a girlfriend. She wanted to be with him, and she didn't care how or what she had to do to accomplish that end. Her sister told her she was crazy and should let him go, but Rachel ignored her. She decided she would go to the Mann farm and find him. She knew he liked her and if she could talk to him, he might change his mind. At the moment she had no idea how she would accomplish that, but somehow she planned to do it.

20

Sister was happy. She'd been with Brooks for two weeks and each day was a learning lesson for her. There was so much that he took for granted that she'd never experienced. She'd never lived in a house with electricity, running water and an inside bathroom. Brooks was patient with her, smiling when she didn't know about something and explaining everything to her. She'd never had anyone be so kind and her love for him grew each day.

On Sunday they went to church, her first time to ever be in a house of worship. The ladies in the church treated her as a curiosity item. They had been surprised that Brooks had gotten married. He was a well-off farmer and many of them had put their daughters forward as a potential wife, but he'd not been interested. And now he had brought this very young woman in as his wife; some had suggested she wasn't over sixteen.

Sister was herself as she always was. She'd never tried to put on airs when around different people. In fact, she had no idea what that meant. What you saw with Sister was what you got. Brooks stayed close and when he saw her getting into trouble, he would gently herd her away.

She liked the service, especially the singing. She knew none of the songs, although she'd heard some of the tunes on guitars and fiddles when people played on the river. Brooks picked up a songbook, turned to the page of the song they were singing and put the book where they could both see it. When Sister looked up at him with big sad eyes, he realized she couldn't read. He closed the book, sat it on the pew and put his arm around her.

They sat down and the preacher got up. He had a big book that he read out of about people she'd never heard of. Then he started his sermon. He was a big man and he talked with a loud voice; at times he would yell loudly. The first time he yelled out Sister jumped. Brooks smiled at her and pulled her close.

As the preacher talked and slammed the big desk with his fist, people in the congregation would talk back to him, seeming to agree with what he was saying. Sister looked at Brooks during this, but he never said a word. She didn't know if he agreed with the preacher or not.

The service ended, everybody filed out of the church and went down a hill to a creek that ran close to the church. Sister followed Brooks and the crowd to the edge of the creek where they all gathered. She had no idea what was about to happen. Brooks looked at her. "They're gonna baptize some folks," he said.

Sister had no idea what that meant. She frowned and looked up at him.

"I'll tell you about it later," he said.

Then she saw two small boys and a woman all dressed in white standing by the creekbank. The preacher was standing with them; he was also dressed in white. Then the preacher waded out in the creek to where the water was up to his waist. Then he motioned to one of the boys and he waded out to him. The preacher took hold of him, leaned him back and dunked him under the water. When the boy came up all the people laughed and clapped. They were all happy about the boy being dunked.

Sister watched but didn't say anything as the second boy waded out and was dunked. Again, the people laughed and clapped.

Then the woman waded out. She was a large woman, almost as

tall as the preacher. The preacher took her by the arm, said some words to her and then leaned her back and dunked her. The next minute was exciting as the woman's feet slipped out from under her and the preacher was hard pressed to keep hold of her. Finally, he wrapped both his arms around her and pulled her up. The woman got her feet back under her and stood up. When she surfaced, she was coughing and spitting.

The crowd about lost control while this was all going on and there was laughing and talking until the preacher held up his hand and started praying. This settled the crowd down.

Sister knew she had to ask Brooks about this on the way home. She had no idea what she had just witnessed but she had enjoyed it.

When they got in the truck and started toward the farm, Brooks told her he would teach her to read and do figures. He explained that when they had children, it would be her job to help the children with their lessons. In order to do that she had to know how to read.

That made sense to Sister, and she told him she would learn if he would teach her. When they walked in the house, she asked him if there was anything wrong with trying to get pregnant on Sunday. He told her there wasn't anything wrong with that and she led him into the bedroom.

The next morning Floyd got in the truck and headed out the gate. In a few minutes he pulled into the driveway at the Hurt farm. He got out, walked up on the porch and knocked on the door.

In a minute the door opened, and a woman was looking at him. He figured she must be Ron's mother. "May I help you?" she said.

"I'd like to talk to Ron," he said."

"May I say whose calling?"

"Tell 'im Floyd is here."

She stared at him for a minute. By the look on her face, it seemed she had heard his name. She closed the door.

Floyd stepped back on the porch and watched the door.

The door opened and Ron was standing in the doorway staring at him. "What do you want?" he said gruffly.

"I want to talk to you."

Ron shook his head. "I don't have anything to say to you."

"Either you come out on this porch and talk to me, or I'll talk to yo' daddy," said Floyd. He watched Ron's face.

Ron glanced back in the house, pushed the screen door open and walked out. He walked down to the far end of the porch and stopped.

Floyd followed him.

Ron turned and looked at him. "What do you want to talk about?"

"You know what I want to talk about," said Floyd. "I know you're involved with the Atlanta people. The man I caught gave me your name." This wasn't true but Ron didn't know it wasn't true.

Ron shook his head. "That's a lie. If that was true, you'd have already gone to the sheriff."

"Mr. Mann kept me from tellin' the sheriff. He don't want to hurt yo' daddy, they been friends for a long time." Floyd walked over close to him. "You tell them Atlanta people to back off and stop right now and there won't be nothin' more said bout what you done."

"I can't do that," said Ron. "I don't know nothing about all this."

"Let me tell you this then," said Floyd. "If we have one more bad thang happen on the Mann farm, I'm gonna come git you. Won't nobody see me git you but you'll sho' be gone." He looked at Ron. "They won't never find you. I got places all on the river where I can hide yo' body. You know I'll do it." Floyd saw the fear in Ron's eyes, and he knew he believed him.

Ron's face turned red, and Floyd could see the hatred. "You can't threaten me like that" he said. "I'll have you arrested."

Floyd smiled. "I tell you what, Ron. I'll drag yo' ass out in the yard right now and beat the livin' shit outta yo' ass and then you'll have somethin' to arrest me for." He shook his head. "You ain't gonna do nothin' cause I'll tell 'em what you been doin'."

Ron took a deep breath. "What do you want me to do?" He knew he had no choice."

"Just what I said," said Floyd. "Tell the Atlanta people the deal be over. You ain't payin' them no more."

"They ain't gonna like it."

"That's yo' problem."

"All right," said Ron. "I'll tell them but give me some time."

"Tomorrow," said Floyd. "Don't go down there. Call 'em and tell 'em."

Ron nodded. When he looked up at him, Floyd saw the hatred in his eyes, and he knew what Ron was going to do.

Ron turned and went back in the house.

Floyd got in the truck and went back to the Mann farm.

W hen Floyd got to the farm he walked over to the big house and knocked. In a minute Virginia opened the door and looked at him.

"I want you to tell the man in charge of the boats to take me down the river in the morning," said Floyd. "I've already talked to 'im and he'll do it if you tell 'im to."

She closed the door and stepped out. "I'll go down there with you. What are you going to do?"

"I know where Doc's house is and I'm gonna visit 'im tomorrow."

She looked at him. "Won't that be dangerous?"

"Sho will be for 'em."

Virginia glanced at him, shook her head and walked on. At the dock she told the man to take Floyd wherever he wanted to go in the morning and in the days to follow.

"Thank you," said Floyd as they walked away. "I've got to go see Woody. I want him to go with me in the mornin'."

She looked at him. "I was planning to stay with you tonight."

"That's good," he said. "But I'll be getting' up early. I'll try not to wake you."

She frowned. "In that case I'll just wait until tomorrow night."

He laughed. "That's up to you." He turned and started toward Woody's room.

. . .

Woody was in his room and Floyd told him to be ready at daylight to go downriver. "Brang yo' pistol," he said, "and I have a rifle for you in case we have to shoot our way out. Also, in the morning go to the mess hall and get some water and some ham biscuits."

Woody didn't ask any questions. He knew where they were going.

Floyd started walking back toward the house.

21

When Floyd walked out of the house the next morning it was still dark. He walked to the dock and Woody was waiting. Floyd handed him a rifle and a pair of binoculars. They walked out to the boat. The motor was idling, and the driver was already on board. They got in. Floyd noticed there was another man standing in the back of the boat holding a rifle. Floyd looked at the man and then back at the driver.

"You didn't tell me what you're gonna do," said the driver. "But based on what I've heard about you, I didn't thank you're going squirrel hunting. I wanted to protect my boat in case there was trouble."

Floyd nodded. "That be good thanking. I'll tell you when we want to land," Floyd said. "When I tell you, just run the bow up to the bank and we'll jump out. Then you get out of there fast. Go down a ways and wait. If you hear a lot of shootin', you come runnin'."

The driver nodded that he understood and revved the engine. The boat quickly planed off and they headed downriver. The boat was much faster than Floyd's boat so they would make better time. The sun was just lighting the eastern sky when they rounded a bend and saw the ferry ahead. The driver slowed down and approached the ferry at idle speed.

The old man was sitting in his chair on the ferry and watched them approach. The driver knew the driver because he made runs most every day and he spoke up as they got nearby. "Hey, Lester," he said, "doin' much business?"

Lester shook his head. "Ain't doin' much, Joe." He looked at Floyd and the other man, then at the driver. "You runnin' fast today, Joe and you ain't loaded. Where you be goin'?" Before Joe could answer, Lester saw Woody sitting in the back. "Damn, Woody," he yelled out. "Where you been hidin'? There's been men here bout ever day lookin' fir you."

Woody stood up and looked at him. "I been workin' upriver, Lester."

"Them folks lookin' fir you ain't been friendly one bit," said Lester. "They went in yo' house and give yo' folks a hard time bout you not bein' here. Do you know who they be?"

Woody nodded. "I know 'em, Lester. You don't need to say nothin' bout seein' me."

Lester shook his head. "I ain't gonna say nothin' to 'em, Woody. I don't like the way they done."

Floyd walked out, his rifle over his arm. "Anybody ask you about us, Lester, you ain't seen us this morning goin' or comin'. He stood and stared at him.

Lester looked at Floyd's face. "I ain't seen nobody all day."

Floyd nodded. "That be good, Lester." He turned to the driver and nodded.

The driver revved the engine, they pulled away from the ferry and soon the boat planed off. They headed downriver as the light was creeping over the trees to their left.

Floyd watched through the trees on the east bank, tapped the driver on the shoulder and signaled for him to slow down. "If there's a boat docked down below here, when you come back up sink it. But if you don't hear any shooting, don't sink the boat and come get us bout four o'clock."

The driver nodded

About a hundred yards later he signaled him to slow down and go into the bank. As soon as the bow hit solid ground and stopped, Floyd and Woody jumped out and ran into the trees. The boat backed out and headed downriver.

F loyd stopped at the edge of the trees and knelt down. He looked at Woody knelling beside him. "If I be right, we're at the corner of the big field on the north side of the house. We'll go up through the trees on this side and set up. I want to git where I can cover the front and the back of the house."

Woody looked at him. "What good would that do? It's a long way cross that field."

"I got a 1903 Springfield rifle," Floyd says. "I can hit 'em at a thousand yards, maybe longer. I ain't worried bout how far it is."

Woody shook his head. "I ain't never seen nobody hit nothin' that far away."

Floyd chuckled. "Them folks ain't never seen it neither." He got up and started through the trees with Woody behind him.

It didn't take long for them to get in position in the edge of the trees where Floyd could see the front and back entrances. He set a log in front of his position to rest the rifle on. He looked through the binoculars toward the house.

"Does Doc live in the house, or does he come from somewhere else?" Floyd asked.

Woody shook his head. "I don't know. When I was there it was up in the day, and he was always there."

"I don't see his big car," said Floyd. "There's only one car there now."

Floyd got his binoculars and looked. "I don't see it neither."

"Maybe he'll come, and we'll get a shot at him," said Floyd as he settled down to wait.

Thirty minutes later they saw another car come up the dirt road toward the house. It parked and two men got out. Floyd was watching. "Damn," he said. "There's that man with the mustache that was with you the night I got Gus."

Woody was looking too. "You're right. That's Gil. If he's here, I'm sure Doc will be here."

Later a large truck drove up to the house. Two men got out, opened the back doors of the truck and carried packages into the house. They made several trips with more packages, closed the doors and drove away.

In a few minutes they saw three cars coming toward the house. One car was leading, then Doc's car followed by a third car. They parked side by side in front of the house. Doc's car was between the other two.

Floyd got his rifle ready and looked through the scope. He propped on the log, got the rifle steady and focused on Doc's car. He couldn't see the side doors since the other car was blocking his view. People started getting out of all three cars, he counted six people in all. They were in a group and for an instant he saw a larger man smoking a cigar, but he was blocked by another body and then the entire group was up the steps and in the house.

"Looks like we're going to have a long day," said Floyd.

The sun was leaning to the west, and they hadn't seen anything when they saw a single car coming down the road. Floyd looked through the binoculars. The car was familiar. It parked, Ron Hurt got out and walked in the house.

"That what I thought he would do," Floyd muttered. He looked at Woody. "Ron is down here to tell them they have to kill me before I tell everybody what he's done. I didn't thank he had enough guts to tell 'em he was through with 'em."

"What you gonna do now?" asked Woody.

We gotta kill Doc and bust this crowd up," said Floyd, "but it ain't gonna be easy."

An hour later Ron came out with two men. They stood on the front steps and talked. Ron seemed to be upset, waving his arms and gesturing as he talked.

Floyd looked at Woody who was watching through his binoculars. "Do you know 'em?"

"I've seen 'em before," said Woody. "They do Doc's dirty work for 'im."

Floyd watched as they talked for several minutes. It seemed Ron was giving the two men instructions. Finally, whatever the discussion was about seemed to be settled. The men went to their car, got in and drove off. Ron got in his car and followed them.

Floyd knew Doc was still inside, so he waited. An hour later the front door opened, and two men came out, then another man. They stood and looked back inside and then Doc stepped in their midst. They walked to the car with Doc in the middle. Floyd tried to get a bead on him, but he couldn't get a clear shot. They all got in the cars and drove off.

Floyd looked at Woody. "We'll have to come back tomorrow. We can't let them get inside the house next time. When Doc comes down the road, we'll have to stop 'em on the road and I'll kill 'em in the cars."

They gathered up their gear and headed for the river. The boat wasn't there when they got to the edge of the trees but came up the river in a few minutes and landed. They got in and headed upriver. They passed the ferry, waved to Lester and kept going. It had been a long and wasted day, but they did know enough to be ready tomorrow.

When they got to the dock Virginia was waiting for them. When he walked off the boat, she ran to him. "You all right?" she asked as she hugged him.

He put his arm around her as they walked to the house. "We'll have to go back tomorrow," he said, "and finish it."

"I worry about you doing this," she said. "Those are bad people."

"We was watching the house today and Ron Hurt drove up." He watched her face as he said it.

She looked up at him, her face looked like he had hurt her. "Ron was there?"

"He was. He went in the house and talked to 'em. Then he came out and drove off."

She shook her head. "I can't believe he would do this. What are you going to do about him?"

"Nothin' right now. I got to take care of the Atlanta people first," he said as they got to Floyd's house.

She opened the door and took his hand. "You haven't seen me in two days. It's time you paid attention to me." She pulled him in the house and closed the door.

$\sim$

R on Hurt was not in a good mood when he got to Doc's house. He went in and asked Doc to do more to get rid of Floyd Wimms. He argued that Floyd knew he was supporting them and if he wasn't eliminated, there would be no more business from him.

Doc took this statement as a threat and didn't like it. Doc looked at Ron over his glasses and puffed on his cigar. "We have other problems right now. We haven't gotten anything out of dealing with you. We had a truck burned and damn near got our people killed that one night trying to get those cows. It was supposed to be easy money, but it didn't turn out that way. We expect you to continue to pay us as you have been. Your payments will not stop." He stared at Ron. "Once all this settles down, we'll see what we can do then."

That didn't satisfy Ron, but he didn't want to push Doc too far. "What if I pay a couple of your men extra money to get rid of him?" asked Ron.

Doc shrugged. "I don't give a damn if they want to do it."

Ron nodded and asked two of the men to go outside and talk to him. They walked out on the steps, and he told them what he wanted. They agreed, got in their cars and left.

Ron followed them out the road.

$\sim$

R achel had thought about going to the Mann farm, find Floyd and talk to him. But she wasn't familiar with the farm, didn't know where Floyd lived and the possibility of getting to him wasn't good. If she went there, she was probably more apt to run into Virginia than Floyd. She didn't want that; she'd already been humiliated enough already.

Then, as she thought more about it, she thought about Dib's. She knew Floyd went there, that was where she met him. Maybe he still went there, she thought. Anyway, she didn't have much chance of seeing him by accident, so going to Dib's might work. That evening she got in her car and went to Dib's.

She walked in and looked around. The tables were half full, and three men were at the bar. She didn't see Floyd. She walked to the table where she'd always sat and waited for him. She sat down facing the door so she would see him if he came in. A waitress came over. Rachel knew she couldn't sit there without ordering, so she ordered a drink. The waitress left and returned quickly with her drink.

She sat and sipped on the drink. Thirty minutes passed. Half her drink was gone, which was more than she usually drank, and she was feeling the effect. She was relaxed and feeling less nervous. She actually felt more confident about herself.

She saw someone in the door. She could tell it was a man, but the doorway was darker, and she couldn't see him clearly. He walked in and her spirits fell, it wasn't Floyd.

But the young man was good looking, and he was dressed nice. His eyes scanned the crowd. He looked at her briefly, then passed on but came back to her. Their eyes met for a second, then he turned, went to the bar and sat on a stool. Rachel's eyes stayed on him. The more she watched him, the more she liked what she saw.

He ordered a drink, took the glass and turned around. His eyes immediately went to Rachel. She met his stare and locked on his eyes without blinking. He stood up and walked to the table and looked down at her.

"May I join you?" he said.

"Yes, you may," she said, her eyes still on his face. She was impressed with his manners.

He sat down, put his glass on the table and turned to her. "I'm Ron Hurt," he said, "and you are certainly pretty."

Rachel nodded and smiled at him. "I'm Rachel and I thank you for saying that."

"It's true," he said. "I haven't seen you before, Rachel. What do you do?"

"I teach school here in town," she replied. "Are you from here? I've never seen you before."

"I live on my family's farm outside of town toward the river," he said.

The fact that his family had a farm impressed her. That was in his favor because as far as she knew, Floyd Wimms owned nothing. They sat and talked. She emptied her drink and he ordered her another. She'd never drank this much alcohol in her life, but he was nice, she liked him, and she relaxed.

R on had come to Dib's to scout the place out. He had told the two men at Doc's that he would meet them here tomorrow night and they would come up with a plan to deal with Floyd Wimms. He'd thought it best to meet them in a public place. He didn't know if Floyd was watching him or not, but he wanted to be careful. Floyd's threat to get him and he'd never be seen again was real to him. He didn't doubt that Floyd would kill him without a second thought.

He looked at Rachel. He was impressed with her, and she seemed to be open to being with him. After his disastrous parting from Virginia, he was ready to be with another woman. Rachel seemed to be perfect for him.

They talked on. Ron slid his chair over as close to her as he could get and had his arm on her shoulder.

"I've drank too much," she said. "I feel tipsy and should go home."

"Are you all right to drive? I can take you home."

She smiled. "I'm not that bad and I don't live far. I'm sure I can make it."

"I'll follow you home," he said, "and make sure you get there safely."

"That would be nice," she said.

They got up, he took her arm to steady her, and they walked out. He put his arm around her and pulled her to him. He liked the way she felt.

Rachel appreciated his concern and was impressed with his manners.

She got in her car, pulled out of the parking lot and he followed her to her house. When they parked, he jumped out, went to her car and opened the door for her. He took her arm as she got out and walked her to the door.

She fumbled with the keys as she tried to unlock the door. He finally took them from her, unlocked the door, pushed it open and stepped inside with her. He had his arm around her.

"I thank you for seeing me home," she said, looking up at him. "You about got me drunk and I never do this."

He laughed and kissed her. She was surprised, pulled away and looked in his eyes. He leaned over and kissed her again. This time she responded and kissed him back. There was a couch behind them. As they kissed, he gently pushed her back and down on the couch. She let him guide her and continued to kiss him.

Then she realized he was undressing her and had his hands all over her. She pushed him away. "I can't do this, Ron," she said. "I'm not in my right mind and I can't do this."

He turned her loose and moved away. "You're right, Rachel. I'm sorry but I just got carried away."

Rachel buttoned her dress and looked at him. "It was my fault too. I got carried away."

He looked at her. "I have to be at Dib's tomorrow night to meet some men. Why don't you come and meet me there? When I get through with my meeting, I'll take you to a nice place for dinner."

"I would like that," she said. She reached up and kissed him.

He got up. "It's a date. I'll see you tomorrow night."

She walked him to the door, kissed him again and he walked out.

As Ron went to his car, he was sure where he would spend tomorrow night.

F loyd slipped out of the bed, being careful not to wake Virginia. He went to the front room, dressed, got his rifle and other gear and went out the door. When he got to the dock Woody was waiting. As before the driver and the other man were in the boat with the motor idling.

"It'll be the same as yesterday," Floyd said to the driver. "I plan on shootin' today so y'all be ready. If there is shootin', make sure you sink that boat."

The driver nodded, revved the motor and they headed downriver.

When they got to the ferry, it was just light enough to see. Lester was sitting in his chair watching them. Floyd told the driver to pull in, he wanted to see if there was any news.

"What's going on, Lester?" said the driver.

Lester looked at Woody. "Them two men was back here yesterday. They still be lookin' fir you. They want to find you sho'nuff bad. They said they were comin back this afternoon."

Woody looked at Floyd. "When we git back today, I'm gonna stay here and wait fir them folks. It be bout time that I stop this."

Floyd nodded. "When we git back, I'll stay with you, and we'll take care of 'im."

Woody nodded. "I'll be ready."

"I'll watch fir 'em," said Lester, "and let you know if they be here."

"We'll check with you when we git back," said Floyd. He motioned to the driver, and they headed downriver.

They got to the place where they had landed the day before and they jumped out. The boat pulled out and headed down the river.

Floyd started through the trees with Woody behind him. He stopped where he' been the day before and looked across the field. "I ain't gonna let Doc git to the house today. If he does git to the house, all the men'll git around 'im and I can't git no clear shot. We gonna go up a ways where I have a better angle on the car. I'll shut the car down and he'll be in the middle of the road." He got up and went another hundred yards through the trees and set up.

An hour later a single car came down the road, went on to the house and parked. Woody was looking through the binoculars. "That's Gil," he said as two men went in the house.

Thirty minutes later they heard cars coming. Floyd got ready as the three cars came into view. As it was yesterday, Doc's car was in the middle. Floyd looked through the scope at the driver of the first car and fired. The glass in the side window shattered and the driver slumped over. The car stopped and two men in the back seat jumped out and huddled on the other side of the car.

When the lead car stopped, the other two cars slammed on their brakes and stopped. With all three cars sitting still, Floyd shifted his attention to Doc's car and emptied the remaining bullets in the clip into the engine. Steam and smoke started pouring from under the hood.

Floyd quickly reloaded and turned his attention to the back seat of Doc's car where he figured Doc was. The windows were dark, and he couldn't see anyone inside, but he knew Doc was in there. He fired as fast as he could work the bolt and throw out the spent cartridges. All the glass in the car windows were shattered. The two men in the front seat of Doc's car were trying to get out the driver's door and Floyd knew he hit one of them.

The driver of the third car pulled around to the far side of Doc's car and three men got out. They were trying to help somebody lying on the ground that came out of Doc's car. Floyd opened fire on them. One of the men fell down. He put several rounds in the engine of the third car.

Now all three cars were disabled, and the men still left alive were huddled in the middle of the road with no place to go. They were trapped. The person shooting at them was eight-hundred yards away so the weapons they had were useless.

Floyd looked toward the house. He saw one man run out on the porch and look up the road. Floyd fired in his direction and the man ran back inside.

Woody was lying beside Floyd watching all this through the binoculars. He looked at Floyd in amazement. He'd never seen anything like this in his life. Damn, he thought, those people are in one hell of a mess.

Floyd stopped firing and watched. Suddenly one man jumped up from behind the cars and started running toward the house. Floyd watched him and let him go. He had no interest in him. The man made it to the house and rushed in the front door.

Floyd put in a fresh clip and emptied it into the back seat of Doc's car. Some minutes later he heard the sirens. He looked at Woody. "We gotta go. The law's comin.'" They got up and headed through the trees toward the river.

When Floyd got to the corner of the field he stopped and looked back toward the house. The smoking cars were surrounded by cars with flashing lights, both police and ambulances. He turned toward the river and ran on through the trees.

The boat was waiting. They jumped in, the boat backed away and they headed upriver. When they reached the ferry, they pulled in and Woody got out.

"I can't stay," said Floyd. "There's liable to be a lot of law around so you be careful, but I doubt them people will be here today." he said.

Woody nodded. "I know but I'll check on the folks." He turned and headed into town.

The boat backed away from the ferry, they waved to Lester and headed upriver. Floyd knew he had to get back to the Manns before they heard about the shooting. He had no idea how much damage he'd done; he hoped he'd killed Doc, but he hadn't seen any proof of that. He didn't know how the Atlanta people would react to what had happened, but he had to be ready for any event.

When they landed Floyd went to the man in charge of the dock and told him to double security for the night. He didn't believe anyone would come in from the river, but he didn't want to take a chance. He also had them close the farm gate and place extra guards there.

Virginia had expected him to be gone all day and when he returned before noon she was surprised. "What happened?" she asked.

"I'm not sure," said Floyd, "but we did do some damage. Now we'll have to wait and see how they react."

"Are you worried?" she asked, watching his face.

He shook his head. "Ain't no need to worry. We'll deal with what comes."

22

Doc wasn't dead. He was wounded and hurt badly but was expected to survive. He had a bullet in his leg and in his back. The shattered glass from the windows had cut his face and arms. The ambulance had taken him to a hospital outside Atlanta and he immediately was taken into surgery.

Doc's organization was decimated. Four of his people were dead and two were wounded in the shooting. Gil had been Doc's main lieutenant, so he took over command until Doc had a chance to heal and get better.

Gil had little involvement and experience in the business end of the organization. He had been Doc's enforcer and he was good at it. Now that he was in charge, he intended to do one thing: eliminate Floyd Wimms.

Nothing about the shooting was in the news or the newspapers. Doc's people didn't want it printed and the local law didn't care. They had been trying to catch Doc for years and they didn't care if he and all his people got killed. They treated the matter as in-fighting between two lawless groups.

. . .

Gil already had a meeting set up with Ron Hurt for that night. Despite all that had happened that day to Doc, he felt he should still meet with Ron. He knew little about Floyd Wimms, so he needed information. Ron did know Floyd, so he would talk to him and hoped to find out where he stayed, where he went and his habits. So far, they had underestimated him, and he didn't want to make that mistake again.

He was impressed with Floyd's attack that day. Obviously, Floyd was not the regular hillbilly clod they had thought he was. His attack had been well planned, like a military operation. He had caught Doc in the open, he had superior firepower and he had punished them. They would have to be more careful in the future.

Gil didn't like being tied up with these farmers anyway. They were better suited to work around Atlanta. He'd been opposed to the operation from the beginning, but Doc had overruled him. Now he had no choice but continue since Doc had been shot. There was no way Doc would allow Wimms to damn near kill him and go free. He hoped that somehow by the time Doc recovered, Wimms would be dead. As he thought of that possibility, he also hoped that he would survive the hunt.

Ron had heard nothing of the shooting as he prepared to go meet Gil at Dib's. His thoughts were on getting Gil and his people to take care of Floyd. If Floyd was out of the way, then he could rest easy. Right now, he didn't feel easy about anything. He knew he was afraid of Floyd.

Then his thoughts turned to Rachel. She had promised to meet him tonight when he finished with Gil. Their initial meeting had gone well, and he had high hopes for tonight. She had been responsive when he'd kissed her and tonight, after a few drinks, she would be more responsive. He had no doubt he would spend the night in her bed. He was ready for her after the disappointment with

Virginia. He'd had high hopes for Virginia also, but she'd rebuffed him. Then Floyd had shown up and she wouldn't even talk to him. He got dressed, went outside to his car and headed to town.

R achel was excited. She'd been so disappointed with Floyd and so embarrassed at the hospital, but now, after meeting Ron her spirits were up. He was nice-looking, dressed well and his family owned a farm. All these were credentials she valued in her search for a husband.

She was concerned about how she'd acted when he came home with her. The alcohol she'd drunk that night had messed up her mind and she'd allowed him to take advances she'd not planned on. While she was with him tonight, she'd watch what she drank and keep control of her senses. She didn't intend to let him get the advantage on her again. However, when she'd asked him to back off the other night, he'd backed off. So, she was sure she could control him until he was interested in her and not just going to bed with her. She got dressed and headed for Dib's.

F loyd had spent the afternoon with Virginia. He'd been surprised that everything was quiet. He'd half expected to have Sheriff White show up and ask him questions about the shooting. Now the sun was almost down, and he'd heard nothing and seen no activity of any sort. The quietness bothered him.

"I can't stand not knowing what's going on," he said. "I've got to go find out.

Virginia shook her head. "You'd better stay here. Those people are going to be looking for you."

He got up. "Don't matter. I'll be back in a while." He got his pistol, stuck it in his belt and walked out. He got in the truck and headed to town.

. . .

Rachel got to Dib's, parked and went in. She looked around but didn't see Ron. He'd said he had to meet some men there and he'd get with her after the meeting. She looked around but didn't see anybody that didn't look like they were local. She sat down, told the waitress she was expecting somebody else and ordered a soda.

She was sipping on the soda five minutes later when another man came in. He stood at the bar, looked around, then walked across the floor to a back table and sat down with his back to the wall. Rachel knew he was not a regular customer. He glanced at her briefly and then watched the door.

It wasn't three minutes later when Ron walked in. He stood in the door for a minute looking around the room. He saw her, smiled and waved, then his eyes went to the back table where the man with the mustache was sitting. He looked at him, nodded, then walked to Rachel's table.

He sat down in the chair beside her, took her hand and leaned over and kissed her. "I told you I have to meet this man for a minute and then I'll be back," he said.

She smiled at him. "I'll be here waiting," she said.

He got up, walked to the back table and sat down. Rachel watched. They were soon in a conversation. She wondered what that was about.

"He shot Doc?" said Ron after Gil had told him what had happened that afternoon.

Gil nodded. "Doc's in the hospital in surgery. He's damn lucky he didn't get killed. Four others there wasn't so lucky. Wimms had them set up and poured it to them. I was in the house and couldn't do a thing."

"He shot them from the other side of the field," said Ron. "That's a long ways."

"It is a long ways," said Gil, "and he was accurate, like a sniper. Somebody said to do that he must have had a rifle like a Springfield with a scope." He looked at Ron. "We ain't never dealt with nobody like Wimms."

Ron nodded. "I told you the son'bitch was crazy. I told Doc that." He stared at Gil. "What are you going to do?"

"We got to kill him, but how do we get to him? Where does he live?"

"He lives in a house on the Mann farm," said Ron. "I know where he lives but it won't be easy to get to him there. Somehow you got to get him off the farm to have a chance at him."

"I thank you're right," said Gil. "Does he have a girlfriend or family?"

"He has a girlfriend, but she lives on the farm," said Ron. "He doesn't have any family here that I know of."

"Well, somehow we got to get him away from the farm." He looked at Ron. "You think about that and let's see what we can come up with."

Rachel had been watching Ron and the mustached man as they talked. By the expressions on their faces, they were talking serious business.

Gil looked at Rachel. "Who's the woman?"

"That's Rachel," said Ron. "I'm supposed to get with her after we get through talking."

Gil stared at her. "Damn good-looking woman. Why don't you go get her and bring her over?"

Ron shook his head. "She don't know nothing about all this."

"We're through talking," said Gil as he stared at Ron. "Go get her. I like to be with good-looking women."

Reluctantly. Ron got up and walked over to Rachel's table. "Gil would like for you to join us for a drink," he said. "It would be good if you would."

She looked up at him. "Do you want me to?"

"Yes, I do. It would be good." He reached and pulled her chair back as she got up. He took her hand as they walked to the table. "Gil, this is Rachel," said Ron.

Gil took her hand and pulled her chair out for her. He smiled at her as she sat down. "You're a good-looking woman, Rachel," he said, as he reached over and patted her on the shoulder.

Rachel looked at him and immediately disliked him. His manner, beneath the smile, made her flesh crawl. She didn't know why Ron was with him, but she didn't like being around him.

"Thank you," she said. She didn't know what else to do.

Gil called the waitress over and ordered a round of drinks. She tried to tell him she was drinking soda, but he insisted otherwise and ordered her a drink.

Floyd pulled into the parking lot at the joint across the road from Dib's and went inside. He wanted to see if the bartender had any information. The bartender saw him come in. Floyd glanced across the crowd, didn't see anybody of interest and went to the bar. He pulled out a bill and laid it down.

The bartender walked over, picked up the bill and looked at him. "Somebody damn near killed all of Doc's people this morning." he said. His eyes were on Floyd's face. "I don't reckon you know anything bout that?"

Floyd just stared at him and waited.

"Docs in surgery but they say he'll live."

Floyd continued to stare at him.

"I just heard that one of Doc's men is at Dib's right now talkin' to somebody."

Floyd put another bill on the table and walked out. He got in the truck, drove across the street and parked at Dib's. If one of Doc's men was at Dib's, he couldn't let this opportunity pass to meet them one on one. They undoubtedly were looking for him.

He got out and walked in. He stood in the door in the dark and looked around. He saw Gil and Ron at the back table, then he saw Rachel sitting with them. Seeing her surprised him. What the hell is she doing with them, he thought? He put his hand on his pistol and started across the room toward them.

T he waitress brought the drinks to the table. Gil picked up his glass and started to take a drink when he quickly sat it down. He put both his hands palm down on the table. He glanced at Ron. "Put both your hands on the table."

Ron puzzled, looked at him.

"Hurry, damn it. Do it." Gil was looking toward the door and saw Floyd coming toward them.

Ron was still confused, but he finally looked around and saw Floyd. He put his hands on the table.

Rachel had heard what Gil said but didn't understand what he was saying. Then she saw Ron's reaction and saw the fear in his face. She had no idea what was going on. Then she looked up and Floyd was standing beside her with his hand on his pistol. Wide-eyed she looked up at him. "Floyd," she started to say.

He interrupted her. "Why are you with these people, Rachel?"

"I was with Ron," she said. "We were going to have dinner."

He looked at her. "Get yo' purse and get up," he said. "You're leaving here right now."

"But," she started to say.

He looked at her. "Hush! Don't you say another word." He looked at Ron. "I told you if you got with these people again, I'd have yo' ass." Then he looked at Gil. "You didn't git enough this mornin'? You come up here to git some more? You were damn lucky to be hidin' in the house."

Gil nodded, his eyes on Floyd's face. "You're right, I was glad I was in the house."

"You ain't in the house now," Floyd said, shaking his head. "You sho' stupid to git caught like this."

Gil smiled and shook his head. "I don't think so. I don't have a weapon."

"You oughta got you one."

Gil smiled. "You're not going to shoot me."

"Why do you thank I ain't?"

"I'm unarmed and there's too many witnesses," said Gil. He looked around. "You have the attention of everybody here. You've made too much noise."

"You better leave us alone," said Ron, as he stood up. "I'm not going to sit here and have you talk to me like this.

Floyd looked at him. "You say one more word and I'm gonna put yo' lights out."

Ron glanced at Gil and slowly sat back down.

Floyd looked at Rachel. "Rachel, you go git in yo' car and wait for me. I'm parked right beside you. When I come out, I'll explain this to you."

Rachel frowned. "Why should I do that? I don't understand this."

Floyd looked at her. "These are bad people Ron is messed up with and somebody might git killed here tonight." He cut his eyes at her. "You do what I say right now."

Rachel, white faced, looked at him, then at Ron, got her purse and walked out the door.

The other customers at the tables had become bored with all the talk, and when Rachel left, they went back to drinking.

Floyd looked at Gil. "I told you it was stupid for you to come up here. Do you think I'm gonna let you go back, get with yo' folks and come after me again?"

Gil shook his head. "I'm just going to sit here till you leave. I won't go anywhere with you."

Floyd looked at him. "You have a choice. You can walk out of here with me through that back door. Or I'll hit you like I did before, you'll be knocked out, and I'll carry you out."

Gil knew then that he had made a bad mistake by coning here and he had no way out. If he tried anything here, Floyd would kill him, and nobody here would care. He stood up.

Floyd looked at Ron. "You come with us."

Ron shook his head. "I'm staying here. I'm not going anywhere."

Floyd pulled his pistol and cracked him on the head with the barrel.

Ron winced and grabbed his head.

"Next time you ain't gonna wake up," said Floyd as he stepped behind him.

Ron got up holding his head and started toward the back door.

Gil followed him. Floyd grabbed Gil's shirt. "If you try anythang, I'll kill you out here in the dark."

Gil walked out the door into the parking lot.

Floyd looked at Ron. "You are one stupid shit." Suddenly his arm came up and he hit him on the side of his face and head with the pistol. Ron crumpled to the ground and didn't move.

Gil looked at Floyd and then at Ron lying on the ground. He didn't comment.

Floyd pushed him toward the parking lot. "There ain't nothin' I'd like better than beat the hell outta you," he said as he stuck his pistol in his belt. "You make one move and I'll damn well do it."

Gil looked at him for a moment and then walked over to the truck.

Floyd reached in the back of the truck and got a piece of rope. He tied Gil's hands behind him. "Git yo' ass in the truck and sit there. I gotta talk to Rachel."

Floyd walked over to Rachel's car. She opened the door and looked up at him. "What is this about, Floyd?" she asked, her eyes on his face.

"The man in the truck is a killer, Rachel. He was sent here to kill me, and Ron was workin' with 'im."

She shook her head. "I can't believe that. Where is Ron now?"

"He's gone home."

"Did you hurt him?"

"I thank he has a headache."

"What are you going to do now?

"Take this man with me to the farm."

She stared up at him. "Will you take me home with you?"

"I have a woman, Rachel. You go home. I told you before to get a

fine young man and marry 'im. I ain't never been no good for you."
He leaned over and kissed her." You stay away from Ron, he's
probably gonna git hisself kilt. You don't want to be messed up with
'im." He smiled at her. "If I didn't already have a woman, I'd take you
with me." He patted the top of the car. "Now you git yo' self home."
He closed the door and walked to the truck.

Rachel started the car and drove away.

Floyd opened the door and got in.

"What are you going to do with me?" said Gil. "I can pay you a lot
to let me go."

Floyd laughed. "Did you really thank you could come up here
and walk away?"

"I made a mistake. I didn't think you'd be out after this morning. I
should have brought more people with me." He shrugged. "I
misjudged you."

Floyd nodded. "You don't git to do that but once in this game." He
drove on toward the farm. He went through the gate and to the dock.
He got Gil out, locked him up in the gated room and told the man in
charge what to do with him. He went to the house.

Virginia was waiting at the house when he walked in.

"What happened," she asked.

"I got Gil, one of their main men, locked up at the dock. With Doc
in the hospital, this should shut them down for a while."

She frowned. "But, when Doc gets well, they'll be after you again."

He nodded. "That might be true."

"What was this Gil doing there?"

"He was meeting with Ron."

"So, Ron really was with those people?"

"I told you he was."

"I still can't believe he could do that." She looked at him. "What
did you do with Ron?"

"I left him at the club," said Floyd. He didn't see any sense in
going into how he left him.

"So, just Gil and Ron was there?"

"Do you remember the girl that came to the hospital to see me?"

She stared at him; her lips tightened. "What does that have to do with this?"

He could tell that he had hit a nerve. "Her name was Rachel, and she was there with Ron."

Virginia was surprised at this news. "She was with Ron?"

"I asked her what she was doing with them," said Floyd, "and she said she was going to have dinner with Ron."

"How did she know Ron?"

Floyd shook his head. "I don't know. I didn't know she knew 'im."

Virginia turned up her nose. "I expect whores know lots of men," she said. "She knew you."

Floyd didn't comment, there was no use to it. "You need to go to sleep," he said.

"That what I intend to do," she said as she turned over with her back to him.

23

R on Hurt came to his senses with one of Dib's clean-up men kneeling over him. "What happened to you?" asked the man.

Ron sat up and stared at him, trying to remember what did happen to him. Then he remembered standing with Floyd and Gil and then his lights went out. He felt of his head, it hurt and felt wet. He looked at his hand, there was blood on his fingers.

"You got a gash on yo' head," said the man. "Looks like somebody done hit you."

Ron nodded. The man was right, Floyd had knocked the hell out of him. He struggled to get to his feet. The man grabbed his arm and steadied him. He stood there for a minute to get his balance, then walked to his car. He got in and looked in the mirror. He did have a gash in his head and dried blood was all over the side of his face. He started the car and pulled out of the parking lot.

He drove to his farm, pulled into his drive, got out and went in the house. He went straight to the bathroom and cleaned his face. His right eye was already turning black. He went to his room and went to bed.

. . .

The sun was up when he was awakened by his mother. She was looking at his face. "Ron," she said, "what happened to you? You've been cut and you face is black and blue."

He sat up. "I fell and hit my head on the concrete at Dib's," he said.

"Were you drunk?" She shook her head. "I told Charlie that you've been hanging out at those beer joints too much lately."

"I wasn't drunk. I just tripped and hit in the wrong place. I'll be alright."

She stood up. "Anyway, there's a man at the door to see you. He said it's important."

Ron frowned. "Who is it?"

"I don't know. I've never seen him before," she said. "He said it has to do with Gil." She looked at him. "Who is Gil?"

"I don't know," Ron said as he jumped out of bed and slipped on his pants. He walked to the front door. The man was standing on the porch. He had seen him before with Gil. He knew his name was Tonk.

Ron walked out on the porch.

Tonk stared at him. "What the hell happened to you?" he said.

Ron ignored his question. "What do you want? You know you're not ever supposed to come to my house."

"You was with Gil last night and nobody has seen him since," said Tonk. "What happened to him?"

Ron shook his head. "We can't talk here," he said as he walked out in the yard.

Tonk followed him.

"Floyd Wimms has him," said Ron. "At least he had him the last I remember, before he knocked me out."

Ron told him about Floyd coming into their table and what developed afterward.

"The man at Dib's said there was a girl at the table with y'all?" said Tonk.

Ron nodded. "There was, but she had nothing to do with what happened to Gil."

"Who is she?"

"She's a schoolteacher in town I had a date with."

"They said she left before y'all left. Why did she leave?"

"I'm not sure," said Ron. "I didn't know that Floyd knew her, but he did. He told her she didn't need to hang around with me and sent her home."

Tonk studied on that for a minute. "Sounds like he was concerned about her."

Ron shrugged. "Maybe so, I didn't think much about it. I was worried about what Floyd was going to do."

Tonk nodded. "He is sho' bad. I'm glad I wasn't in them cars yesterday. He damn near killed everybody."

"That's what I heard," said Ron. He looked at Tonk. "What are you gonna do?"

"We gonna get Gill back," said Tonk as he walked to his car.

Ron chuckled. "Good luck with that." He turned and went back in the house.

~

Sister wasn't pregnant and she wasn't happy about it. She woke up that morning and had started her period. She lay in the bed and cried she was so disappointed. She went to Brooks with tears rolling down her face and told him the news. He smiled and hugged her.

"Sister," he said, "it's only been one month. We have plenty of time to have children. You're young and healthy so stop worrying about it."

She heard what he said but it still bothered her. She knew he wanted children and she wanted to please him. This feeling was new to her. She had never in her life been concerned about pleasing another person. But Brooks had been good to her and that was a new experience for her from a man. All the men she'd met before Brooks, except for Floyd, had been mean to her.

He life had been going well. She was learning to read; Brooks was teaching her, and she found she liked reading. It had taught her about places she never knew existed and people she'd never heard of before.

The same was true for going to the church. After going several times, she was beginning to understand a bit of what the preacher was talking about. Some of the things he said made her have questions and Brooks had to explain it to her. Some she didn't think Brooks understood. But she liked the talk about doing good and loving people, she could understand that. However, as she thought about it, she decided that most people she knew hadn't ever heard this sermon. Or if they had heard it, they didn't pay any attention.

She loved Brooks and liked being with him, but she missed the excitement of being on the river. She had thought about talking to Brooks about her going up the river and seeing Virginia. He would probably let her go, but she hesitated about it. They had only been together for a month, and she didn't want to have him think she was unhappy. So, she didn't say anything to him.

But as the days went on and she spent time in the kitchen and Brooks was working all day, she could still hear the call of the river. As much as she liked being with Brooks, she missed the independence of being on her own. While she knew these thoughts were crazy, she had all any woman could want, they were now with her every day.

She asked Brooks to let her go to the cabin and stay for a couple of days by herself, thinking that would satisfy her longing. She went to the cabin and stayed but it didn't. She went back home with the same thoughts that had been bothering her.

~

It had been three days since Floyd had brought Gil to the farm. Every day they had watched and waited for some retaliation, but nothing came. They kept guards on the river and the main gate.

Floyd had eaten supper and was walking back to the house when he saw one of the guards on the gate running toward him. He stopped and looked at him. "There's two men down at the gate that want to see you," the man said.

"Who are they?" said Floyd.

"They said to tell you they was from Doc."

"Are they armed?" he said, staring at the guard.

"I didn't see no weapons. They come up in a car, got out and now they be standing at the gate. Another thang," he said, "there's another car behind them. It be about twenty or thirty yards away, just sitting there."

Floyd frowned. "So, there be people in that car too."

The guard nodded. "I can see people in the car, but I don't know who they are."

Floyd frowned. "I don't like that," he said. "Let me git my truck and you can ride back down there with me."

Floyd ran to the truck and the guard got in the passenger seat. They went down the road to the gate. He saw two men were standing on the other side of the fence. As the guard had said, another car was parked on the road about thirty yards away from the gate.

He got out, walked down to the gate and looked at the two men. "What do you want?"

"We understand you have Gil," said one of the men.

"What if I have?" said Floyd.

"We want him back."

Floyd looked at the car on the road. "Who's in that car?"

The man glanced back at the car and then at Floyd. "They're with us. Do you have Gil?"

Floyd nodded. "I have 'im and I be gonna keep 'im. Why would I ever give 'im to you?"

"We have something to trade for 'im," the man said.

Before Floyd could answer he heard a car drive up behind him. He looked around. Virginia got out of the car and came walking up behind him. "What's going on?" she said.

Floyd looked around at her. "I'm not really sure right now, but you ain't got no business down here. You might git hurt."

She shook her head. "Don't worry about me. What do they want?"

"They want Gil. I'm talking to 'em."

"You go ahead. I'll just listen."

Floyd looked back at the man. "What are you talkin about, havin' somthin' to trade.?"

"We got somebody you want, and we'll trade her for Gil," said the man.

Floyd stared at him. "What the hell are you talkin' bout."

The man turned and waved to the car in the road. The back door opened, and a man got out. Then Rachel got out with another man holding her.

Virginia walked up beside Floyd. "Who is that girl?"

"It's Rachel, the girl you saw at the hospital," said Floyd. "I told you she was with Ron the other night when I got Gil."

She looked up at him. "I don't understand why she was with Ron at Dib's?"

Floyd nodded. "I don't neither, but she was there and I sent her home." He looked back at the man. "You hurt that girl and I'll kill ever one of you bastards."

"We ain't gonna hurt her," said the man. "We'll give her to you when you give us Gil."

Floyd pulled his pistol, walked to the gate and stared at the man. "Listen to me, you stupid sons'abitch, I don't give a damn bout that girl. I ain't gonna trade Gil. The first thing I be gonna do is kill you two if you don't give me the girl. I've got you outgunned here, and then we'll kill everybody in that car too. I ain't gonna give you Gil and have to fight you bastards from now on." He pointed his pistol right in the man's face.

The man held up his hands. "Wait a minute. I'm not stupid. I knew when I come up here that if you didn't deal, you'd kill me.

You give us Gil and we'll be gone. You won't never see us up here again."

"Why the hell should I believe that bull shit?" said Floyd.

"Doc said we're pulling out," the man said. "He said we never should have been up here to start with. This wasn't our business."

Floyd shook his head. "They tell me Doc's bout dead. How could he say that?"

"He is hurt some but he's out of surgery and he told us that today," said the man. "I talked to him today myself. That's what he told me."

Virginia walked up beside Floyd. "We can't let them hurt that girl. She has to be scared to death."

Floyd looked at her and then back at the man. "We don't know he be tellin' the truth."

The man stared at Floyd and then looked at Virginia. "I done told you I ain't stupid. I wouldn't have never walked out here if I weren' tellin' you the truth." He looked back at Floyd. "Doc say you give us Gil and we give you the girl. Don't nobody want to hurt her."

Floyd looked around at the guards. "Y'all keep yo' eyes on him. If he tries to leave, kill 'im." He looked back at the man. "I'm gonna talk to Gil. What's yo' name?"

"I'm Sam," he said.

Floyd took Virginia's arm and they walked to his truck.

Rachel had been upset for three days since the confrontation with Floyd at Dib's. She didn't understand all that had happened and didn't understand all Floyd had told her either. But based on what he'd said, Ron was mixed up in something bad and with bad people. Floyd said that Gil was a killer and had been sent to kill him. She found all this hard to believe, but she'd seen Floyd's eyes when he told her, and she believed him.

She was really disappointed in Ron. He had impressed her, and she thought he had all the attributes she was looking for in a man. Floyd had used her and walked away. Thankfully she hadn't taken that next step with Ron, but if they hadn't been interrupted by Floyd, she probably would have. Now she had to forget about Ron and Floyd and go on with her life. She vowed to stay out of Dib's from now on.

She walked out of school that afternoon, got in her car and drove to her house. She noticed a car was following closely behind her, but she didn't think anything about it. She pulled into her drive and got out. She was getting her papers out of the back seat when she noticed the car was stopped behind her car. She stood up with the papers in her arm as two men jumped out of the car and rushed at her.

She screamed as they grabbed her, a bag was put over her head and she couldn't see, everything was black. She felt herself picked up, then she was in the car, and it sped away. She was kicking and struggling, hitting out at whoever had her. The thought was in her mind, these men have me and she expected the worst. She expected her clothes to be torn off at any minute.

She could feel a man's arms around her holding her arms tight. "Be still," said a man's voice. "We ain't gonna hurt you, quit fighting before you hurt yo' self."

She knew it was useless to continue fighting, they were too strong, so she quit.

"That's better," said the voice. "You be quiet, and you'll be all right."

"Why do you have me?" she asked in a trembling voice.

"You'll find out," said the voice. "Just stay still and be quiet."

She did as he said. She could feel that they were riding on a bumpy road. Then the car stopped. She heard doors opening and closing and then people talking. This went on for several minutes and she wondered what was happening. At least they hadn't molested her to this point, and she was thankful for that.

She heard the door open beside her, somebody had her arm and pulled her out of the car. The she was standing outside the car, and somebody was holding her. Then the bag was pulled off her head and she could see. It took her a minute to get her eyes adjusted to where she could see clearly.

There was a car parked in front of her and then there were men standing at a gate across the road. There were people on the other side of the gate. They were all looking at her. Then she saw Floyd and the girl she'd seen at the hospital, Virginia. What was happening and why were they looking at her?

Floyd was talking to the men, and they seemed to be talking about her. She didn't understand what was happening, but it seemed the men that had her weren't planning to hurt her. She didn't think Floyd would let them hurt her if he could help it. Then Floyd and Virginia turned and started walking away and it scared her.

She looked at the man holding her. "Where are they going?"

He shook his head. "I don't know. They gonna talk some more I reckon."

Floyd looked at Virginia. "I'm goin' to talk to Gil. This is still dangerous here. Somebody might do somethin' stupid and start shootin' and git people hurt. You go back to the house, and I'll let you know what's happening."

"You can't let them hurt that girl," she said, looking in his face.

He shook his head. "They don't want to hurt her. She'll be all right."

"Why did they get her?" she asked. "Did they think she was special to you?"

Floyd looked at her. "They didn't know anything about me and her. The only people that knew Rachel knew me was Gil and Ron. He thought for a moment. "Gil's been locked up here so he couldn't tell 'em. Ron had to tell 'em that I knew her, and they thought they could use her."

She looked at him. "You mean Ron did this to her?"

"I spect he did," said Floyd. "They wouldn't have ever knowed 'cept for 'im."

"I was wrong about Ron," she said. "He is a sorry bastard."

"You go to the house. I gotta go talk to Gil."

She got in her car, turned around and headed toward her house. Floyd got in the truck and followed her.

F loyd parked at the dock, got out and went to the room where they had Gil locked up. He opened the door.

Gil was lying on the bunk. He got up when the door opened and looked at Floyd.

"Seems Doc wants you back," he said, watching Gil's face.

"Reckon how he plans to do that?" said Gil.

"Do you remember the girl with Ron at the table the other night?"

Gil nodded. "Rachel, I remember her." He frowned. "What does she have to do with me?"

"Doc's men have her and they've offered to swap her for you."

Gil half-smiled and pursed his lips. "Is she something special to you? Why do they think you'd make that trade?"

"She ain't special and I wouldn't trade you fir her," said Floyd.

"So why are we talking?"

"The man that's doin' the talkin', he says his name is Sam, told me Doc will pull out if he gits you back." Floyd watched Gil's eyes. "Sam said he talked to Doc this mornin' and he told 'im that."

"Where is Sam now?"

"He's down at the gate," said Floyd. "My people have 'im covered. I done told 'im if anything goes wrong, I'm gonna kill 'im right off."

Gil nodded. "Sam's telling you the truth. He wouldn't have never let you get him in the open like that if he didn't think you'd make the trade."

"How did y'all git mixed up in this to start with?" asked Floyd.

Gil shrugged. "Ron Hurt sold it to Doc. He said it would be easy money. I was against it, but Doc went with him." He cut his eyes at Floyd. "It was easy money till you showed up."

"So, you believe Doc will go away, even though he bout got killed."

Gil nodded. "If he said that he will. He don't like to go against the odds."

Floyd looked at him. "You come with me. We'll go talk to Sam." He walked to the truck and Gil followed him. They got in and started toward the gate. When they passed the big house, Virginia was sitting in her car. Floyd signaled her to follow him.

"That your wife?" said Gil.

Floyd chuckled. "Ain't got no wife. Ain't never had one. Ain't never gonna have one." He rode on to the gate and Virginia followed.

They got out and walked to the gate. Sam was standing on the other side of the fence watching them.

"You talked to Doc?" said Gil.

"I talked to him this mornin'."

"How was he?"

"He was hurting but he talked alright. He said we'd pull out if he turned you loose."

Gil looked toward the other car. "If anybody has hurt that girl, I'll have his ass."

Sam shook his head. "Ain't nobody done nothin' to her. Bout scared the hell out of her though."

The man holding her had pushed Rachel back in the car when Floyd had walked away. She had watched him leave and then watched him come back. He had that Gil with him now. They stood at the gate talking.

The man grabbed her arm and pulled her out of the car again. She stood and watched Floyd and the others talking. She couldn't hear what they were saying.

Gil turned to Floyd. "You let me go and I'll go see Doc tonight. It seems he feels we don't have any business up here and I'll tell him I feel the same way. We'll pull everybody back and you won't see us again."

Floyd stared at him.

Gil laughed. "You made a believer out of everybody when you

shot from the next county and hit what you shot at." He looked at him. "You'd done that before, I figure."

"I was a sniper in the war in France."

"Figured that," said Gil. He stepped back. "It's your call now as to what happens next."

"What you gonna do bout Ron Hurt?"

"We're done with him. You can do what you want with him," said Gil as he stepped closer to Floyd. "Let me tell you something and make it clear. We don't make deals with people that kill our people. We kill them. We're dealing with you, not because there's honor among thieves, but because we don't want you after us."

Floyd stared at him.

"If you come after us again, in any way, the war will be on." Gil looked across at Rachel. "If you start the war again, there won't be any more deals made. People will get hurt and people will die. Do you understand what I'm saying?"

Floyd smiled and stared at Gil. "You be standing here tellin' me that. Let me thank about that. Doc's all shot up and I don't know how many people y'all got besides what's right here. I figure if I was to kill you and Sam and this other fellow here. And then I kill all of them in that other car. All y'all be dead and all I lose is one girl that I don't give a damn about." He stared at Gil. "I figure that would bout wipe out Doc's gang." He stared at Gil and waited for an answer.

Gil smiled. "You act like a damn hillbilly but you ain't. Tell me what you gonna do?"

"Tell 'em folks in that car to send Rachel over. When she be halfway, you can go." He turned to the guard. "Unlock the gate and push it open."

Sam had listened to everything that was said. He turned and yelled to the man in the car. "Send the girl over."

R achel had watched the talking. It seemed to last forever. Then the man turned and said to send the girl over. The man holding her turned loose and said, "You can go. Don't run."

Rachel started walking toward the gate as Gil came through the gate and started toward her. They passed in the middle of the road. She glanced at him as he went by. His eyes were straight ahead. She walked on and went in the gate.

Floyd took her arm but then Virginia rushed up and wrapped her arms around her. "You poor dear," she said. "You come with me, and I'll look after you."

Rachel stopped and looked up at Floyd. "You go with Virginia," he said. "She'll look after you."

Floyd turned as Gil and Sam got in the car, turned around and drove away. He looked at the guards. "Y'all be careful tonight. Keep yo' eyes open. I ain't never trusted the Devil."

He got in his truck and headed to the house. He parked, got out and opened the front door. Virginia and Rachel were sitting on the couch. Both their eyes were on him as he walked in. He walked over, sat down by Rachel and put his arms around her. Virginia stared at him but didn't say anything. Rachel looked up at him. He could tell she'd been crying.

"I be sorry you got caught up in this, Rachel," he said. "It didn't have nothin' to do with you."

"Why did they get me?" she said. "How did they know about me?"

Floyd frowned. "The people at Dib's saw you with Gil and Ron the other night." He looked in her eyes. "Ron had to tell 'em bout you."

She shook her head. "I can't believe he'd do that to me. I thought he was nice."

"I thought the same thing," said Virginia. "I dated him, and he asked me to marry him. I'm glad I didn't fall for him. He just wanted me to get our farm."

"Did they hurt you?" asked Floyd.

Rachel shook her head. "They didn't hurt me, but they scared me. I didn't know why they had me, but I thought something bad was going to happen to me to start with."

"I would have thought the same thing," said Virginia. She looked at Floyd. "You know how men are about women."

"Well, you be safe and all right now," said Floyd. He looked at Virginia. "What have y'all talked about doin'?"

Virginia looked at Rachel. "I told her she can stay with me tonight if she wants to. It's up to you, Rachel. I thought you might be afraid to go back home tonight."

"You've been very nice to me, Virginia," Rachel said. "I really appreciate it, but I can go home. I'm not afraid now." She looked at Floyd. "They wouldn't bother me now, would they?"

Floyd shook his head. "I don't thank so. I don't know why they'd bother you again noway."

Rachel looked at Floyd. "Would you take me home?"

"We'll take you home," said Virginia, her eyes on Floyd's face.

Rachel looked at her. "I didn't mean anything by that, Virginia. I just didn't want to bother you."

"It's not a bother for me," Virginia said as she got up. She looked back at Rachel. "I know you slept with Floyd, Rachel. If he took you home and asked to stay with you tonight, would you?"

Rachel looked at Floyd and then back at Virginia. She smiled. "If he wanted to I would."

Virginia nodded. "That's what I thought." She walked to the door and opened it. "We've had enough excitement for one night," she said. "We don't need anymore. Y'all come on." She walked to Floyd's truck.

Rachel looked at Floyd and they walked to the door. "Virginia's real sweet. You should have told me she was your girl."

"She weren't then. I hadn't made her no promise" He looked at her. "Fore long I'm going up the river. Would you go with me?"

"She laughed. "You surely don't want me on the river. I wouldn't be any good to you."

"You would at night," he said, smiling at her.

She shook her head. "Virginia's right not to trust you, Floyd." She stopped and looked up at him. "If she didn't go with us; would you get in the bed with me?'

Floyd nodded. "Sho' would. I couldn't help myself."

Rachel turned and went to the truck. "Virginia," she said, "it's good you're going with us. You can't trust Floyd."

"I told you that," said Virginia.

They got in the truck, Virginia in the middle, and headed to town. They got to Rachel's house. She hugged and thanked Virginia. Floyd walked her to the door. He reached down, picked Rachel up and kissed her. She wrapped her arms around him and kissed him back.

He sat her down and looked at her. "You be one hell of a woman, little girl. I may see you again."

She looked up at him. "I surely hope so." She opened the door and went in.

Floyd walked to the truck and got in.

Virginia looked at him. "Was all that kissing necessary?"

Floyd nodded. "I wanted to make sure she remembered me."

Virginia looked out the window. "You're sorrier than gulley dirt, Floyd Wimms."

24

The next morning Woody Sharpe showed up at Floyd's door. It was the first time he's seen Woody since they'd shot up the cars at Doc's place.

"Where you been, Woody?" Floyd asked him.

"I been at the ferry since you let me off and I ain't seen none of Doc's people there. I was ready fir 'em but they didn't none show up."

"Let me tell you what's been goin' on," said Floyd. He brought Woody in and told him about what had happened.

"Damn," said Woody. "Do you thank Doc will do that?"

"We'll see but I feel like he will."

"What you gonna do bout that Ron Hurt?" asked Woody.

Floyd shook his head. "I ain't gonna do nothin' cept he bother me. If I hear anything from him, I'll handle it."

"If there ain't no trouble going on, there won't be nothin' for us to do," said Woody.

"Well," said Floyd, "you can work at the dock. Fir me, If I don't have nothing to do, I'll go on up the river. That's what I was doin' when I stopped here."

"It ain't none of my business," said Woody. "But I thought you were set pretty well with Virginia. I thought you done found a home."

Floyd stared at him. "You be right, it ain't none of yo' business. I ain't never been one to be in one place fir long."

Woody didn't mention it again.

F loyd and Virginia were in the bed that night talking. She was lying close to him, her head on his arm.

"Rachel is a sweet girl," she said.

"She is sweet. I done told her she oughta find a good boy and marry 'im."

"She likes you."

Floyd turned and looked at her. "Why you be talkin' bout this? I'm here with you."

Virginia didn't say anything for several minutes. "If Doc keeps his word, then the troubles we've had on the farm from them will be gone."

"Probably will be."

Virginia raised up and looked in his face. "I still have this farm here to look after by myself for the most part. Daddy helps what he can but not like he used to."

Floyd watched her face.

She was looking in his eyes. "I know what you said when you came here. I know what you said about getting married. That was clear at the start."

He saw the first tears pool up in her eyes and start to flow down her cheeks.

"But that was before I fell in love with you," she said as the tears flowed. "I know you were headed to the mountains, you told me that. I know you have feelings for me."

Floyd reached up and pulled her to him. He wiped her tears. "Why are you talkin' like this?"

"Because I know if there's no trouble for you to get into, one morning I'll wake up and you'll be gone. I know you'll do that, and I'll be left alone." She looked at him, questioning.

"We don't know there ain't gonna be no trouble," he said. "We gotta wait and see if Doc keeps his word fore we worry bout that. How come you all stirred up bout this right now?"

"Because I'm in love with you and I'm afraid you're going to break my heart. I didn't intend to like you, but I did." She laid back down and turned over with her back to him.

He reached over and pulled her to him. "I ain't never made no woman the promise I made to you. You never know what's gonna happen. There be a first-time fir everthang."

"That ain't what I want to hear," she said.

Floyd turned over. He didn't know how to deal with this. In a little while he was asleep.

~

The next week went by quickly. Nothing was heard of Doc or any of his people. Floyd took the extra guards off the dock and the gate. It seemed the peace they had negotiated was holding. Virginia had said no more to Floyd about his leaving.

~

Ron Hurt hated Floyd Wimms. Never had he burned with such hatred for any person in his life. He felt this way for several reasons. He had planned to take over the Mann farm by marrying Virginia and he thought that was going well until Floyd showed up and that plan fell apart; Virginia wouldn't even talk to him now. Then he'd hired Doc and his gang to bankrupt the Mann farm so he could take it over and Floyd had got in the middle of that. Now he was told that Doc had decided to back away and not do anything more to help him. Without Doc's help, he could do nothing.

Then there was his physical and emotional hurt. Floyd had humiliated him in public at Dib's and he had physically hit him with his pistol. He still had the scar from that attack.

Lastly there was Rachel. He had her set up to do his bidding and Floyd had stepped into the middle of that too. He had told her slanderous lies about him and now she would have nothing to do with him.

At night, he lay awake and thought of ways to kill Floyd, but he knew he wasn't capable of doing that. He finally admitted to himself that he was terrified of Floyd and didn't want to face him ever again.

Finally, he decided he would go to Doc and insist he support him as he had agreed to do. He would remind him he had paid him a lot of money and he hadn't finished the job. If Doc didn't agree, he would go to the law and tell them all he knew about his operation.

The next morning, he got in his car and went to the hospital to see Doc. He went to Doc's room, told him what he wanted to say and gave him an ultimatum. Doc listened to what he had to say, told him he understood his point and told him he would take care of it. Ron walked out of the hospital feeling good and headed home.

That evening he went to Dib's to celebrate. He pulled up in the parking lot, parked and got out. He didn't notice the car pulling up behind him or the man with the gun getting out. The man fired three times, all three bullets hit Ron in the chest, and he was dead before he hit the ground. The car sped away. Nobody saw the car nor the man.

Virginia was eating supper with her daddy when she got the call. "Somebody shot and killed Ron Hurt in front of Dib's tonight, Daddy. They say they don't know who did it."

Mr. Mann looked at her. "I feel sorry for Charlie and Coleen, Virginia. Ron should have known better than to get mixed up with those people."

Virginia nodded. "Excuse me, Daddy. I need to go tell Floyd." She got up and ran across the street.

"He oughta never got in with them folks," said Floyd after she told him about the call. "He must have got 'em sho'nuff mad for 'em to kill 'im. They don't usually do that."

She looked at him. "They wanted to kill you."

Floyd smiled. "I spect they still do. They just be scared to try it and mess up cause they know I'll be comin' after 'em."

"Do you really believe that?"

He nodded. "Sho' I do," he said. "They'll jump all over anybody they ain't scared of."

She stared at him. "The more I'm around you, the less about you I understand."

25

Sister had cooked breakfast and had it on the table when Brooks came in the kitchen. It was still dark outside; the sun was thirty minutes away from first light. He walked over, put his arm around her and kissed her as he always did every morning.

"I'll be plowing in the south field all day today," he said. "I probably won't be back till about dark."

"I have yo' lunch and a gallon of sweet tea all fixed," she said. "I figured you'd be gone bout all day."

He nodded. "I thank you for that." Then he noticed she was looking at him in the way he'd learned indicated she had something on her mind. He stopped eating and looked at her. "You got something bothering you?"

She nodded. "I wanted to ask you somethin'. If you don't thank it be right to do, I won't do it. But I was goin' to ask you."

He frowned. "Sister, you know you can always ask me anything you want. What is it?"

"I been thankin' bout goin' upriver and seein' Virginia," she said, her eyes on his face. "She was sho' good to me and I ain't seen 'er in some weeks." She rushed on, her eyes watching for his reaction. "I figure I could leave this mornin' and be there before dark. I'd spend the day with 'er and come back on Saturday. Then I could go to church with you Sunday."

Brooks stared at her. "You talking about going by yourself? You know I'm in the middle of plowing and can't go with you."

"Ain't no problem me goin' by myself," she said. "You know I been on that river all my life. I wouldn't have to spend the night."

"You been thinking about this?" he said. "I thought you had something on your mind, you been sorta different lately."

"I just thought it'd be good to see Virginia."

He looked at her. "I'll be worried about you but if that's what you want to do, you go ahead."

She jumped up and kissed him. "I won't be gone but a day, so I won't need much. I already got my bag ready."

He got up. "Go get your bag and I'll take you to the cabin." He looked at her. "You sure you want to do this?"

She nodded and ran to get her bag. He took it and they walked to the truck. They started down the road to the river.

"I reckon you have plenty of gas?"

"The can is full. I'll have plenty."

They got to the cabin. He got her bag and they walked to the boat. He put the bag in the boat, turned around, put his arms around her and looked in her face.

"I'll be worried about you until you get back," he said. "You be careful." He kissed her.

"Ain't no need to worry bout me. I got my pistol." She looked up at him. "When I git back we gonna work on gittin' me pregnant."

Brooks laughed. "I thought that was what we'd been working on."

Sister laughed and ran to the boat, got in and started the motor. She turned, waved to Brooks and started up the river.

He stood on the bank and watched until she went out of sight around the bend. He stood there for a minute, then went to the truck, got in and started back to the house.

. . .

S ister looked back and saw Brooks standing alone on the bank watching her. She felt sad to leave him. But then the excitement of being on the river on her own and the thought of seeing Virginia again took over. She also thought of Floyd as she had several times in the past few days and the thought of seeing him also excited her. She'd never completely cleared her mind of the thought that she was supposed to be his woman. She'd settled the debt she owed for him saving her in that one night, but the thought had never gone away. She knew that if he wanted her, she would go with him. Having that feeling bothered her. She was married now.

She pushed these thoughts aside and looked at the riverbanks and the water as she rode. This was her place on the river, and she enjoyed it. For the next three days she was on her own. What happened after then was to be found out. Right now, she had no idea how it would end up, but she was looking forward to the trip.

The sun came up and warmed the air. Animals and birds on the river woke up and began their day. She flushed wood ducks as she rounded a bend and caught a deer swimming in the middle of the river. She always enjoyed seeing the wildlife. You never knew what was going to be around the next bend.

An hour later she came around a bend and saw a boat in the middle of the river. Two men were in the boat fishing a trotline. They were about halfway across with the line, so she slowed down to allow them to fish on across. With the line pulled up as they were fishing it, the line on both sides of the boat was on top of the water. She didn't want to get too close and hit the line with her propeller and cut it.

They had their eyes on her. They started talking and laughing as they watched her. She couldn't hear what they were saying over the noise of her motor, but by their looks, she could imagine. They were rough looking, bearded and dirty. They had stopped fishing the line and were watching her. The one in the front of the boat fishing the trotline pointed at her and said something to the one at the motor. Then he turned the line loose and dropped it over the front of the boat into the water. The line sank and both men's eyes were on her.

Sister reached in her purse, got her pistol out and put it in her lap. She knew they were going to come after her.

The man at the motor cranked up and headed toward her. The man in front had his eyes on her and was directing the driver. She steered toward the bank and increased speed, but she saw they had a larger motor, and she knew that she couldn't outrun them. She had her motor wide open, but they were gaining on her. The man in front was laughing and talking to the driver. They were enjoying the chase.

She tried to turn and keep them behind her, but they were too fast. Finally, they came up alongside and the man in front grabbed the gunnel on the left side of her boat. He held on, looked at her and grinned. "You might as well stop, Missy," he yelled. "We gonna have a good time with you."

She turned the boat sharply to the right and he lost his grip. For a few seconds she was loose, but the driver turned with her and again was alongside. This time the man in front grabbed hold and pulled the gunnel tight against his boat. The driver started turning and pushed her toward the bank.

The man holding the gunnel looked at her and grinned. He wasn't over five feet away from her when she raised the pistol and shot him in the shoulder. He was knocked back but held on. The second shot was in his face. He turned her boat loose and fell back in the boat.

Surprised when she shot, the driver looked at his partner lying in the bottom of the boat with blood pouring from his face and started veering away. She turned with him. He was looking back at her, she saw the terror in his eyes as she shot him in the back. He fell forward in the boat. Driverless, the boat headed straight across the river and ran aground on the far bank. She followed right behind and landed beside it.

The driver was struggling to get up and was on his knees when she shot him in the back of the head. He fell forward, his body draped over the boat gunnel, his head in the water.

She turned to the man in the front of the boat. His face was bleeding, but he was alive. Lying on his back in the bottom of the boat, he was choking and gasping for breath. She walked to the front of the boat, stood over him and shot him in the chest with the last two bullets.

She beached her boat and tied it up. She got out, got in the other boat and after a struggle, dumped the man in the front of the boat into the water. She walked to the back of the boat. The driver was lying half out of the boat over the gunnel, and she had less trouble pushing him into the river. They both drifted down in the current for a bit and then sank. She pushed their boat away from the bank and let it drift down the river.

She got back in her boat, got bullets out of her purse and reloaded her pistol. She cranked up and headed upriver. When she passed the ferry, she went to the far side of the river, hunkered down low and kept going. She saw the old man sitting in the chair, but she didn't want him to know who she was.

It was late afternoon when she rounded the bend and saw the big warehouse and docks. She was relieved that she'd got there without any more trouble. She went on up to the dock and beached the boat where she'd landed before. She got her bag, got out and walked up the steps to the dock. She didn't see anybody, so she headed to Virginia's house.

Virginia and Floyd had eaten supper with Mr. Mann and had just got back to his house when somebody knocked on the door. Virginia jumped up from the sofa, ran and opened it. She stared at Sister.

"Sister," she screamed and hugged her, "where did you come from?"

Sister hugged her back. "I come up the river. I come to see you." Then she saw Floyd walking up. She turned Virginia loose, grabbed him and kissed him. He picked her up and kissed her back. Virginia stared at him and shook her head.

Sister held up her hand and showed it to Virginia. "I be married. I even got a ring," she said.

"You said you had a man waiting for you when you left," said Virginia. "You didn't waste any time it seems. You have to tell us all about it."

For the next thirty minutes they sat on the couch and Sister told them about Brooks and the farm and trying to get pregnant. Both Virginia and Floyd were amazed as she told her story. So much had happened to her in such a short time. "I be learning to read," she said, "cause Brooks say I got to help the chillun with their lessons." She frowned. "But we ain't got no chillun yet,"

Virginia laughed and patted her arm. "You have plenty of time for that."

"I go to church now," she said. "Brooks be a Baptist and them folks like to dunk people in the water. Brooks say I gotta be dunked, but I ain't done it yet." She looked at Virginia. "You be here in Floyd's house. You be his woman now?"

Virginia nodded. "I be his woman now."

Sister stared at Floyd. "She be yo' woman?"

Floyd nodded.

"She stay with you here in yo' house?"

Floyd nodded.

Sister looked at Virginia and then at Floyd. "I don't reckon I can stay here tonight?"

Floyd looked at Virginia. "What do you think?"

Virginia hugged Sister. "You've already been with him once. I think that's enough." They all laughed. "Have you eaten? I bet you are starving having been on the river all day."

Sister shook her head. "I gotta tell y'all somethin', "she said. "I was comin up the river and two men tried to git me. I kilt 'em both."

Both Floyd and Virginia stared at her and then she told them the story about what happened.

"Where was you?" asked Floyd.

"It be fore I got to the ferry." said Sister.

"You put 'em in the river?"

Sister nodded.

"That's good," said Floyd, "it'll take a while fore somebody finds 'em." He looked at her. "It's good you know how to shoot that pistol."

"Those men were going to harm you, Sister," said Virginia. "You did the right thing."

Sister nodded. "It don't bother me none killin' 'em. They oughta left me alone."

"Did anybody see you when you came by the ferry?" Floyd asked.

"The old man was sittin' on the ferry, but I stayed on the other bank and got down low." said Sister.

"How long are you going to be here?" asked Virginia.

"I be gonna stay tomorrow with y'all and then go home Saturday," said Sister.

"Saturday we'll go home with you, Sister," said Floyd. "We'll make sure you don't have any trouble gettin' back home."

Sister frowned. "Ain't no need doin' that. That be too much trouble fir y'all."

Floyd looked at her. "Don't argue with me. We gonna take you back."

"There's no need to argue with him, Sister," said Virginia. "You know how hardheaded he is." She looked at Floyd. "I've got to run over to the house. I promised Daddy I'd get those papers for him to sign." She looked at Sister. "I'll be back in a minute, and we'll talk about tonight and tomorrow." She jumped up and ran out the door.

Sister looked at Floyd. "You gonna marry Virginia?"

He shook his head. "You know I ain't the marryin' kind of man."

She slid over on the sofa up against him and kissed him. He put his arm around her, pulled her to him and kissed her back.

She looked up at him. "You know I wanted to be yo' woman."

"But you done got yo'self married."

She ignored that statement. "You gonna leave and go on upriver?"

"That was where I be goin' when I stopped here. I spect I will."

"Take me with you when you go," she said, staring in his eyes.

"You'd leave yo' husband?"

"I would to go with you."

Floyd got up and looked down at her. "I wouldn't never do that,

Sister. I ain't never been worth a damn, but I wouldn't do that. You need to stop talkin' bout that and git yo' ass back to yo' husband."

She smiled up at him. "Virginia be yo' woman. I be thankin' you ain't never gonna leave here."

He shook his head. "Don't you say nothin' to Virginia bout this."

Sister smiled. "I be talkin' to her tonight."

The door opened and Virginia walked back in. "Come with me, Sister and I'll get you something to eat." She looked at Floyd. "Sister will sleep in the guest room tonight and I'll stay over there too. You'll have to sleep by yourself tonight."

Sister looked back at Floyd and grinned as they went out the door.

Virginia took Sister upstairs and got her set up in the guest room. Then she took her to the kitchen and fixed her something to eat. Afterward she took her into the den and introduced her to Mr. Mann.

"I understand you're married now, Sister, and your husband has a nice farm," he said. "Virginia tells me he's a good church-going man."

"He be a Baptist," said Sister. "I reckon I gonna be a Baptist like Brooks but I ain't one yet cause I ain't been dunked."

Mr. Mann smiled. "I think there's a bit more to it than being dunked, Sister, but you'll find that out in time." He smiled at her. "I think you're very fortunate to have your husband."

Sister nodded. "He say he be lucky to have me."

Mr. Mann laughed. "If he said that, then he's a smart man."

Virginia stood up. "Come with me, Sister. We have a lot to talk about." She took her hand, and they went back upstairs. They went in the guest room and sat on the bed.

Sister looked at Virginia. "You be Floyd's woman now. I thank he gonna marry you."

Virginia looked at her and frowned. "Why do you say that? What did he say to you?"

"I offered to go up the river with 'im if he left here," said Sister. "He told me to git my ass back to my husband."

Virginia looked at her. "Sister, you have no shame. You'd leave your husband and go with Floyd?"

Sister nodded.

"You're supposed to be my friend and now I have to watch you all the time around Floyd," said Virginia.

Sister shook her head. "Ain't no need fir you to watch me. He wouldn't do nothin'. He say he done made you a promise."

Virginia lay back on the bed. "Well, that's good to know."

They talked to late in the night. When Virginia got up the next morning, she went through her closet again and filled a box with clothes she had outgrown. She knew Sister could use them.

She walked in the guest room and Sister wasn't in the bed. Then she heard her in the bathroom. She walked to the door and Sister was kneeling on the floor over the commode throwing up. She ran to the cabinet, wet a washcloth and handed it to her. She knelt by her. "Sister, what happened to you?

Sister wiped her face. "I don't know. I woke up and I got sick at my stomach, and I been throwin' up." She looked at Virginia. "I done the same thang yesterday mornin', but then I got better."

Virginia took the washcloth and rubbed her face. She looked at Sister. "Have you had your period this month, Sister?"

Sister cut her eyes at her. "I don't thank so," she said. "I ain't sure."

"I think you're pregnant," said Virginia.

Sister stared at her. "How come you say that?"

"It looks like you got morning sickness," said Virginia. "Many pregnant women have that, and it seems you have it."

"I ain't never heard of that," said Sister. "You thank I be pregnant?"

Virginia nodded. "It would seem so."

"We sho been tryin," she said.

Virginia laughed. "Well, it sho' looks like it worked." She hugged Sister. "I know you'll be a good mother."

Sister nodded. "If it be a boy baby, I gonna name 'im Floyd."

"Lord, Sister," said Virginia, "you can't do that."

Sister frowned and stared at her. "Why come I can't do that?"

"You don't name your son after an old boyfriend you slept with. What would your husband say?"

Sister was puzzled. "Brooks don't know Floyd. How come he be carin'?"

"I'm not sure I can explain this," said Virginia. "You take my word that you don't need to name him Floyd, Sister. If you do, you'll end up hurting Brooks."

"I don't want to hurt Brooks," she said. "That wouldn't be good."

Virginia nodded. "Maybe you should talk to him about names for a boy or girl?"

Sister nodded. "I thank you be right."

They went across the street to Floyd's house and told him the news. He laughed, hugged Sister and kissed her. She kissed him back.

Later Virginia pulled him over to the side. "It may be right to hug these women and kiss them on the cheek. But now I've watched you kiss Rachel and Sister like you were about to go to bed with them. I think that's a little much."

Floyd looked at her and scratched his head. "I weren't hiding nothin'," he said. "You thank that was too much?"

She nodded. "If you feel the urge to kiss somebody like that, you kiss me."

He smiled. "I'll remember that."

They spent the rest of the day talking and having supper with Mr. Mann. They all enjoyed Sister being with them and made plans to go downriver with her on Saturday.

They were up early the next morning, loaded the box of clothes for Sister in the big boat and tied Sister's boat on behind. They could all get in the larger boat, talk and enjoy the ride. It would take less time to make the trip too.

They started downriver. The fact that Sister said she had killed two men somewhere below the ferry was on Floyd's mind. She'd said she'd not seen anybody but the two men so she should be all right, but he didn't want to take a chance.

When they got to the ferry, Lester, as usual, was sitting in his chair. He watched them pull up alongside the ferry.

"Hey Lester," said Floyd. "You doin' all right?"

"I be good," said Lester. "What y'all be doin' down this way."

"We be just goin' downriver a bit." Floyd looked at him. "Day before yesterday, late in the day, did you see any boats come upriver and pass here?"

Lester rubbed his hand across his face as he stared at Floyd. "I seed one boat come by late. It stayed on the far bank, and I couldn't tell who it be. Whoever it be sorta squatted down."

Floyd reached in his pocket and pulled out a bill. He handed it to Lester. "That was probably my man," he said. "I sent him down here to check on somethin' fir me. If anybody was to ask you about seein' somebody. I spect you ain't seen nobody."

Lester nodded. "That was just what I been tellin' you. I didn't see nobody go by."

"That's right," said Floyd as he pushed the boat off, they started the motor and headed downriver. They hadn't gone far when they rounded a bend and saw several boats in the river ahead of them. When they got closer, they saw one of the boats had a Sheriff's emblem on the side. They slowed down and pulled up to the boat with a deputy in it.

"What's going on?" asked Floyd to the deputy.

"We got two men missing," said the deputy. "We found their boat with blood all over it but there ain't no sign of them."

"That sho' be strange," said Floyd. "What do you thank happened?"

The deputy shook his head. "I ain't got no idea. Them two men were river folks so I can't imagine anybody killin' 'em, but it looks like that might have happened. We ain't seen no bodies so we don't know."

"That's too bad," said Floyd. He signaled the driver, and they went on down the river.

Sister walked over to Floyd. "I thank you fir lookin' after me."

He hugged her but didn't kiss her. He cut his eyes at Virginia.

She nodded and smiled.

S ister was getting excited as they got closer to her home. She could hardly wait to tell Brooks about the baby. She'd told him she'd be back on Saturday, and she hoped he was at the cabin waiting.

When they got in sight of the cabin he was standing on the porch. He'd expected to see Sister in her boat, and he stayed on the porch and watched the larger boat until he saw Sister waving at him. He ran down the steps to the riverbank and waited until the boat landed and Sister jumped off. She ran and grabbed him. "I'm gonna have a baby," she yelled as she hugged him."

He stared at her and then looked at Floyd and Virginia. It took him several minutes to understand who all the people were, and that Sister was pregnant. When everybody was introduced and Sister again told him she was pregnant and Virginia backed her up, it all finally settled in. It was evident to everybody that he loved Sister very much.

They decided that it was so late that they would stay the night at the cabin. They would get an early start on Sunday morning. Sister insisted that they get in Brook's truck, and all go to see her house and their farm, which they did. They were all impressed and happy for Sister.

They came back to the cabin and talked until late. They said their goodbyes that night because they were leaving at daylight and Brooks and Sister were going to church. It was sad when Sister left, Virginia especially hated to see her go. She hugged Floyd, kissed him on the cheek and headed to the house with Brooks.

At daylight they got in the boat and headed upriver. They talked about Sister as they rode. They agreed that she had a great situation now with Brooks and they were glad for her.

26

Floyd was walking back to the house on Monday morning when he saw one of the gate guards coming toward him. He stopped and waited.

"There's a man at the gate that says he wants to see you," said the guard.

Floyd stared at him. "Did he say who he is?"

"He didn't say, but I know who he is," he said. "He's Doc's man, Gil, that you had here."

This news surprised Floyd. "You're sure it's him?"

The guard nodded. "I took him his food sometimes when you had 'im locked up at the dock."

Floyd went to his truck. "Come with me and we'll go down there." They got in the truck and headed to the gate. When they got close, Floyd could see that the guard was right. It was Gil. His appearance set off all sort of alarms in Floyd's head. Why would he be here?

Floyd got out and walked to the gate. "Well, Gil, this is a surprise."

Gil nodded. "I'm sure it is." He stepped close to Floyd. "I'm going to make this quick because I don't have much time. I've left Doc and I'm leaving town. But I wanted to tell you some things before I left. I gave you my word when we made a deal and I'm not going back on my word to you."

He looked at Floyd. "Doc promised he was going to leave you alone, but he's changed his mind. He's been stewing about you shooting him since it happened. After it happened, he was afraid of you but since then he's got braver. Now he's brought in two men from up north to get rid of you."

Floyd shook his head. "Why you be tellin' me this?"

"I thought Doc was telling the truth and I believed him. I gave you my word about it. I've told him this wasn't right, but he's set to get rid of you. I'm not going to go along with what he's doing so I'm leaving. I'm tired of this business anyway. I have a friend in Texas and he's going to give me a chance to make a honest living. But before I left, I wanted to warn you."

"Are these men he's brought in here yet?" asked Floyd.

"I'm not sure," said Gil, "but I don't think so. I didn't see them before I left so I don't know who they are or what they look like. All Doc said was they were from up north. He wanted me to help them when they got here, but I'm not. Doc doesn't know I'm gone."

Floyd looked at him. "Why did y'all kill Ron Hurt?"

Gil shook his head. "That was Doc's doing. Ron threatened him and Doc had him killed. I didn't know about it until it was done. That was when I decided to get out."

"I appreciate you tellin' me this," said Floyd.

"One other thing," said Gil. "There are guards around the house where you ambushed us before. Every morning before daylight a truck comes in the field, a man gets out and goes in the trees where you were. He stays there all day to make sure nobody is there. Then the truck rides around the field with a man with a rifle in the back. They don't plan to get caught in the open like they did before."

"Anything else?" asked Floyd.

Gil nodded. "They're going to have a meeting at the house, probably tomorrow, when the two men get here. Doc knows you stay here on the farm and you're careful about going anywhere. He wants to draw you out so they can get to you. He mentioned using that girl

Rachel again. If that doesn't work, he plans for them to come on the farm at night after you."

Floyd shook his head. "Doc is sho' serious about gittin' me this time seems like."

"He's dead serious," said Gil. "I don't agree with all this so that's why I'm here. Doc ain't worried about you right now because he expects you to honor the deal we made. Once they start after you, Doc will hide behind gates until you're dead. When he goes to the house in the field tomorrow is your best chance to get him."

"How many people does Doc have now?"

"Five or six," said Gil, "but they're just handling the business side. If he wants any rough stuff done, he hires outside people. He does have two men that stay with him all the time. They live in his house with him and drive him around. He don't go anywhere without them."

"Does he live close to that house where he got shot?"

Gil nodded. "In the town not far from there. His house is surrounded by a fence with guards on the gate and would be hard to get close to."

Floyd looked at him. "So, you be leavin' now?"

Gil nodded. "Right now."

Floyd thanked him again and shook hands with him. Gil turned, got in his car and drove away.

Floyd got in his truck and headed back to the house. Damn, he thought as he walked in the house. I thought all this was settled and but now it's not. He decided not to mention this to Virginia. It'd just get her upset and wouldn't accomplish anything. He did have one thing in his favor. Doc didn't know that Gil had told him about his plan, so he had a little time to move first. How should he do that was the question?

He left the house and went to the dock. He found the boat captain and told him to get ready for a trip downriver about midnight. Then he went to Woody's room and told him to be ready to go that night. He told him to get two cans of gasoline to carry with them. Then he went to his truck, got in and headed to town.

When he reached town, he turned south and, in a bit, crossed the county line. He had to have information about what was going on. He pulled into the parking lot at the joint across from Dib's, got out and went in. His source, the bartender, was on duty and saw him when he walked in. Floyd walked to the bar, sat down and put a bill on the bar.

The bartender filled a mug with beer, walked over and sat it in front of him. He picked up the bill and looked at Floyd.

"I hear there's a couple of new people in town," said Floyd as he took a drink of the beer. He watched the bartender's eyes.

"They ain't here yet," he said, "but they supposed to be here tomorrow, so I hear." He leaned over and looked at Floyd. "All this has been mighty quiet, and I had a hard time findin' out bout it. Word is these people are pros. You sho' better be careful this time."

"Do you know where they be stayin'?"

He shook his head. "I ain't heard nothin' bout that. They might be stayin' with Doc, but I don't know that."

Floyd nodded. "I might send another man in here tomorrow to see if you have anything else. I'll tell him to come in, sit here and put a bill on the bar. You tell 'im anything else you find out."

The bartender nodded that he understood.

Floyd got up and walked out. He got in the truck and sat there for a minute. Then he started the car, pulled out of the parking lot and went into town. He turned down a street where he'd been before and pulled into the drive. He got out, walked up to the house and knocked on the front door.

In a minute the door opened, and Rachel was standing there. Wide-eyed, she stared at him. Then she caught herself and got control. "Floyd, what are you doing here?"

"Rachel," he said, "I ain't got time to explain all this, but the men that got you before might try it again. I want you to go to the farm and stay till we git it all settled."

She stared in his eyes. "Can I get me a bag with my things?"

"You git what you need. I hope it just be for two nights."

"Am I to stay with you?" She cut her eyes at him.

He smiled. "I thank you be stayin' with Virginia."

"I'll be back in a minute," she said as she turned and ran in the house. It wasn't much more than a minute when she came to the door with a bag. He took the bag, and they went to the truck. They got in and started toward the farm.

She slid over against him as close as she could get, picked up his arm and put it around her shoulder. She looked up at him. "Virginia is not with us now."

He smiled and pulled her close. She didn't move away until they got to the gate. They parked in front of his house and got out. He took her bag and walked to the big house and knocked on the door. Rachel was standing beside him.

The door opened and Virginia was looking at him, then she looked at Rachel and then back at Floyd. Her lips tightened.

"Virginia," he said, "I found out somethin' a while ago and I need to tell you about it." He stared at her. "Let me talk and don't say nothin'." Then he told her about Gil's visit and what he'd said about Doc's plans. "I figured it best that Rachel stays here tonight. She done been through enough already."

"Yes, she has," said Virginia as she put her arm around Rachel and pulled her in the house. "I'll take care of her. You go and do what you have to do."

"I'll be gone tonight and most of tomorrow," said Floyd.

Virginia nodded. "You be careful," she said as she closed the door.

Floyd turned and went to his house.

F loyd was at the dock a little before midnight. Woody was there along with the boat driver and his guard.

"We be goin' to the same place we went before," said Floyd as he looked at the driver. "We ain't gonna have no lights, it be dark all the way. You know the river, so you oughta be alright."

"Won't be no problem," said the driver. "I done it too many times."

"Me and Woody gonna git out like we had done before. Y'all go downriver and wait till you hear shooting and then come git us. They got guards out this time so it gonna be tougher than it was before."

The driver cranked the motor, eased out of the dock and started downriver. It was a clear night with a three-quarter moon. The form of the trees along the banks could be seen against the sky.

Floyd talked to Woody about what Gil had told him about the man in the trees and the two men in the truck patrolling the field. "I'll take care of 'im in the trees and then when you hear me shoot, you kill the driver in the truck. I don't want him chasing me."

"What about the man in the back of the truck?" asked Woody.

"You stay in the trees and keep 'im in the truck. He ain't gonna be close enough to me to be no problem," said Floyd. "I gotta make sure I git Doc this time so I gotta be where I can git a clear shot at 'im. So, I'm gonna git closer.

"How you gonna do that?" asked Woody. "You know he's gonna have people with 'im."

"I ain't sure," said Floyd. "He ain't specting us to come after 'im so maybe he won't be watching so careful."

Floyd sat and watched as the boat moved down the river at half-speed. He knew he'd have this one chance at Doc and if he failed, he might not ever have another. He knew he had to settle it today.

They passed the ferry. Lights were on in the small town, but they didn't see anybody moving about. The driver increased speed as the river widened. They still had three hours to first light.

They got to the drop-off point without incident. The driver nosed the prow against the bank and kept the boat steady there as Floyd and Woody jumped out. They ran into the trees. The driver backed the boat out and headed downriver.

Floyd moved into the trees with Woody behind him. They got to the corner of the field. "You stay here," said Floyd. "I'm gonna move on up the field and wait for the truck to come and let the guard out. I'll take care of 'im and you watch the truck. I'm gonna set up in the trees right by the road and git Doc when they come by."

Woody nodded.

Floyd moved out of the trees into the field where the walking was easier. He walked on up in the field until he was past the house. He moved back into the trees and waited for daylight.

It was still dark when he heard a truck and the saw the lights coming down the road toward the house. Midway to the house the truck turned and came across the field directly toward him. Floyd squatted in the trees and watched.

The truck stopped and a man got out of the passenger seat. Floyd could see that the man was carrying a rifle. He said something to the driver, closed the door and walked toward the trees. The truck pulled away and went down to the corner of the field and stopped. Another man got out; he also had a rifle. He climbed in the back of the truck.

In a few minutes the first light lit up the sky over the trees to the east. Birds in the trees started moving around and chirping. The man standing near Floyd moved from the field into the edge of the trees. He was about twenty yards away when Floyd unsheathed his knife and started creeping forward.

The man stopped, leaned his rifle against a tree and unzipped his pants. He started peeing. In three steps Floyd was on him. He grabbed him by the shoulder, jerked him around and stabbed him in the neck. The man grunted and fell forward as blood spurted onto the ground. Floyd pushed him away, walked to the edge of the trees and looked down the field to where the truck was parked. It hadn't moved.

Floyd sheathed his knife, picked up his rifle and headed through the trees. His plan was to stay in the trees, move around the field and set up in the edge of the underbrush as close to the road as he could get. Based on what he had seen, he wouldn't be over twenty yards from the road and the cars would have to pass right by him. It didn't take him long to get in position. He glanced across the field. The truck hadn't moved. If Woody was in the position where he had left him, he was within fifty yards of the truck. At the right time, he should be able to easily hit the driver.

The sun was now just over the trees to his left and lighting up the house down the road to his right. He made sure the rifle and his pistol were loaded, sat down and waited.

.   .   .

Woody was in the trees at the corner of the field and the truck was just in front of him. The driver got out and talked to the man standing in the back of the truck. They both lit up cigarettes and stood talking and smoking. Woody had been watching when the truck had first stopped in the field and a man with a rifle had got out and walked in the woods. He hadn't seen him since and figured Floyd had taken care of him by now. He settled back in the bushes with his rifle ready and waited.

Floyd heard a car coming and he got ready, but it was one car with two men in the front seat, and he let it go. The car passed him and went on down the road and parked in front of the house. The two men got out and went inside. All the inside lights came on. One of the men came out the door carrying something and went to the trash can at the corner of the house. He took the lid off, dumped his load in and replaced the lid. He turned and went back inside.

He heard another car coming and he got ready. Again, it was a single car and as it passed, he saw a woman sitting in the passenger seat. This was a surprise to Floyd; he'd not seen a woman in his earlier visit. He wondered about her. Maybe she was a secretary or an office worker. Like the first, this car drove down the road to the house and parked. Two men and the woman got out and went inside.

In a few minutes he heard more than a single car coming. He figured there was a good chance this was Doc, and he was right. When the cars came in view, there were three as there had been before. Doc's car was second in line. The first car passed with two men in the front seat. He let it pass.

Doc's car was almost in front when he fired and killed the driver. He quickly ejected the cartridge and fired again at the back window, shattering the glass. He ejected the second cartridge and killed the driver of the third car. He put his rifle down, pulled his pistol from his belt and charged out of the trees toward Doc's car. The man in the passenger seat in Doc's car was opening the door to get out. He was trying to get his pistol out when Floyd shot him. knocking him back into the front seat.

Floyd got to Doc's car and looked through the shattered window into the back seat. Doc had opened the back door on the other side and was getting out. He was halfway out of the car when Floyd shot him three times, the last shot in the back of the head. Doc fell out of the car onto the ground.

Floyd glanced at the third car and saw three men getting out. The man getting out of the passenger seat was the closest and Floyd shot at him. The bullet hit him in the leg, and he collapsed. The other two men were behind the car's doors and firing at him. Floyd turned and ran for the trees.

As he ran, he glanced down the road. The first car was almost to the house when the driver looked in his mirror and saw what was going on behind him. He had turned around and now was on his way back toward Doc's car. Floyd picked up his rifle, knelt on one knee and fired at the oncoming car. The bullet shattered the windshield and the car stopped. The two men inside got out and huddled behind the car.

The two men in the third car ran to Doc's car. When they looked at him, they knew he was dead. One looked at the other. "The sonsabitch is in the woods."

The other man looked at him. "Damn if I'm going in there after him. That bastards like a damn snake. He'd be done killed you before you could get ten feet."

"I ain't goin' after him neither," his partner said. "As soon as we can get out of here, we need to go back to Chicago.

They both holstered their pistols and sat down beside the car.

Woody had watched the cars come down the road and park at the house. He could see that the driver and the man on the back of the truck were watching them too. Then he heard the first shot and several more that followed. He raised up and as he fired the driver gunned the engine and moved forward. The bullet hit right behind the driver's head, and he mashed the gas pedal and leaped forward.

The man in the back of the truck heard the shot behind him and turned to fire toward the trees. He was off balance and as the truck went forward his feet went out from under him, and he fell into the truck bed. It was a struggle for him to get his rifle in his hands and get up. He yelled for the driver to slow down as he got to his feet, grabbed the side of the truck and regained his balance.

Woody had emptied his clip at the truck but did no good, it was still going across the field. He reloaded and looked across the field. He could see the three cars stopped in the road and figured Floyd had done his job. He could see two men huddled behind the first car but didn't see anybody else. He watched the truck as it headed across the field.

Floyd ran through the bush away from the cars. He looked in the field and saw the truck coming toward him. A man was standing in the back with a rifle; Woody hadn't done his job. Floyd knelt, brought the rifle stock to his shoulder and fired. The windshield in front of the driver shattered, the driver mashed the gas and turned the steering wheel sharply to the left. The truck headed out of the field at full speed and crashed into a large oak. For the second time the man in the back of the truck was thrown down and slid hard against the side of the truck. He staggered unsteadily to his feet and crawled out of the truck. He walked around and looked at the driver who had a bad gash on his head and seemed to be unconscious. He turned and went into the woods.

Floyd had watched the truck crash into the tree and saw the man jump out of the back and go into the brush. That was a problem. The man was between him and the river where he had to go. He figured the people in the office had called the police by now and he didn't want to be here when they came. He had to do something about the man in the woods in front of him. He took out his pistol and started forward.

He was almost to where the truck had hit the trees. He knelt down and looked to his front. He knew the man had gone into the woods in this area and he didn't want to make a stupid mistake and get shot. He stayed down and listened. Then a movement to his right caught his eye. The man with the rifle was walking slowly toward him, his eyes jumping back and forth as he walked. Floyd waited until he was no more than ten feet from him.

"If you move, I'll kill you," said Floyd. "Drop the rifle."

The man's head turned slowly around, and he stared at Floyd and the pistol pointed at him.

"Drop the rifle," Floyd said again.

The rifle hit the ground. The man kept his eyes on Floyd

Floyd got up. "Come here," he said.

The man walked over to him, sweat was pouring down his face. "I weren't gonna shoot nobody, mister. I ain't never shot nobody."

"Shut up," said Floyd. "You git yo' ass across that field and you tell 'em other people over there that if I ever hear of 'em again, I'm gonna come back and kill you all." He looked at him. "Do you understand what I just said?"

"Yes'suh. I understand what you say. You ain't never gonna see me down here again."

Floyd walked over and looked in the truck at the driver who was sill unconscious. He looked across the field and saw four men standing by the first car. He looked at the man. "You go tell 'em what I said."

The man nodded and headed across the field at a trot.

Floyd turned and started toward the river. When he got to the corner of the field, Woody was waiting for him.

"I messed up, Floyd. I missed 'im," said Woody.

"It don't matter," said Floyd. "We done what we come to do."

'You killed Doc?"

Floyd nodded. "He be dead." He looked toward the field. He could hear the sirens. "We need to go," he said. They both headed toward the river.

The boat was already against the bank with the motor running when they got to the river. They climbed aboard and the driver backed out. He looked at Floyd. "I heard a lot of shootin."

Floyd nodded as the boat pulled away from the bank into the current. "We done what we come to do."

The driver didn't say anymore, headed the boat upstream and revved the motor to full speed. Floyd got the sack of ham biscuits Woody had brought and a mason jar of sweet tea and ate the first food he'd had since supper the night before.

Woody munched on a biscuit and looked at him. "Do you reckon this ends it?" he asked.

Floyd looked at the riverbank as it sped by. "I thank it does," he said. "Doc be dead, and Gil gone, that bout wiped 'em out. Ron Hurt be dead so ain't nobody up here gonna cause no more trouble with 'em." He looked at Woody. "I figure they be done."

"Reckon the law's gonna be lookin for us?" said Woody.

Floyd shook his head. "I don't thank so. Them folks what be at the house ain't gonna say nothin' and I don't thank the law gives a damn that Doc got kilt."

They got to the ferry, slowed down and pulled alongside. Lester had been watching them as they approached. He leaned over and spat a wad of tobacco into the water. He cut his eyes at Floyd. "Y'all musta traveled early," he said.

Floyd took a bill out of his pocket and handed it to him. "How many folks you seen pass here today, Lester?"

He looked at him and shook his head. "I ain't seen nary a soul go past here at all today."

"That be right," said Floyd as he pushed the boat away from the ferry. He nodded to the driver, he backed away, turned and headed upriver.

. . .

The sun was straight overhead when they reached the dock. They pulled in and tied up. Floyd and Woody got out. Woody headed to his room and Floyd walked up the road to his house. He was tired, it had been a long night.

Virginia was standing at her bedroom window looking out. Rachel was sitting on the bed behind her. She had looked toward the dock a hundred times looking for Floyd. Then she saw him walking toward the house. She turned and started toward the door. "He's back," she said. Rachel jumped up and followed her out the door, down the stairs and out the front door.

They ran into the road and headed toward Floyd. He was carrying his rifle and had his pack over his shoulder. He stopped and waited when he saw them coming. He put his pack down and laid his rifle on it as Virginia rushed up, wrapped her arms around him and kissed him. She finally turned him loose and looked in his face. "We've been worried about you. Are you through? Is it over?"

He nodded. "I thank we be through." He looked at Rachel. She was watching him with sad eyes. He walked over to her, put his arms around her and kissed her. "I be sorry you got messed up in all this," he said.

She smiled up at him. "I appreciate you looking after me."

He picked up his rifle and pack and looked at Virginia. "I'm bout wore out. I be gonna take a bath and sleep for a bit."

"You do that," said Virginia. "Rachel and I are going to eat with Daddy, and I'll wake you up later. We'll take Rachel home then, I'm sure she's ready to go."

Floyd nodded and walked in his house.

Floyd was sleeping soundly when he awakened and realized someone was in the bed with him. It took him a few seconds to get his mind to working correctly and his eyes open. He looked up and realized Virginia was kneeling on the bed beside him, staring down at him. He finally got his eyes focused on her and saw she had nothing on; she was naked.

"What are you doin'?" he asked as he looked at her.

She leaned over and kissed him. "We're going to take Rachel home and before we do that, I wanted to remind you of what you have here. I don't want you to be thinking of any other woman or wishing you had somebody else." She reached down, pulled the covers back and crawled in beside him.

He laughed and pulled her to him. "You be a shameless woman," he said as he pulled her to him and kissed her.

They pulled into the drive at Rachel's house. Virginia hugged her and Floyd walked her to the door. She looked up at him. "You know you're breaking my heart," she said. "I wanted to be with you."

"I done told you I ain't no good for you," he said. "You need to find somebody that will love you and you can depend on." He looked at her. "That ain't me and I done told you that. I ain't never been somebody to stay in one place."

She shook her head. "You're with Virginia and you made her a promise to just be with her. She told me you did."

"She be right. I did promise her that as long as I'm with her," he said. "But she knows how I be too. I done told her what I told you; one day I'll be gone."

"She thinks she's going to marry you." Her eyes were searching his face.

He leaned over, kissed her, turned and walked to the truck.

Virginia looked at him as he got in the seat. "Have you ever thought about just shaking a woman's hand when you meet them or say goodbye to them?"

He frowned and shook his head. "Sometimes I shake a man's hand. I ain't never thought bout that with a woman."

Virginia turned and looked away. "That's what I thought."

They rode on toward the farm. "Tell me what happened," she said. "All you said was that it was over." She slid over against him. "What does that mean?"

"Doc is dead," he said. "Gil is gone so I figure there ain't nobody left that's gonna mess with y'all."

They rode on as she thought about what he said. "Was Doc the only one killed?"

He cut his eyes at her. "Probably was some more but I ain't sure."

"They ran their business in that house?"

"That be what Gil said."

"And when you left there were still people in the house running the business?"

He cut his eyes at her. "What's yo' point?"

"Most people in a business have records. If they worked in that house every day, I expect there were records in that house. Another person could take those records and continue the business."

He looked at her. "Somebody else could pick up Doc's business?"

She nodded. "I would think so."

He drove in the farm gate and parked in front of his house. He turned and looked at her. "I'll be back early in the morning."

"I'll be waiting," she said as she leaned over and kissed him. She got out and walked in the big house.

He sat in the truck for a minute then turned and headed toward town. In a few minutes he was pulling up to the joint across from Dib's. He walked in and sat at the bar.

Several people at the tables were looking at him and talking. The bartender came over with a beer. He put a bill on the table and looked at him.

"Everybody's talkin' 'bout you," said the bartender. "Doc's people that be left be scared of you and what you gonna do."

"You put the word out that I ain't after nobody," said Floyd. "Doc come after me and he be dead, so it be over."

The bartender nodded. "There be two or three of Doc's folks that are arguing over who's gonna take over the business. There might be trouble bout that." He thought for a minute. "They say that a woman worked for Doc, and some say she' gonna take over. I don't know if she was Doc's woman or not, but the word is that she's smart."

"What about Doc's two bodyguards that stayed with 'im?"

"They both be dead." The bartender chuckled. "The two men from Chicago packed up and left this morning." He wiped off the bar and then looked up at Floyd. "The word is that Doc's business is worth enough that somebody will want it, so it'll still be around."

Floyd got up and looked at him. "Find out all you can about these people, especially the woman, and let me know." He got up and headed for the door. He got in the truck and headed for the farm. He parked at his house and went to find Woody. He was in his room and Floyd told him to get two cans of gasoline and met him at the dock.

He found the boat driver and told him they would be going downriver in an hour. He went to the house, got his gear and headed back to the dock. Woody was there with the gasoline. The driver had the engine idling. Floyd got aboard, they backed out and headed downriver.

"What we gonna do?" asked Woody.

"We gonna burn that house down," said Floyd.

Woody cut his eyes at him. "Do I have to shoot anybody?"

Floyd laughed. "I hope they all be gone, and we don't have no trouble."

I t was dark when they got to the ferry. Lester was nowhere to be seen so they ran slowly past along the west bank. The riverbank toward town was deserted. Once past the ferry the driver revved up the engine, the boat planed off and they headed downriver.

The driver nosed the boat into the bank as he had done the day before. Floyd and Woody both grabbed a gas can and jumped out. The disappeared into the woods. The boat backed out, turned and headed downriver.

Floyd headed into the trees toward the field with Woody behind him. When they got to the edge of the field he stopped, sat the can down and looked across the field at the house. All the lights in the house were on. There were two cars parked outside.

Woody came up beside him. "How come the lights be on?"

Floyd shook his head. "I don't know." He knelt on one knee and watched for several minutes. He didn't see anybody outside the house. Through one of the windows, he could see people moving around inside, but he couldn't tell how many there were.

"You stay here," he said to Woody. "I'm goin' to see what's happening and why these people are here." He got up and started trotting across the field. He hadn't expected people to be in the house and had no plans as to what to do about them. He slipped up to the window and looked in. There were two men moving boxes and papers around. A woman was sitting at a desk. That must be the woman the bartender was talking about. She was young and attractive.

As he watched she seemed to be telling the men what to do. There were several desks in the room and file cabinets lined the wall like in a regular office. He watched for several more minutes. They continued what they were doing.

He didn't know how long they intended to be here; it was already past midnight, and he was running out of patience. He had no intention to stay here all night, so he had to do something. Finally, he ran around to the front of the house, walked up on the porch and grabbed the doorknob. It was locked.

He pulled his pistol out of his belt, reared back and kicked the door. The doorframe splintered and the door flew open. He stepped inside and looked across the room. The two men were standing on the far side holding boxes which they quickly dropped. They were staring at him; he could see the fear in their faces.

He looked at the woman sitting at the desk. She was calmly staring at him. She got up, her eyes on his outfit of leather and beads. "Floyd Wimms, I presume," she said as she stepped out from behind the desk. "They said you looked like an injun and now I see why they said that." She walked toward him, her eyes on his pistol.

"We're not armed," she said, "so you have the advantage, Mr.

Wimms. You haven't killed us yet, so I assume you're here for another reason."

Floyd stared at her. Up close she was really pretty. "I come to burn the house down," he said. "Y'all need to get out."

Her brow furrowed and her lips tightened. "Why would you do that, Floyd? May I call you Floyd? Calling you Mr. Wimms sounds pretentious. My name is Elsie. I assure you there's no need to burn the house."

"This was Doc's house," he said. "I'm gonna clean it all up."

She shook her head. "Doc is dead, Floyd. He is no longer a threat to you. Nobody here is a threat to you now. I'm an accountant so I'm certainly not."

"Doc had other people. They tried to kill me."

She nodded. "He did have other people; some were bad people. You killed several of them yesterday and the others left. All that's left are people like me trying to run the business that remains. Doc had some shady, illegal businesses but he also owned two banks and several grocery stores. Nothing we do is a danger to you."

He thought for a minute as he stared at her. "Do you be in charge?"

She nodded. "The people still involved here asked me to run things. Like I said it's just a business now with Doc gone. He was the one that did things that caused trouble, like stealing the Mann's cows. Trying to kill you was all Doc's doing."

"How do I know you be tellin' me the truth?" he said.

"You don't, but it's true," she said. "We all knew Doc made an agreement with you. We knew he was going to break it and come after you. You got him first and he deserved it. Nobody blames you for what you did: I figure Gil warned you." She stared at him, questioning.

He didn't answer her.

"It's all over now. But if you burn the house down and all our records, some people are going to be pissed." She nodded. "That could start trouble again. I don't want that, and I don't think you do either. Walk away and let everything settle down."

"How do I know the others will agree with you?"

"Here's what I'll do," she said. "I run the office and a man named Scott Battle runs the daily business. Scott and I will meet you tomorrow night at seven at Dib's or wherever you want to meet. We will both assure you that we don't want any more trouble."

He stared at her for a moment. "I'll be at Dib's at seven."

"We won't be armed," she said.

He smiled, put the pistol in his belt and walked out. He got outside and trotted across the field. Woody was waiting for him.

"What happened?" he asked as Floyd walked up.

"I'll tell you about it on the boat," said Floyd. He started toward the river. The boat was waiting, they got on and headed upriver. Floyd got Woody to the side as they rode and told him what happened.

"Do you thank she means it?" he asked.

Floyd nodded. "I thank she does. When we meet tomorrow night, I want you to be at Dib's and watch us. You be armed and have my pistol for me in case I need it. Also watch the people there and see if there's any people we don't know."

They landed at the dock, Floyd got out and headed to the house. It was well after midnight. He wondered where Virginia was. He went in, took a quick bath and walked to the bedroom. She was lying in his bed. He pulled back the cover and slipped in beside her.

Virginia raised up and sleepily looked at him. "You got back?" she mumbled.

"I got back," he replied.

"Good," she said as she turned over and went back to sleep.

27

S ister had settled in to being a farmer's wife and she was happy. Being pregnant had given her a purpose, something she'd never had before. She was looking forward to having the baby. She'd never had anyone be as good to her as Brooks had been. He couldn't do enough for her.

She'd been lonely at times when they first married. Brooks was in the field much of the time and she was in the house by herself. Brooks had been an only child; his parents were dead, and he had no other family. But then she met Katherine Hayes at church. Katherine was older, she and her husband Thomas had four grown children and a number of grandchildren. They lived on a neighboring farm. They were leaders in the community and well thought of by everyone.

Katherine saw that Sister was somewhat lost in her new surroundings. It was obvious she wasn't reared in a home where her parents had taught her how normal people live and act. So, Katherine adopted her and took her under her wing. As she had with her own daughters, she showed Sister by her example how to be a good wife and mother.

The Hayes family were close-knit. They all were involved in

working on the farm. After church on Sunday, they all gathered at their parents' house for dinner. Katherine would get up early, prepare the meal and keep it warm in the wood stove. She asked Sister and Brooks to join them each Sunday.

So, Sister now got to see a home where the family loved each other and got along. The house was filled with children running around doing what children do. This was all a new experience for her, and she learned from it. She decided this was the way she wanted her house to be.

Sometimes she would think of her earlier life and experiences on the river, but most of those experiences were fading. Much of her earlier life she didn't want to remember. She no longer felt any urge to relive any part of that life.

The fact that she had shot and killed people didn't bother her. She thought of the two fisherman that had come after her that day when she was going up the river. All they had to do was let her pass and nothing would have happened. But since she'd been going to church, she'd learned that they were sinful people.

The same was true for the two young men that came after her at the bridge. They were full of the Devil and were going to have their way with her. If she hadn't had the pistol, they would have raped her and probably killed her.

She tried not to think of Trip and Whit, the two men Floyd had killed in Nell's place. Her daddy had sent them after her when she ran away from home. They were supposed to take her home, but they took their time about it. Each night they would camp and use her. She would fight and scream but it did no good, they were too strong.

Thankfully, they grew thirsty for a drink of whiskey and stopped at Nell's.

When they went inside, she hoped she'd find somebody to help her. She didn't realize it at the time, but she was praying for help. She didn't know who she was praying to, she just felt the need and said it.

She'd looked at the three men at the table, but they wouldn't be any help.

Then she'd turned and looked at Floyd. When their eyes met, she knew he would help her. She'd never seen him before and didn't know who he was, but she knew he would help her. That was the reason he was here, as surely as if he had told her so.

She asked to go pee and Trip sent Whit with her. When she heard the shot, she knew Trip was dead. And then Whit had rushed in, and Floyd killed him. In the blink of an eye, she was free. Then she knew what she had to do; she had to go with Floyd. But he wouldn't let her go, so she had followed him. She was indebted to him and would always be until the debt was paid. Finally, that night in his house in his bed, she paid the debt.

That was why she was now Brooks' wife and carrying his baby. She had been freed to live her own life. She knew it all happened that way for a reason. She didn't understand it all, but she knew it was so.

She remembered that Virginia had been good to her. Every time she wore one of the dresses she'd given her, she remembered her kindness.

She also thought of Floyd at times. Since the day he saved her, he had a special place in her heart. During the time she felt indebted to him and had chased him up the river, he seemed larger than life. But now she saw him as just a man, with flaws that all people have. He was still special to her, but in his proper place.

She and Brooks hadn't talked about possible names for the baby, but she knew it wouldn't be Floyd. She smiled as she thought of that idea. When the time came, they would sit down and think of names. She thought they should think of several because she planned to have more children.

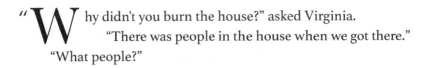

"Why didn't you burn the house?" asked Virginia.

"There was people in the house when we got there."

"What people?"

"There was a woman and two men in the house. They had worked for Doc, and I reckon they was trying to get all the paperwork together. Anyway, that's what she said."

"You talked to her?"

Floyd nodded. "I busted in the door and was gonna run them out before I set the house on fire." He looked at her. "She said they weren't after me or y'all anymore. Doc was dead and it was over. They just want to run Doc's businesses and not bother us."

"Who was the woman.?"

"She said her name was Elsie and she was a accountant. She run Doc's office and did the paperwork."

"What did she look like?"

"She was young and seemed smart."

"Was she pretty?"

He nodded.

"Was she Doc's woman?"

He shrugged. "I don't know bout that. She didn't seem to care much that Doc was dead. She said he brought all this trouble on his self."

"So, you didn't run them out and burn the house?"

He shook his head. "She said they weren't gonna bother us but if I burnt up the house and the records, some folks wouldn't like it. That could cause trouble." He looked at her. "I thank she be right."

Virginia stared at him. "So, what do you do now?"

"She wanted me to meet her and another man at Dib's tonight at seven and settle everything."

"You think that's the thing to do?"

He nodded. "I thank so. We done had enough fightin' and killin'"

"So, you're going to meet them?"

"I thank that be best."

"All right," she said. "If you're going to meet them, I'll go with you." She stared at him, waiting to see if he objected.

He shrugged and said nothing.

. . .

Floyd and Virginia were at Dib's a few minutes before seven. Woody came by the house earlier and got Floyd's pistol. If he'd done what he'd been told, he was already inside at a table.

They walked in and Floyd looked around. He saw Elsie and another man at a table across the room. She'd been watching the door and was looking at him. He saw Woody at a table to the left of Elsie. He scanned the room but didn't see anybody that looked out of place. He took Virginia's arm and they walked past the bar to Elsie's table. Elsie and the man stood up as they approached.

"Elsie, this is Virginia," Floyd said. Elsie then introduced Scott Battle, they all shook hands and sat down. A waitress came over and they ordered drinks.

Elsie smiled at Virginia and looked at Floyd. "How many of your people are in the room, Floyd?"

Floyd smiled and looked at her. "Ain't got but one," he said.

She chuckled. "I saw Woody when I came in. You know he used to work with us."

"Yes, I knew that, but I didn't know if you knew 'im," replied Floyd.

Elsie looked at Virginia. "Have you ever noticed, Virginia, that sometimes men think we women are really stupid?"

Virginia glanced at Floyd. "Yes, I have noticed that, on more than one occasion."

After that they all settled down and talked.

"I've talked to Scott about what we talked about last night," said Elsie. "We both agree that we have no reason to bother y'all at all and we hope you will now feel the same way. The troubles we've had in the past were due to decisions Doc made and have no bearing on us now. We won't get involved in things like that in the future."

Floyd looked at Virginia and then back at Elsie. "We feel the same way."

"Good," said Elsie. "Then that's settled." She signaled to the waitress. "I ordered steaks for everybody. Just tell her how you want them cooked." She looked at Virginia. "I'm going to freshen up. Maybe you'd like to go?"

Virginia nodded, got up and followed her to the bathroom.

"Floyd is a remarkable man, Virginia," said Elsie. "Y'all are lucky to have him. Otherwise, Doc would have ruined y'all."

Virginia looked at her, wondering where she was going with this. "You're right, he is special."

"As I understand it, he works for y'all," she said. "He's not family or anything, is he?"

Virginia shook her head. "He's not family. He's just a friend that came to our rescue when we were in trouble."

"I would like to have someone like him in our organization," she said. "He is a remarkable man. But I didn't want to offend you by talking to him about a job, if there was a special relationship."

Virginia stared at her. "Let me explain something to you, Elsie, since you don't seem to know him very well," she said. "Floyd is not employed by us. We've never paid him a dime; he doesn't need it. He made a fortune in the gold field, so he doesn't need money. What he did for us against Doc was on his own, for his own reasons."

"I'm sorry, I didn't know that was the case," said Elsie. "I thought he was an employee."

"Floyd is a free spirit, Elsie. Nobody has a hold on him, that's the way he is," Virginia said. "But he and I do have a special relationship. Since he's been with us, I decided to be his woman and sleep with him every night. I do it because I want to. He's made me no promises about the future, and it wouldn't surprise me if I wake up tomorrow and he's gone. I assure you that there's no chance in hell he would work for you."

Elsie looked at her and smiled. "You are one lucky woman, Virginia. I admire you for your honesty. I will say no more about it to him."

They walked back to the table. The dinner went well, and they left feeling good about the meeting. They were riding back to the farm when Floyd looked at Virginia. "I saw Elsie talking to you when y'all went to the bathroom. What was she talkin' bout?"

"She asked me about you, she thought you were an employee," said Virginia.

Floyd's brow furrowed as he thought about what she'd said. "What did you tell her?"

"I told her you were a friend and you helped us as a friend. We'd never paid you any money."

"What was her point in this?"

"She was very impressed with you and wanted to offer you a job. She didn't want to offend me if there was a special relationship."

"What did you tell her?"

"I told her that the special relationship was that I slept with you every night," said Virginia. "Then I told her that you would never take a job with her. She thanked me and said she wouldn't mention the job to you."

Floyd smiled, leaned over and kissed her.

They got to the farm, parked and went in the house.

The next week was quiet. Floyd felt the meeting with Elsie had been successful, but he'd not talked to anybody outside the farm since they'd met, so he wasn't sure. That afternoon he got in the truck, headed to town and turned south. In a few minutes he was at the joint across from Dib's. He pulled in, parked and went inside. As usual he went to the bar and sat down. His bartender was at the other end of the bar. Floyd put a bill on the bar and waited. The bartender saw him, poured a beer, walked over and sat it in front of him. He looked at him.

"Everthang's been quiet this last week," said Floyd. "What do you hear?"

"It is quiet," he answered. "Elsie is in charge now, that's all been settled." He nodded and stared at Floyd, choosing his words carefully. "She wants to talk to you."

Floyd frowned. "Bout what?"

"I'm not sure, but the word is she likes you and would like to have you work with them. There be some people in Atlanta that have their eyes on parts of Doc's business. I thank she's worried they gonna move in on her." He stared in Floyd's face, questioning.

Floyd thought for a minute. "Can you get word to her?"

The bartender nodded.

"Tell her we've already talked, and everything is settled as far as I'm concerned. But if she needs to talk to me about something, I will talk to her."

"So, you do want to talk to her?" asked the bartender.

"Tell her I'll be at Dib's at seven tomorrow night," said Floyd as he got up. "Tell her to come alone." He walked out, got in the truck and went to the farm.

Virginia was at her window in the big house and saw him drive up and get out. She ran downstairs, out the door and met him. "I saw you leave. I wondered where you went?"

"I went to see the bartender. He said everthang is quiet."

"That's good," she said. "Were you worried about something?"

He shook his head. "I wasn't worried, but I like to be careful. I don't want to be surprised." He looked at her. "Didn't you say that Elsie said she wouldn't talk to me about a job after y'all talked?"

She nodded. "That's what she said."

"The bartender told me that she wants to talk to me. He said the word is she wants me to go to work for her."

"Then she lied to me?"

Floyd nodded. "It would seem she did."

"What did you tell the bartender?"

"I told him to tell Elsie that I'd meet her at Dib's at seven tomorrow night. I want to see if what he said about a job is true. I need to know what she has on her mind."

"That all bothers me," said Virginia.

Floyd hugged her. "Don't worry bout it. I'm gonna git her straight." He had his arm around her as they waked in the house.

T he next morning when Floyd walked out of his house, he was surprised to see Mr. Mann standing by the road in front of his house. He walked across the road to him. "Good mornin', sir," he said. "It's good to see you up and out."

"It's good to be up and out, Floyd," he said. "I'm feeling some better and I wanted to ride over the farm. I haven't been out in a while."

"Would you like me to take you, sir?"

Mr. Mann shook his head. "Thank you, Floyd, but my man is going to take me." He looked at him. "I want to thank you for all you've done for us. Virginia has kept me informed about what has gone on. I'm afraid that if you hadn't been here, we would have been in real trouble. You did what you did at great personal risk.""

"I was glad I could do it, sir," he said.

"Do you think it's all settled?"

"Yes, sir, I think it is."

Mr. Mann frowned as he struggled to say the right words. "I know that Virginia has a relationship with you, Floyd. She is a grown woman and can do as she pleases, but I hate to see her get hurt. After all she is my daughter."

Floyd nodded. "I ain't never lied to Virginia, sir. I told her to start with that I ain't the marrying kind and one day I'll probably be gone. She knows that; we've talked about it."

"I understand that is the way it is, Floyd. All I'm asking is that you be honest with her."

"I intend to do that," he said.

The door to the big house closed and Virginia came out. She ran over and put her arm around her daddy. "Isn't it great to see him out?" she said. "He wants to look over the farm and I'm going to ride with him."

As she finished the truck drove up. They helped Mr. Mann get in.

Virginia got in beside him and they started down the road. Floyd watched them for a bit, then he went back in the house.

F loyd thought about the meeting with Elsie and how to approach her. Finally, late that afternoon he dressed in what everybody called his injun outfit, stuck his pistol in his belt and headed to town. He'd told the bartender he'd be there at seven, but he was going early to be there before she came.

He got to Dib's, parked and walked in. He looked around and didn't see anybody that bothered him. He walked to a back table, sat down with his back to the wall and ordered a drink. His glass was half filled when he saw Elsie walk in. She stopped and looked around. When she saw him, her face showed her surprise at the way he was dressed.

She walked across the floor toward him. He got up and waited for her.

She stared at him. "Gracious, Floyd," she said, "I thought this was a social visit and you look like you're ready for a fight, carrying a pistol and dressed like that."

"Well, the word was you wanted to talk to me, and I didn't know what it might be about, so I wanted to be ready." As he talked, he watched her face.

They sat down, the waitress came over and she ordered a drink. "I was glad we got together the other night," she said. "I enjoyed meeting Virginia."

The waitress came with her drink. She took a sip and looked at him. "I've been impressed with how you handled the situation with Doc. I don't think anyone else could have done it."

He took a drink and looked at her.

"I thought that you worked for the Manns," she said. "But Virginia told me that wasn't true; she said you weren't an employee. They'd never paid you any money. She said you helped them because you were their friend." She stared in his eyes.

Floyd nodded. "That be true. Virginia told me that y'all talked about that."

Ellsie smiled. "Virginia also told me there was one benefit that you had. She said she slept with you every night." She looked at him. "Now that's not any of my business but she did tell me that."

Floyd nodded. "She said she told you that." He sat his glass down. "What did you want to talk to me about?"

"I told Virginia that I was impressed with you and how you operated. I told her that I'd like to have you help me as you've helped them. I have people that are probably going to give me trouble because they want part of our business. I need somebody to deal with them." She stopped and looked at him for a minute.

Floyd waited, watching her face.

"Virginia said that you wouldn't work for us, and I told her I wouldn't say anything to you about it," she said. "I realize me talking to you is not what I told her, but while she might be right, I wanted to hear it from you. She said you didn't need money, but what could I offer you that would make you interested?"

Floyd thought he knew where she was going with this, but he wanted to hear her say it. "What exactly are you sayin?" His eyes never left her face.

"If money isn't important to you, there are other things that might interest you. I could offer you a position of part ownership in the company, some valuable property and a large house." She leaned over toward him. "I would work closely with you at all times. I would be available to you day and night for whatever you wanted." She smiled. "I'm certain I could please you in every way."

He nodded. "I expect you could do all that, Elsie." He stared at her. "You are a good-lookin' woman and I like women, but I already got all I need. Virginia said she told you that I wouldn't be interested in working for you and she was right. I be happy with her and the Manns."

Elsie nodded and smiled. "I thought that would be your answer, Floyd, but I wanted to hear it from you. You tell Virginia that I didn't mean to lie to her, but I wanted to talk to you. It seems you affect people that way."

He laughed. "Sometimes I do affect 'em, but not in the right way."

"That is certainly true," she said. "We've talked now, I told you what I wanted to say, and you've given me you answer. We have an agreement as we talked about the other night. As far as I'm concerned, that is still our agreement."

He nodded. "That be what I thank."

She stood up and shook his hand. "I appreciate you meeting with me," she said. "If you ever change your mind, you know where I am." She turned and walked out the door.

Floyd sat down and finished his drink. Then he got up, went outside and drove back to the farm.

When he got out of the truck and walked in the house, Virginia was waiting for him. She took his hand, led him to the couch and sat down, pulling him down beside her. "Tell me everything she said."

"She wanted to talk to me about a job, but she did apologize to you that she did it. She said she wanted to hear me say that I wasn't interested."

She stared in his face. "What did she offer you to come with her?"

He thought for a moment. "I thank she said I could be a partner, git property and a big house."

She stared in his eyes. "What else did she say? You better tell me the truth."

Floyd smiled. "She said she would work close with me all the time, day or night."

Virginia's lips tightened. "That bitch," she said. "I knew she would do that. What did you tell her?"

He reached and grabbed her, pulling her down on the couch. "I told her I had all I could handle at home."

She reached up and kissed him. "I guarantee you that's the truth," she said as she wrapped her arms around him.

. . .

Later she lay on the couch beside him, her head on his arm. "Do you think she will do what was agreed to?"

"I think she will," he said. "She don't have anybody left to protect her so she don't want no trouble. From what she said she's worried bout some folks from Atlanta getting' her business. I ain't worried bout 'em no more."

She raised up and looked at him. "You remember I told you I knew Karen Hogan from Shoal Creek. I went to school with her in Atlanta."

"I remember you talkin' about Karen. I told you I'd met her."

"She called me yesterday and we talked. I told her I was with you now."

Floyd watched her face, wondering where she was going with this.

"Karen told me that when you lived in River Bluff, you went with a schoolteacher there, I don't remember her name, but it seemed pretty serious, according to Karen." She leaned over and looked in his eyes.

Floyd raised up, pushed her legs off him and stared in her face. "Her name was Alva Tinney, and we dated some. She was nice." He pursed his lips. "When we talked and I promised to just be with you and no other woman, do you remember that we said we wasn't gonna talk bout nothin' or nobody in the past? Do you remember that?"

Virginia frowned. "Did we say that? I can't remember."

He nodded. "You remember it."

She smiled. "Yes, I remember. But I have one question. Why did you leave her? If you don't want to answer, I won't mention it again, but I am curious."

He cut his eyes at her. "Alva had knowed me for a long time; she knew how I was, just like you do. I told her how I was, just like I told you." He looked at Virginia. "She wanted to git married but told me I couldn't roam the river no more and be gone fir days. I'd have to quit dranking and cursing, I'd have to live in town and go to church ever Sunday. I couldn't do all that, so I left."

"Did you love her?"

His lips tightened as he stared at her. "I done said all I be gonna say bout 'er."

"So," she said as she reached over and kissed him, "I can be with you as long as I let you do exactly as you want to do?"

"I didn't say that. I weren't talkin' bout you."

"But one day I'll wake up in the morning and you'll be gone."

He frowned. "Why come you be brangin' all this up to cause trouble? I be here with you right now."

She smiled and kissed him. "You're right. I was just being a jealous woman because I love you so much."

"You worry too much," he said as he hugged her.

She looked at him, waiting to hear a reply to her saying she loved him, but he didn't. She got up, picked up her clothes and walked to the bathroom. As she dressed, she thought that he had told her how he was, and it didn't seem he had changed. If she stayed with him, she would have to deal with it.

F loyd watched Virginia walk out. He knew what she wanted, what she was waiting to hear from him, but he wasn't ready to make that commitment. He had made it clear to her that her being with him was her choice. She had agreed without any papers being signed and without any legal involvement. He had told her that he could leave whenever he pleased.

She had brought up Alva Tinney out of the blue and questioned him about her. He thought back to Alva. Of all the women that he had been with, she was the only one that he'd ever seriously thought about marrying. He knew that if he married her, there would be changes he'd have to make in his life, but he couldn't deal with a complete makeover. He remembered that someone had told him years before that they didn't understand how a woman could fall in love with a man as he is, but after the wedding she wanted to change him to something else.

He was still drawn to Alva and thought about her often. Several times since he'd left River Bluff, he'd thought about going back and seeing her. But as he'd studied on it, he knew that her convictions ran deep, and he doubted she would change. Since he didn't think she would change, there was no need to return to River Bluff.

He was very fond of Virginia and that fondness had grown deeper as he was around her more. Physically she was everything a man could want in a woman, and he knew she loved him. He also knew she was tied to this farm and wouldn't leave, especially as long as her daddy was here.

He knew he could marry her; she had indicated as much, and he would have a good life. But he wasn't a farmer and he'd never thought about being a farmer. In fact, he'd never thought about being anything other than what he was, a free spirit that if he felt like leaving and traveling, he left and traveled.

He also knew that with Doc's gang torn apart and Ron Hurt dead, the threat to the farm was gone. Now they would settle into a daily routine where this Monday would be like last Monday and so forth. He wasn't sure he could deal with that for long.

That afternoon, wearing his injun outfit, Floyd walked over to the big house and knocked. In a minute the Virginia opened the door. "What are you doing," she asked. She looked him up and down.

He took her arm and pulled her outside. "I'm gonna take my boat and go up the river for a few days. We been doin' a lot lately and I'd like to get away for a while and be by myself."

She frowned. "You're leaving. Are you coming back?"

He shook his head and laughed. "All my stuff is in the house, even my rifle. I be comin' back."

Her brow furrowed. "What is this about?" She turned and walked halfway across the street, then came back and stared in his face. "Where are you going?"

"I told you where I be goin'. I be goin' up the river."

She rubbed her hand across her face, her eyes on him. "How long will you be gone?"

"Like I said, a few days."

"When are you leaving?"

"My gear is in the boat."

"So, you had already decided to go, without saying anything to me about it?"

Floyd looked pained as he stared at her. "Virginia, I be a grown man. I ain't askin' you if I can go. I be tellin' you I be goin'. I ain't keepin' nothin' from you."

"I know you're a grown man, Floyd. You've certainly proved that." She turned, walked in the house and slammed the door.

He stood in the street and looked at the door for a minute. Then he turned and went to his house and went inside. He was getting his pistol and the last of his gear when heard a knock on the door. He walked over and opened it. Virginia was standing there.

"You make me act like a damn fool," she said. "I just despise you."

He smiled and hugged her. "I'll be back in a few days, and we'll go to the mountains to the restaurant where we went."

She looked up at him. "You promise?"

"I said I would." He took her hand. "Come walk with me to the boat." They walked to the dock and down to his boat.

She looked at him. "Floyd, please don't get into any trouble. I know how you are."

He laughed and kissed her. "I ain't gonna git in no trouble," he said as he got in the boat and pushed off. He waved to her, cranked up and headed up the river.

Virginia watched until he was out of sight and then walked back to the house.

28

F loyd felt good to be on the river. He'd slept in a house for several
weeks now and he was glad to get outside. He knew he didn't
have far to go before the river got too shallow for his boat, but he
would go as far as he could. The leaves on the hardwoods were
beginning to turn as the weather got cooler. A sprinkling of red and
yellow leaves was mixed in with the green.

He rode until the sun went behind the trees to his left. He found a
small stream emptying into the river. He landed, found a level spot to
put down his ground cloth and stretched his tarp out. He spread out
his blankets and a heavy quilt and was ready for the night.

He had brought a sack of fried chicken and biscuits from the mess
hall, so he didn't have to bother with a fire and cooking. When he
finished eating darkness had closed in, so he burrowed under the
cover and went to sleep.

H e was up at daylight, packed his gear and was on the water.
The second night was like the first. On the morning of the
third day, he knew he wasn't far from a small settlement, and he
arrived there about noon. He'd been there before and remembered

there was a small general store there that had a bar on one side. He hadn't had a drink in days so he thought that would be a good idea.

When he got to the landing, there were several boats already tied up there. He got out and walked up the road to the store. He walked into the general store side, on through the groceries, canned goods and clothing into the room on the other side. He stopped in the door and looked around. The bar was to the right with stools in front. An older man was behind the bar looking at him. He remembered him from being there before. There were three tables and chairs in front of the bar. Two young men sat at one of the tables with beers in front of them. They were watching him.

Floyd walked over and sat on one of the stools. The old man came over and looked at him. He stood back and stared at him.

Floyd stared back at him, wondering if he was going to wait on him.

The old man finally stepped to the bar and faced him. "I didn't thank I'd ever see you again," he said. He didn't look or sound friendly.

Floyd nodded. "Why'd you thank that?"

The old man chuckled. "I figured that if you kept wearin' that injun outfit, somebody'd be done kilt you by now."

"There has been some that tried," said Floyd, "but I ain't kilt yet." He looked at the old man. "Brang me a beer." He put a bill on the table.

The old man brought the beer. "I just hope you don't start nothin'. The last time you was here I got two windows busted and blood all over the floor."

Floyd shook his head. "All I want is a beer."

One of the young men got up from the table and walked up to the bar and ordered a beer. He looked at Floyd and then at the old man. "You serve injuns in here, Walt?" he asked as he took a swallow of the beer.

The old man leaned over the bar and looked at him. "Do you remember Arch Smith?"

The young man nodded. "Yeah, I remember 'im. He got killed here in yo' place two years or so back."

The bartender nodded. "You be right." He glanced at Floyd. "That be the injun that kilt 'im. It be best you go sit yo' ass down and don't say nothin' else."

The young man looked at Floyd, picked up his beer and walked to the table. He said something to the other young man, he got up and they both went out the door.

The old man walked over to Floyd. "I hope you finish yo' beer and git out of here fore somebody else comes in."

Floyd laughed and drank the last swallow. "I ain't said a word."

"You don't have to," said the old man. "Trouble just finds you."

Floyd got up and walked out. He went to the landing, got in the boat and went up the river. He spent one more night on the riverbank. When he got up the next morning, he packed his gear and started back downriver. It had been good to get away. He'd had time to clear his head and think about what he should do. He spent two more nights under the tarp and mid-afternoon of the next day he landed at the dock.

He left his gear and his tarp in the boat and headed to the house. He'd been on the river for a week, hadn't had a real bath during that time and not only was he dirty, but he felt dirty. He must be getting soft, he thought. In the past he'd gone for weeks without a bath, and it had never bothered him.

He went in the house, stripped off all his clothes and got in the tub and ran it full of hot water. He soaked for a while, then soaped and scrubbed all over. He got out, dried off, dressed in his best clothes and went across the street to the big house. He knocked on the door.

He heard somebody running inside and the door opened. Virginia ran out, grabbed him and kissed him. Then she looked in his face. "Don't you ever leave me for a week again and not let me know you're all right." She kissed him again.

He was overwhelmed by her greeting. "I didn't have no way to let you know anythang," he said. "Anyway, I'm home."

She took his hand and led him across the street to his house. She walked to the couch, sat down and pulled him down beside her. "Now you tell me everything that happened," she said.

He shook his head. "Didn't nothin' happen 'cept I went up the river. I did stop at one place and had a beer and then went on up the river. That be bout all that happened."

"Did you see any women?" she said, watching his face.

"What do you thank?" he said staring back at her.

She shook her head. "I don't know what I think about you," she said.

He stood up and looked down at her. "I told you when I said you was my woman that I wouldn't have nothin' to do with no other women." He pursed his lips. "How come you keep askin' me bout that?"

She got up and hugged him. "You're right," she said. "I won't ever mention it again. You said you would take me to the mountains when you got back. Are you going to do that?"

He nodded. "You go git yo' stuff. I be ready now."

She kissed him and ran out the door. He stood at the door and watched her run in the big house. He walked to the bedroom and packed.

In a few minutes she came out with her bag. They got in the truck and headed toward town. In the center of town, he turned on the main road and headed north. As they rode, he could see the color changes in the trees. By the late afternoon they were in the foothills and the hardwoods were a mixture of red and yellow.

It was almost dark when they got to the inn where they had stayed before. They went into their room and left their bags. They both were hungry; Floyd hadn't had a real meal in several days. They went to the restaurant and ate their fill. They came back to the room, got in a tub together and then went to bed together for the first time in days. It was way into the night when they finally turned over and went to sleep.

They slept late, got in the truck and went further up in the mountains. They stopped and ate in a place overlooking a long valley. While they were eating a light snow started falling.

Virginia looked out the window at the flakes. "It's going to get cold before long back at home," she said.

Floyd looked out. "You be right," he said. "Ain't long fore the snow comes."

They rode back down to the inn, went in and lay with each other until supper time. They ate, then came back to the room and did as they'd done the night before.

Virginia looked at Floyd as she lay beside him. "I wish we could do this forever."

He kissed her. "Sometimes we'll do it again." He held her as they both went to sleep.

They slept late and then headed home. Virginia sat right beside him all the way back She looked up at him. "I had a wonderful time. I appreciate you taking me and being so sweet."

He pulled her close. "I had a good time too."

It was dark when they got to the house. They carried their bags in and Virginia ran across the road to see about her daddy. They were both tired, so they went to bed early. She went to sleep in his arms.

Sometime during the night, he eased out of bed. She was sound asleep. He dressed in his injun outfit. He picked up the bag from his trip and the other bag he'd packed earlier, got his rifle and headed to the dock. When the sun came up, he was several miles upriver.

Virginia slept later than usual. She woke up and saw that Floyd was already up. She eased out of bed and went to the bathroom. She brushed her teeth and walked to the kitchen but didn't see him. She walked to the bedroom and saw that his bag was gone. She rushed to the closet, and it was empty. She ran to the front room and looked over the mantle. His rifle was gone.

She walked back in the bedroom and sat down on the side of the bed with her head in her hands. "I'm not going to cry," she said to herself. "He told me that one morning I'd wake up and he'd be gone. Now he's done what he said he was going to do."

She sat on the bed for a few minutes, then got up and dressed.

She left the house and walked to the dock. Despite what she knew, there was a chance that he had gone in the larger boat somewhere. However, she knew that he wouldn't have taken all his clothes if that was what he had done. Her main reason for going to the dock was to see if his boat was indeed gone. If his boat was gone, then he was gone.

She walked past the end of the dock to the steps leading to the river. She looked down the bank to the tree where his boat was usually tied up. It was gone. She turned and walked back toward the house.

I am a grown woman, she thought as she walked. *I fell in love with a man and did everything I could to make him love me. I don't know what else I could have done. He has left me so obviously he didn't feel the same way as I did. If he chose not to love me, there's nothing else I can do except accept his decision as it is and go on with my life.*

She walked on toward the house. *I will not cry and feel sorry for myself, but damn it hurts.* She walked in the big house; her daddy was eating breakfast. She walked in and sat down.

He took one look at her and knew something had happened. "What's the matter?" he said.

She looked at him. "Floyd has left, he's gone."

He watched her face and saw the hurt. "You're sure?"

She nodded. "He took everything, even his rifle is gone. I went to the dock and his boat is gone."

"Did you argue or have a disagreement?"

She shook her head. "Everything was perfect this weekend." She looked at him. "From the day I met him, he consistently said that one day he would leave. Regardless of what I did for him, he never said anything different." She smiled ruefully. "He meant what he said."

Mr. Mann nodded. "Floyd was indeed a man of his word." He looked at her. "I'm sorry, Virginia. I know you're hurting."

"Yes, I'm hurting and I'm afraid I'll be hurting for a long time." She got up, kissed her daddy and went upstairs. That afternoon she went across to the guest house and gathered up all her belongings and took them back to her room. She lay on her bed and stared at the ceiling.

Later she ate a bit of supper and spent a restless night trying to sleep. She got up early and went down to breakfast. Her daddy looked at her when she walked in and knew that he couldn't do anything to ease her pain. She had to deal with it herself.

She was on her second cup of coffee when she heard a knock on the door. She got up and walked to the door, wondering who could be here so early. She opened the door and Floyd was looking at her.

"I tried to leave but I couldn't do it," he said as he shook his head. "I come back to be with you."

She looked at him, her eyes on his eyes. "If you want to be with me, Floyd, there will be papers signed and notarized."

He looked at her and nodded his head. "I figured you'd say that."

She kissed him, grabbed his hand and pulled him inside. "Let's go tell Daddy the news."

29

Don't Forget Lanny Bledsoe's
Exciting Shoal Creek Series
Vol. 1-4

Shoal Creek
Rep's Return
Storm Rising
Rocky Shoals

Times were hard in rural Georgia in the 1930s,
but some people were harder,
especially on the Chattahoochie River.

Made in United States
Orlando, FL
01 September 2022

21875042R00168